He dialed 911 and

where the fire was

Fire was spreading rapi...
gathering fuel as it devoured hay. Beams lay crossed on one side.

That's when he saw Eliza lying under one of the beams, flames beginning to lick at her legs. Brandon hefted the beam off her and threw it aside. Sparks flew and the fire heightened.

Willow neighed in terror, kicking the stall door. Brandon lifted Eliza and ran with her out of the stable, the sounds of Willow's screaming haunting each stride.

Placing Eliza gently on the ground outside the corral, he bent to check for breathing. Worry swallowed every thought and emotion in him. The beam that had fallen on her was big. Had it hit her head, or had she been knocked out when she struck the ground? He couldn't lose her now. He'd already lost her once.

Don't miss the other books in the Vengeance in Texas series:

A WIDOW'S GUILTY SECRET
by Marie Ferrarella—January 2013

A BILLIONAIRE'S REDEMPTION
by Cindy Dees—March 2013

A PROFILER'S CASE FOR SEDUCTION
by Carla Cassidy—April 2013

Dear Reader,

Continue the journey in Vengeance with Eliza Harvey-Reed and Brandon Reed. It's no accident that they share a common last name. Eliza is in love with her husband's brother...and her husband is one of three murder victims. I invite you to follow this intriguing homicide investigation in a town erupting with drama and excitement.

Eliza and Brandon do engage in a scandalous affair, so I let love play a guiding hand in writing this story. The cost of losing a husband and brother is great, and takes great love to overcome. I particularly enjoyed writing the ending. I hope you'll find the twists and turns as satisfying as I did—and may you find yourself reaching for the next book in the continuity!

Jennie

JENNIFER MOREY

A Rancher's Dangerous Affair

HARLEQUIN® ROMANTIC SUSPENSE

Special thanks and acknowledgment to Jennifer Morey for her contribution to the Vengeance in Texas miniseries.

ISBN-13: 978-0-373-27810-7

A RANCHER'S DANGEROUS AFFAIR

This edition published by arrangement with Harlequin Books S.A.

For questions and comments about the quality of this book, please contact us at CustomerService@Harlequin.com.

HARLEQUIN®
www.Harlequin.com

Printed in U.S.A.

Books by Jennifer Morey

Harlequin Romantic Suspense

**Special Ops Affair* #1653
**Seducing the Accomplice* #1657
Lawman's Perfect Surrender #1700
**Seducing the Colonel's Daughter* #1718
A Rancher's Dangerous Affair #1740

Silhouette Romantic Suspense

**The Secret Soldier* #1526
**Heiress Under Fire* #1578
Blackout at Christmas #1583
    "Kiss Me on Christmas"
**Unmasking the Mercenary* #1606
The Librarian's Secret Scandal #1624

*All McQueen's Men

Other titles by this author available in ebook format.

JENNIFER MOREY

Two-time 2009 RITA® Award nominee and a Golden Quill winner for Best First Book for *The Secret Soldier,* Jennifer Morey writes contemporary romance and romantic suspense. Project manager *par jour,* she works for the space systems segment of a satellite imagery and information company. She lives in sunny Denver, Colorado. She can be reached through her website, www.jennifermorey.com, and on Facebook.

For Mom.

Chapter 1

September 5th

Eliza Harvey-Reed always felt better when she was busy planning parties. Just a day into her vacation and she already missed the hustle and bustle of Effervescent Events. She'd made a name for herself in Hollywood and had a reputation for delivering flawless, flamboyantly entertaining service. Fun. Exciting. Newsworthy. That was her business. She'd rather be back in California than in her hometown of Vengeance, Texas, climbing out of the rental car to visit her husband's brother, the object of a teenage crush she'd never quite forgotten.

Except, to her, it had been more than a crush. She hadn't realized how much more until he'd ended their relationship. Things had grown hot and heavy between them. He had begun to rule her world. She'd had so much ambition back then. Still did. He had begun to feel like an anchor, a hot, hard, sexy anchor, but an anchor nonetheless. And then he'd dumped her. Out of the blue. She hadn't seen it coming. If there was to be any dumping going on, she had thought it would have been her. He'd begun to matter more than he should.

Sometimes she wondered if his rejection had elevated him to some unnatural level of importance. People always wanted what they couldn't have. More expensive cars. Bigger houses. Better vacations. More chocolate. When denied these things, they became suspiciously more important. Brandon Reed had become too important.

Walking toward the front porch of the Reed Ranch house on a wide stone circular driveway, Eliza noticed her husband, David, look behind him again. He kept doing that. When they'd turned onto the long dirt road leading to the ranch, he'd checked the rearview mirror more than once. When he'd gotten out of the car, he'd checked the road. Now he was doing it again.

Her long, dark brown hair waved in the slight breeze as she looked toward the road. No cars. No people. No animals. It wasn't dark yet. A winding dirt road disappeared over a hill several hundred yards away. The expensive copper fence lined one side; a carpet of green grass rolled to the edge of a thick stand of trees.

"What's the matter?" she asked.

"Nothing."

His austere profile only stoked her concern. "Is Brandon expecting more company?"

"No."

"Are you?"

"Enough, Eliza."

That meant leave him alone. He'd changed since they'd run into each other at one of her parties and followed impulse to a quick Vegas wedding. He never talked to her about anything that bothered him. She tried to get him to open up, but he always responded with short answers. If there was one thing she'd learned about him in the short time they'd been married, it was that David Reed could keep secrets. Had those secrets gotten him into trouble?

His dark brown eyes scanned the surroundings again. A couple of inches shorter than Brandon's six-two, he was handsome and blonder but not as rugged as his brother. Why she always made those comparisons, she'd rather not examine.

"You're acting like Bruce Willis in one of his *Die Hard* movies."

"I'm not in the mood, Eliza."

"Did you piss off a hacker or something?" She couldn't help her sarcasm. He was nothing like Bruce Willis.

He scowled at her before stepping onto the porch. This was how they spoke to each other now. Why had she married him, anyway? She was afraid the answer was just on the other side of the door.

Brandon Reed had captured her heart when she was sixteen. Try as she might to capture his all those years ago, she'd never succeeded. Absurdly, she thought marrying his brother would trip him up. Get him to realize what a mistake he'd made letting her go. Well, all she'd gotten was a terse congratulations over the phone and a question on where her next party was. He may have been jealous. He may have been unaffected. Eliza had no idea which. With him, reactions were never easy to ascertain. The man wore his personality like a sunken ship, hidden treasure locked away in a deep abyss. He and David had that in common. Except Brandon's mysteries lured her more than David's.

David froze at the door.

Eliza turned. At the top of the hill, a car had appeared. Instead of driving to the house, it made a U-turn and vanished. Who was that? Someone who was lost? Or was it David who'd attracted them here?

"Is someone following you?" she asked.

Turning his grim face away from the road, he opened the door without responding.

"You've been acting weird lately." Inside, she put her purse down on a table against the wall, vaguely aware of another purse there.

"No, I haven't." He quietly closed the door.

She faced him. "David. Talk to me. What's going on with you? Is someone after you?"

"Eliza," he complained, stepping past her with an admonishing look.

"Just tell me."

He ignored her.

Sighing with exasperation, she stepped from the new marble flooring of the entry to the hardwood floor of the living room. Earth tones and splashes of red accents popped out at her. The exposed vaulted ceiling extended to a formal dining room. Brandon must have hired someone to do the decorating. She couldn't picture him doing it. A lot of years had passed since she'd seen him, but he couldn't have changed that much.

As she heard voices in the kitchen behind a partial wall, Eliza's heart jolted with shock. There was a purse on the entry table. Brandon wasn't alone. A woman was in the kitchen with him. Why was she nervous about seeing him, regardless of whether he was with another woman or not? She was married. There was no chance for them. There never had been. So why did she still put so much importance on him?

The woman laughed, flirtatious, warm and soft. Eliza's stomach soured with more churning. "We should have called to let him know we were early." They weren't supposed to be here until tomorrow.

David stopped, turning toward her. "Don't like it that he's with someone else, huh?"

"Why would that bother me?"

"You tell me."

She smirked. He'd started accusing her of marrying him to spite his brother shortly after their wedding. She'd fantasized about making Brandon jealous, that's all. There had never been a time that she actually believed he would be. If only that were possible. Brandon didn't care about her.

"They might want to be alone," she said.

"Maybe you'd like to be alone with him."

Now he was going too far. "Is that why you cheated on me four months after our wedding?"

"Yes." He started toward the kitchen again.

His cruel reply dug deep. He hurt her when he talked to her like that. Did he really think she was still pining for his brother? Why had he married her then? Brandon was her first love. They were kids when they were together. She'd never forget him because he'd been her first. That didn't mean she still wanted him.

Maybe this was about more than David's insecurities where his brother was concerned. David shared her enthusiasm for parties, but he overindulged. Women. Alcohol. Drugs. If she didn't know better, she'd think he was one of her famous Hollywood clients instead of a sports journalist and husband.

Eliza crossed the living room behind David, hearing dishes clanking and the soft tone of the woman's voice. The dread she'd felt ever since boarding the plane in L.A. intensified.

She wished David would have done as she had asked

and taken her to a hotel. She'd planned a big birthday party for her brother tomorrow night and had a lot of loose ends to tie up. She'd rather do that than face Brandon with his latest lover.

The dread wouldn't ease. Normally, when she visited Vengeance, it was for business. She only squeezed in enough time to see her brother, and those visits she always kept deliberately short. Ryker Harvey never missed an opportunity to point out how lucky she was to have escaped this town. She didn't understand why he wasn't happy. He had a really great wife and two adorable children. He ran an auto repair shop in town and had a stellar reputation. Everyone loved him. What more could he possibly want?

She hoped her party would smooth things over between them. He hadn't seemed very excited the last time she'd spoken with him.

"Always partying," he'd commented blandly just before he'd thanked her.

Eliza entered the kitchen behind David. A news program broadcasted from a small television hanging in the far corner. Brandon's deep chuckle ended abruptly when he looked up and saw them, those golden-brown eyes going hard as he spotted her. His thick, shaggy, dark blond hair was a little on the messy side, and stubble peppered his jaw. He'd aged but in an appealing, masculine way. Rugged. Just like she remembered.

The woman he was with had long dark hair like Eliza's and beautiful blue eyes. Eliza's were blue-green. Brandon's tall, muscular body dwarfed her, his broad shoulders sloping and his biceps bulging as he held the woman around her tiny waist. Eliza was slightly taller than her. Did Brandon prefer smaller women? Not that Eliza was big. She had a nice shape.

He stepped back, and the woman's smile slipped as his hands left her. "I didn't hear you come in."

David walked farther into the kitchen, stopping next to the long island. "We decided to come a day early. Eliza has a lot to do before her brother's birthday party tomorrow night."

Brandon continued to stare at Eliza.

"We're planning to attend," the woman said, leaning against him, angling her head as though trying to capture his attention.

"Eliza," Brandon said.

"Hello, Brandon."

The woman with him straightened, eyes taking on the threat that Eliza must present. "I'm Jillian Marks. Brandon's girlfriend."

"Sorry," Brandon said. "Jillian, this is my brother, David."

The woman extended a dainty hand to him.

"And this is Eliza Harvey."

A flash of malice crossed through Jillian's eyes as she extended her hand.

"Reed," David corrected.

Eliza removed her hand from Jillian's, wondering why her husband bothered with the name correction. He'd proven how much he cared for her when he'd slept with someone else. Unless he was jealous of Brandon and that was why he'd cheated on her. Eliza didn't know what to do about that. Had her inability to let go of Brandon really driven him away before they'd even had a chance to get started? She couldn't even feel guilty about that. Brandon didn't want her. Why was David worried?

"You're married," Jillian said, smiling at Eliza.

"Mr. and Mrs. Reed," Brandon said tersely.

"Could have been you, big brother," David said snidely.

Brandon didn't respond. His face became a blank mask as he looked at David.

"You and Brandon were…"

"In high school," David finished her deduction.

While Jillian's eyes went cold, David moved in a circle, checking out the huge, elegant kitchen equipped with every modern amenity imaginable. "The place looks good. Selling a lot of beef?"

It was a poor attempt to sound cordial.

If Brandon took offense, he hid it. "Record year."

"Brandon is a smart businessman when it comes to cattle." Jillian hooked her arm with his and smiled flirtatiously up at him. It was all a forced show, a defensive reaction to Eliza and what her presence meant.

Brandon didn't return the smile. In fact, he moved away. Her arm slipped free of his, and her smile flattened.

"You always were good at taking care of yourself," David said, fingering a bowl of fruit on the kitchen island as though making sure it was real.

Brandon ignored the barb and moved another inch or two away from Jillian. How long had they been seeing each other? Long enough for Brandon to feel cornered, it would appear.

Seeing the way David distastefully regarded his brother, she wondered if she was the sole cause of his unrest. When they were kids, she'd thought they had a normal relationship. Brandon was the older brother and acted that way. But Brandon was also taller, made more money and had stolen Eliza's heart when she was a teenager. He had everything that David didn't. And now he thought she still had feelings for Brandon. Though she'd tried to convince him he had nothing to worry about, he didn't believe her.

That was the only reason she hadn't left him after she'd

caught him between an entertainment reporter's legs. She still wasn't over what he'd done. She wasn't sure she could stay married to him. And she definitely hadn't had sex with him since. He believed she loved Brandon and not him. Did that give him the go-ahead to cheat on her when she denied his accusations?

"Do you have anything to drink?" David headed for the kitchen entry without waiting for Brandon's reply.

He'd had enough to drink on the plane already.

"You know where the wine is," Brandon said drily.

David left the kitchen, no doubt planning on getting more than one bottle. Why was he drowning in alcohol lately? Was it his perception of his older brother and Eliza or something else? The car on the hill gave her some insight, but he wouldn't talk to her. They'd never talked, not the way they should as a married couple. More and more she thought their marriage was a sham, the result of blind impulse. While a deeper part of her had reasoned he was the next best thing to Brandon, reality hadn't been kind. The mistake she'd made expanded and bloomed. As much as it hurt, she was better off alone than marrying the wrong man.

Realizing she was still staring at the empty doorway David had gone through, Eliza turned and caught Brandon watching her. His gaze drifted down her body before going back to her face. He seemed neither hurried nor concerned what she or Jillian would think of such blatant inspection. He hadn't looked at her like that since she was a sophomore in high school; only now he was a man, not a boy. A warm rush swept over her, an instant reaction. He'd always been able to do that to her.

David entered the kitchen with three bottles of red wine and saw them. His steps faltered as he pinned Eliza with an accusatory look. Brandon glanced at Jillian before busying himself with retrieving wineglasses. She missed it, her glaring gaze on Eliza. David passed his wife on his way to the kitchen island, where he put down the bottles.

Eliza wandered past the kitchen island and stopped before the table, trying to dismiss the significance of the way Brandon had looked at her. What did it mean? Had he seen something when she'd been lost in thought? Did he know she wasn't happy?

She spotted a newspaper on the table. The headline read Darby College Professor Melinda Grayson Missing.

"Here you go, darling." David handed her a glass of red wine.

She smirked at the way he'd said *darling* and took the glass, holding the paper in her other hand.

"What are you—" He stopped short when he read the headline. "Professor Grayson is missing?" He took the newspaper from her.

"I heard her housekeeper reported it," Jillian said.

David turned with the paper and kept reading as he strode slowly to the kitchen island, putting down the paper. "It says she might have been on her way to the grocery store when she was taken."

Eliza followed him and put her glass down. David had placed the three bottles of wine on the counter. Brandon and Jillian had yet to pour wine into their glasses.

"She didn't leave willingly," Brandon said. "She had all her material ready for the semester."

"Who would kidnap her?"

David's concern didn't pass by Eliza. If Melinda wasn't so much older than him, she'd wonder if he'd slept with her. Then again, ten years wasn't all that much. Melinda was in her early forties.

"Probably someone who didn't like her views," Jillian said, nearly sneering. She obviously didn't like Melinda.

"Did you go to Darby?" Eliza asked. The woman had to be around twenty-five so it was more than possible.

"Yes. And I hated Melinda's class."

Melinda was known for her controversial teachings. She was a feminist who thought men were superior and women's movements had the wrong approach to gaining equality. Porn stars were true feminists because of the control they had over men. Sociopaths improved society. That sort of thing.

But Jillian's tone hinted at deeper emotion. Brandon and David caught her animosity along with Eliza. Brandon said nothing as he assessed her, and David abandoned the newspaper to do the same.

"That sounds like motive to kidnap and hurt her," David said.

Jillian's chin rose an inch. "Just because she wasn't my friend doesn't mean I'd hurt her."

David let it pass, lifting his wine for a drink.

Eliza saw how Jillian slid a self-conscious glance toward Brandon, as though anxious that he'd think less of her for voicing her opinion of the great Melinda Grayson. The sign of insecurity said a lot about the state of their relationship. Eliza almost felt sorry for her. Brandon must be close to running.

Brandon could tell Jillian wasn't happy that Eliza and David were here at his ranch. Or maybe it was only Eliza she wished would disappear. Sitting at the kitchen table with the third bottle of wine empty, most of which his brother had consumed, he listened to Eliza talk about the Friday parties she used to plan during high school.

"The whole school loved you," David said.

Brandon watched how Eliza remained stiff with the affectionate comment. He hadn't missed how distracted she'd been when she and David had arrived. Something was going on between them. He hated the ray of hope that shot through him the instant he realized it. Why did he always have to fight his attraction to her? She was a stunning woman, but she hadn't changed. She was still the Friday Party Girl. It was what had led to their breakup. It was what had taken her to Hollywood. She frequently appeared in entertainment news and had so many friends it made him dizzy. He often wondered what would have happened if she hadn't always put her social life ahead of him.

Maybe that was what had come between her and David. His brother shared Eliza's passion for a good time, but it was easy for her to forget a man in the process. He'd tried to warn his brother, but he was already headed down the same road as Eliza. Both of them lived for the party. Except for that nagging feeling that she'd somehow changed. The way she dressed. Her hair. Her makeup. All of it was more subdued. Why?

He stifled another ray of damn hope.

Eliza had been the kind of girl who stood out in a crowd. Intentionally. Brandon had been the opposite. Still was. They had never meshed that way. He preferred his secluded life on the ranch. Eliza would never thrive here. She may have matured over the years, but she was still Hollywood's hottest party planner. She shined the brightest when she was the center of attention. She'd wilt away in the silence of Reed Ranch.

"Remember the one you threw at the park?"

Brandon was drawn back into the discussion. Jillian had been awfully quiet. He dreaded finding out why. He was afraid he already knew.

"Which one?" Eliza laughed.

Did she laugh because she was no longer that girl,

or did the memory delight her? Either way, he was entranced. Unwillingly.

"The one that you couldn't break up by ten."

"Oh, yeah." She nodded with the recollection. "You weren't there, were you?"

His face lost its animation. "Yeah. You didn't talk to me, though."

Eliza turned away, rigid with whatever thoughts pressed her.

"I remember that night." As soon as Brandon spoke, Jillian fidgeted beside him, pursing her lips and averting her face. He couldn't reassure her. He had to be honest. And if he was honest, he'd admit he didn't feel enough for her to pretend Eliza didn't matter to him. She did. She just wasn't the right woman for him. She was a friend. But Jillian wasn't the right woman, either. Looking right at Eliza, he continued, "Two of the boys were angry that you kept telling them to leave." He had stayed to make sure she was okay. He'd done that a lot with her. As wild as she was, she'd needed someone to look out for her.

Her striking blue-green eyes lifted, and he found himself back in time with her. Bumping into each other at the Smokin' Burger. Kissing her on her front doorstep. Beating up boys for her…

"He was always rescuing her," David said to Jillian, not hiding his derision.

"Maybe we should talk about something else," Eliza said.

"That's supposed to be your job now," Brandon said to David. "You staying out of trouble?"

Eliza averted her head, and that sparked his curiosity.

"Stop being my big brother, Brandon. I can take care of myself."

He had his doubts about that. Taking in Eliza's profile,

he'd bet she wasn't helping matters. David loved to party and that was her specialty.

"We should get to bed," Eliza said, pushing back her chair to stand.

"It's not that late," David protested.

"Come on, David." Eliza took his hand and coaxed him to stand.

Reluctantly, he did, meeting Brandon's reproving look in defiance as he slipped his arm around Eliza. Refusing to let it get to him, he stood and so did Jillian. He didn't understand why Eliza was affecting him so much now.

"Good night," she said to him and Jillian, lingering the longest on him.

"Good night," he answered.

Jillian said nothing.

Brandon watched them leave the kitchen, David swaying a little against Eliza. He wished he was the one taking her to bed. He'd already shown them to their room, one that was far away from his. He'd be damned if he was going to sleep anywhere near enough to hear them. And that frustrated him. Aside from the alcohol David depended way too much on, he was his brother and Eliza was his wife. The two of them together shouldn't bother him.

Turning to Jillian, he saw how she still watched him the way she had all evening. "I'll walk you to your car."

Jillian didn't move when he took a step toward the living room.

"Can I talk to you first?"

There it was. She was going to grill him now. "Sure."

She breathed out an uncomfortable laugh that he thought might be staged. "I don't quite know how to say this."

"Just say it."

Slipping one of her hands around his biceps, she moved closer. Brandon had to smother the urge to shrug her away from him. How his sentiments had changed so rapidly bothered him.

She tipped her head up to look at him shyly. "I think it might be good if Eliza and David stay in town tomorrow."

Her shyness contradicted her statement. "They're staying here. David is my brother."

"I know, but…"

"What's wrong, Jillian?" He struggled for patience. Was she so insecure that she'd ask him to kick his own brother out of his house?

Sliding her hands over his chest, she leaned against him. "I can tell she still has feelings for you."

Had it been that obvious? Had David noticed? He must have. A tide of guilt overcame him. "She's married to David."

"That doesn't mean anything. She could still try and take you from me."

Take him from her? Alarm bells buzzed in his head. That was taking insecurity to a new level. Brandon stepped back. "I don't belong to anyone."

"But, Brandon…" She angled her head coyly and manipulatively.

"We talked about this, Jillian." He cut her off before she could continue. "I don't want to settle down with anyone. I thought you were okay with that."

"I am." She crowded him some more, clinging, her hands touching too much.

He stepped back farther, feeling a familiar suffocation encroach. Women who demanded too much of him never lasted. Usually he saw this coming a lot sooner and ended the relationship before anyone got hurt. But Jillian was good. She'd snaked her way close to him and now she was striking.

"You better get going," he said.

Something akin to panic flared in her eyes, and then she quickly recovered. "Sweetie, I know you're afraid. So am I. But it will be all right. We're perfect for each other."

Perfect for each other. This was beginning to feel rather warped. "I'm not afraid. I just don't want a serious relationship. I told you that."

"You can't stay single your whole life. At some point you're going to have to get married." She reached for him yet again.

This time he caught her wrists and stopped her. "Maybe we should take a break for a while."

Now anger flowed into her pretty blue eyes, eyes that had enchanted him when he'd first met her. She jerked her wrists free. "You're breaking up with me?"

"No. Let's just take a break." *A permanent one.* He'd just let her down gently. It wasn't his style to use women. He made sure they understood what he was after. He must have missed the signs in Jillian. She definitely wanted more than he could give.

"I'm not an idiot, Brandon. I know when a man is trying to get rid of me."

He bent his head momentarily, trying to think of what to say.

"It's okay, Brandon. I understand. We don't have to take a break. If you'll just give it some time… You're only confused because your old girlfriend came back."

"She's married," he repeated.

"That doesn't matter. I saw the way you looked at her, and her at you."

That was ridiculous. But inside, her words mocked him.

"Please, Brandon." He let her put her palms on his chest. "Please don't give up on us."

"There is no us."

She stared up at him, finally believing him. This was it. He was finished.

"What did I do to scare you away?"

"Nothing." Suffocate him. Try to control him. And the way she'd gone from angry to pleading…

Something wasn't right about her. She was a little too desperate.

"I'm sorry." He moved away from her, backing into the living room. "I don't want to hurt you."

Tears swelled in her eyes.

Damn it.

"Brandon. I love you." She came for him again.

He turned and strode toward the front door, hearing her stumble after him, sobbing, "Brandon."

It made him ill. How could she possibly love him? They'd only dated a few times. He never allowed a relationship to last longer than a few months. Anything longer than that led to more. It had happened once. He'd gotten too close, too far out of his comfort zone. It had ended badly. If he ever settled down, it'd be with a woman who didn't crowd him like that.

He could not be crowded.

After handing Jillian her purse from where she'd left it on the table in the entryway, he opened the front door. "I'll walk you to your car."

She stood there crying. "I don't understand why you're breaking up with me."

"Sometimes I don't understand it myself."

Sniffling, her tears eased. "Then you aren't sure."

No, he was sure. Especially when she kept doing that, misconstruing his words and hanging on to hope that he wouldn't end it between them. She'd probably had other experiences like this and that was why she was taking it so hard.

Reaching for him, she took his hand. "Let's go up to bed. By morning you'll feel better."

He removed his hand from hers and backed up against the open door, giving her room to pass.

She looked through the open space and then back at him. Her eyes cleared of tears and anger seeped back into them. "You can't do this."

He angled his head. *Really?* Was she going to snap on him?

"You can't be loving one minute and then let me down the next!" She marched right up to him and pointed at his face. "Before that bitch arrived, everything was fine. Now you're telling me to *leave?*"

How had he missed this crazy streak in her? "I really am sorry. I didn't mean to hurt you."

The anger melted away. "Oh, Brandon." She pressed her body against his and began kissing him. "I knew you were just confused."

Whoa. Brandon grasped her arms and forced her away. "You need to leave now."

"But—"

"Please, Jillian, just go."

"No."

He moved her so that she was outside his door and shut it.

"You bastard!" she screeched, pounding the door. "I knew you were hiding something from me about that bitch. Let me back in there! I'll make sure she knows where you belong!"

Holy cats! The woman had lost it. Was she referring to Eliza? She'd questioned him about her. Maybe someone in town had let her in on the history between them. That he'd broken up with her, and she'd moved away with a broken heart. Had seeing him interact with her tonight triggered this bizarre tantrum?

A few seconds of silence passed.

"Brandon?" Jillian pleaded. "Please don't do this. Please let me in. I'm sorry. I just didn't expect you to do this tonight. It started out so good, and…Brandon?"

He didn't respond.

The doorbell rang. Rang again. When he didn't answer, she knocked. Pounded.

"Brandon?" she called louder.

She pounded for about a minute longer before she finally gave up.

"This isn't over," she growled from the other side of the door.

There had to be something wrong with her. She was unnaturally angry. Violently jealous of Eliza. What would she do next? Would she come after him? Or Eliza….

Chapter 2

Was that yelling she heard? And someone had pounded on the front door. Who was it? Was someone here for David? Alarmed and worried about Brandon and Jillian, Eliza checked on David. He'd passed out as soon as he lay down. He hadn't even undressed or gotten under the covers.

In her nightgown, she left the guest room that was on the first level and made her way down a long hallway, opposite the kitchen. Stepping into the living room, she saw Brandon looking out the front window.

After a few seconds, he turned and saw her, his unwelcoming face impassive the way she remembered him. She had always wondered what lived beneath that thick wall. Glimpses of a softer man had sneaked out when they were kids. Maybe that was what kept her from being able to forget him and move on.

She stepped closer, searching for Jillian. "Is everything okay?"

He took in her knee-length nightgown with spaghetti

straps and scooped neckline as she stopped before him. "Yes. Jillian just left."

"Is she okay?"

"You should go back to bed." He started for the stairs leading to the upper level.

"Who was at the door? Was it someone looking for David?"

Stopping, he turned and angled his head shrewdly. "Why would anyone be looking for David here?"

"Who was at the door, Brandon?" she insisted. Why did he not want to tell her?

She moved toward him. He undressed her with his eyes as he once again took her in, spending too long on her scooped neckline, which was demure enough to be proper. It didn't hide the movement of her breasts, however. She supposed she should have put on a robe, but the urgent yells and pounding had made her skip that step.

"Jillian," he finally answered. "She was upset."

Upset? "What was she so upset about? And why was she on the other side of the door?" Recalling the way she'd glared at her, Eliza had a pretty good idea already.

"I'd really rather not talk about it." He headed for the stairs again.

"Did you break up with her?"

With a hand on the railing, he turned his brooding gaze on her. "Go to bed, Eliza."

"Was she getting too close?"

He sighed in annoyance and came back to her, standing close. "She didn't want you and David to stay here."

There was only one reason for that. Jillian was jealous. And then she'd gotten angry. Had he kicked her out? He must have. That by itself didn't surprise her. Jillian's reaction did. Eliza was married to David. Brandon wasn't interested in her that way. What had Jillian seen? What had David seen? Were they both overreacting or was there some merit to this?

"She was that mad when you told her we were staying?" she asked.

Slowly, he nodded, his worry showing. And something else.

"You did break up with her, didn't you?" Her original conclusion had to be correct. "She was getting too close."

"Eliza, damn it." He turned again.

Why had he broken up with her tonight, though? She'd heard them in the kitchen before Brandon was aware of their arrival. They'd sounded so infatuated with each other. What had happened to turn him off so quickly?

"You do that all the time, Brandon. When are you going to get over that? Why are you so afraid of commitment anyway?"

"I'm not afraid. I know when it isn't going to work... unlike you."

That gave her a jolt. "What is that supposed to mean?" And why was he so defensive?

"David shows up at one of your fancy parties and you think he's the one. Well, all you've done is make matters worse for him. He had problems before he ran into you again. All you're doing is compounding them."

Why was he so angry? She'd nailed him with the truth and now he was retaliating by bringing it all back onto her. She had to breathe to calm her shock and the aftermath of the insult. "That's not fair! *He* asked *me* to marry him."

"Yeah, and I can see why. With you, the party never ends."

"You're going to stand there and blame me for the way David has been behaving lately?"

"Lately? What's changed? He's still as wild as ever.

More so. I was close to getting him back on track when he met you at that athlete's party and you two started having such a good time together."

David must have told him everything. She certainly hadn't had the opportunity to have a close and personal talk with him.

Eliza folded her arms. "So it was all me. David had nothing to do with it. He didn't have to make any decisions on his own. He just had to do what you told him."

Brandon glanced down to where her breasts had plumped. "Go back to bed."

She refused to move. He was always the one walking away. Not her. Eliza wasn't a quitter. When it came to relationships, Brandon was, and she had a flaming impulse to find out why.

He'd caused her enough grief in her life. Maybe it was time to get to the bottom of it and put an end to it once and for all. Maybe then she could leave him in the past where he belonged.

Eliza left the guest room. She was glad she had to prepare for her party. It kept her mind off Brandon, or more appropriately, her desire to mine through his rock-hard heart to learn what was in there. Uncover the layers, as it were. There had to be some. Many. All of which he kept hidden, especially from women.

David had protected him. Both brothers looked out for each other in different ways. When Eliza had asked about Brandon's inability to stay close to anyone, he'd answered vaguely, guarding Brandon's privacy. Which only made her more curious. What was so important to hide?

She checked her watch. David wasn't here at the ranch. He wasn't answering her calls, either. While that worried her, she'd waited too long already. If she didn't leave now, she'd be late. She'd only come back here to shower and change. The house was quiet. Brandon hadn't come in from the stable yet. Good. She'd enjoy her evening without both men. Because she was pretty sure David wasn't going to show up. He'd taken one of Brandon's ranch trucks and gone God only knew where.

Opening the driver door of the rental car, Eliza stopped when she saw an envelope with her name on it.

Dropping her purse into the rental, she picked up the envelope and tore the paper, slipping out a card with a pretty red flower on the front. Opening it, she read, "You made a big mistake this time." It was a blank card except for that.

An eerie chill chased along her skull and arms. Recalling how David had looked around when they'd first arrived, she did the same now. The sun was low in the sky. Birds chirped. A slight breeze toyed with the curls she'd put in her hair before putting it up.

Someone had come here and delivered the card. She and David had left the car doors open when they'd arrived.

Who had written it?

If someone was after David, it didn't make sense to send it to her. Could Brandon have put it there? He held her responsible for David's recklessness.

"Going early?"

Jumping, she turned. Brandon stood there. Wearing jeans and a long-sleeved, patterned green shirt, boots and a cowboy hat, he made her swoon. The low sun cast him in shadows.

"I need to make sure the caterers set everything up."

She felt him take in her sparkly party dress and her carefully coiffed hair. She always looked her best for her events.

"What's that?" He indicated the card.

Why would he ask if he had been the one to put it in the rental? “A card. Someone left it.”

Frowning, he stepped forward, taking the card from her and reading what was inside.

“Did you write that?” With him so close, the words came out a little too sultry.

His eyes lifted. “You think I wrote this?”

“You think I married David to—”

“I didn’t write it.” He handed her the card. She didn’t want it. She tossed it into the rental, and it sailed over to the passenger seat next to her purse.

Nor was she ready to get into the car and stop looking at him.

His brow creased. “Isn’t David going with you?”

“David hasn’t been home all day.”

Home. This wasn’t their home....

“Maybe you should wait for me.”

He was going to her party? “You want to go?” She was afraid she sounded a little too animated.

“That note is suspicious.”

So he’d go to make sure she was okay. “Just like old times,” she teased. “Are you going to beat up some boys for me again?”

He chuckled, a rare sound from him. She breathed through the spark it caused.

“Just like old times, you’re going to drag me to one of your parties.”

“Who’s dragging?”

Still smiling, he didn’t reply, only touched her with his gaze all over her upper torso and face.

“You look beautiful.”

Tingles seeded and spread. “Thank you.” David never told her she was beautiful.

“It’s really good to see you again.”

Was he really talking to her like this? Eliza felt her face heat from all the tingling arousing her.

"It's really good to see you, too." She wished he'd have said this to her years ago. How could he, when she'd avoided him until now? Married to his brother, this felt a little dangerous. Alluring. Tempting. She was back in time to when she was a teenager. She loved it.

His boots scraped against the stone driveway as he stepped closer. His knee bumped her inner thigh, almost as if he'd nudge her legs apart.

Eliza put her hands on his chest as he leaned in. Her heart raced. Heat scorched her. Instantly out of control.

He kissed her, openmouthed and hungry. His arms went around her, and her body was deliciously pressed against him. He devoured her mouth, and she gave him everything he asked for.

Then he tore away from her, swearing gruffly.

He moved back, breathing erratically like her, dark eyes brooding with fiery lust. She was certain she looked the same. He had her so hot right now she might have a hard time driving.

What had just come over them?

Angrily, he turned and strode toward the house.

The guests were already arriving, and David hadn't even called her yet. Where was he? She was beginning to worry. Who had followed him to the ranch? Was he on the run from that person? Is that why he was staying away? Maybe she should have paid more attention to that. Her husband could be in trouble and all she'd been doing was thinking about Brandon. She still couldn't believe he'd kissed her!

It had been incredible. A kiss had never felt so good. Even when he'd kissed her as a teenager, and those had been potent enough. She thought she'd die. She'd have gladly taken whatever he was willing to give. He could have led her into the house and she'd have gone. He could have thrown her on the hood of the car. In the backseat. Hell, standing right there in the driveway!

It was appalling, shameful and exciting at the same time.

She looked around the banquet room. Everything was perfect. Elegant and color coordinated. She smiled. This was her favorite part. Before people dug in to the impressive display of food. Before the white-linen tables were obscured in the crowd. Before dishes littered every surface. The early conversations. The first glasses of libation. The end of the night would come, but right now, right here, the fun was just beginning.

Senator Merris entered with his wife, he in a suit and she in a conservative cocktail dress. He saw her and waved. Average height and thin, he kept his white hair short. His wife was something of a mousy thing, always in her husband's shadow. A few years younger than his sixty-two, she tried hard to look young, but the look came across boyish. Short, dyed blond hair, minimal makeup and jewelry and rare smiles.

Eliza headed toward them. "Senator." She greeted his wife, too.

"I see you've created another marvel." He leaned in for a brief hug. "Your brother will be happy."

She hoped so. "Thank you."

"The entire town will show up for this one. With an open invitation and you the host, they're all expecting you to bring Hollywood to Vengeance." He glanced around. "And it appears you've succeeded."

"The only thing missing are the stars." She laughed at her quip.

So did he. His wife barely cracked a smile.

"Your party planning company is one of the best, so I wouldn't be surprised to see one tonight."

"I'm lucky that way." Word of mouth and a few mentions on entertainment programs had boosted her business.

She did have Roy Greenwood playing tonight. The *American Idol* sensation was sure to be the real reason attendance would be high. And Eliza had planned it that way.

"Either that, or a natural."

She angled her head at his generous praise, certain he was doing it so that she'd keep giving him discounts on the events she planned for him.

Over his shoulder, she spotted Brandon walking into the banquet room and endured a rush of passion and shock. He'd actually come to her party. In a dark suit and dark pink-and-gray tie, he put a hitch in her next breath. Was he really concerned about the card she'd received? Or was he here for her? Excitement obliterated guilt for a moment or two.

Greeting him would be torture, but if she ignored him that might seem suspicious. He was her brother-in-law.

A cocktail waitress stopped near the senator, and Eliza excused herself, wandering toward Brandon, greeting people on her way.

He saw her, and those brooding eyes darkened.

"This is a far cry from my Friday parties." She hoped to lighten the air between them.

He scanned the opulent room. "I can see that." And then his gaze roamed over her black sparkly cocktail dress again, dipping low in front and ending just above her knees. Her Jimmy Choo shoes brought her closer to his six-two height.

"Nice suit," she said, then immediately regretted it.

She was married to his brother and flirting shamelessly. After that kiss, how could she not? If he weren't her husband's brother, she'd probably have an affair with him.

"Did David make it back to the ranch?"

"No."

She checked the door and the thickening crowd. He'd been doing this a lot lately, abandoning her for his own agenda. Withdrawn and disinterested. Neglecting her. She was afraid that was directly related to her unresolved feelings for Brandon.

"Did he know you were coming?" she asked.

"I haven't seen him."

Her brother wasn't there, either. Since he was the reason for the party, she'd be embarrassed if he didn't show. Another check at the door produced Ryker. Her mood brightened. At least she wouldn't have to worry about explaining why her brother didn't show up at his own birthday party. He and his wife looked stunning. Six feet tall with brown hair and green eyes, Ryker was handsome in khaki pants and a white golf shirt. Aegina looked incredible in her little black dress, red hair up in a stylish clip and green eyes brighter than Ryker's.

Behind them, her mother appeared. She was plump around the middle in a layered and flowing blue dress, and her graying hair was short now. She'd come out of her severe depression after losing her husband but was a quieter version of the mother Eliza had once known. She had her occasional bubbly moments, but losing her husband had devastated her. Her mother never really seemed to move on. Once you loved someone that deeply, there were no replacements.

Seeing her, Ryker led his wife and their mother over.

"Happy birthday." Eliza hugged him, and he stiffly hugged her back.

"You could've stopped by the house. The kids keep asking why we had to leave them at home."

It was a deliberate jab. "I'll make it up to them."

"Eliza, look at you. You're my beautiful girl." Her mother came in for a hug.

"Thanks, Mom."

"I'm so proud of you."

She always said that. Over her shoulder, Ryker smothered a glare.

"Stop it, Ryker." His wife elbowed him. "Eliza went to a lot of trouble planning this fabulous party for you."

Sidling between Brandon and Eliza, her mother took in the room in delighted amazement. "Wow."

"She's come a long way," Brandon said.

Eliza wondered what he meant.

"Where's your husband?" Ryker asked derisively. He had always thought David was selfish and now he was married to Eliza, who was equally selfish in his opinion.

She didn't answer. She couldn't. The truth was too complicated.

Brandon noticed her sinking mood. "I'm going to get a drink. Would you like anything?" he asked everyone.

"A pinot grigio." Aegina Harvey was full of life. "I can't pass up a night without the kids!"

"I'll have the same."

This was the brightest Eliza had ever seen her mother since her father died.

"I'll go with you," Ryker said.

Brandon waited for Eliza to answer. "Nothing for me."

That gave him pause, and then he went with Ryker to one of the four bars. She was glad for the reprieve from both of them.

"He'll get over it, Eliza," Aegina said. "He goes through this every time you come here to visit."

Her mother hooked her arm with Eliza's. "I keep telling him to change his attitude."

"Why does he blame me for leaving Vengeance?"

"You knew what you wanted at eighteen," her mother said.

"And Ryker didn't figure that out for himself until it was too late," Aegina added.

That wasn't enough for Eliza. "He wanted to be a doctor. He always talked about it growing up."

"Yeah, but notice how he never did anything about it?"

Aegina's tone caught Eliza's attention. She glanced at her mother, not sure she should say anything more. Her mother did it for her.

"He feels he was forced to stay in Vengeance because of me. Responsibility isn't part of his vocabulary."

"He moved in with me before you did," Aegina pointed out.

Ryker had fallen in love, and that was why he had stayed. Then why did he resent Eliza?

"He didn't have the gumption that Eliza had. He didn't go to college because he didn't want it badly enough. That's why I don't move out of the carriage house, you know. He's so confused he doesn't even know he's in denial."

Eliza laughed a little and so did Aegina.

"Maybe that's why he doesn't love me anymore," Aegina said.

Though she joked, Eliza could see she was serious. "He loves you. He must. Why else would he have stayed?"

"At first he may have believed he loved me. But as soon as he realized everything he gave up, that all changed."

This was new, alarming news. Didn't Aegina believe

Ryker was only going through a phase? One that had lasted ten years…? "Are you two okay?"

She snagged a flute of champagne from a passing waiter. "Oh, yeah, we're fine. What do you expect after a decade of marriage?"

"Love." The kind her parents had before her dad had died. The kind Eliza never planned to have. She loved David, but he was more of a pal. Pals were safer.

Unless they were Brandon Reed…

She caught the faraway look in her mother's eyes and knew the talk about love had sent her back in time. Eliza never wanted anyone to catch her looking like that.

Ryker returned with the wine. Brandon wasn't with him.

A quick survey found him talking to a stacked brunette just south of the bar. Why that chafed her, she'd rather not explore.

With a scowl, her brother handed their mother her wine and then his wife's, watching in disgust as she drained the champagne glass with one hand and took the pinot with the other.

The band started playing. Many in the crowd cheered. Even Eliza was impressed with the turnout. If only Brandon could appreciate it as much as she did.

"When are you going back to Hollywood?"

Ryker sounded as though he couldn't wait for her to go. "We planned a week here."

"Can you handle being away from all that excitement for so long?"

"It's not excitement, Ryker. It's my job. My business."

"You have a fascinating job. You get to meet rich and famous people," Aegina said, sipping her wine and taking in the party.

"She craves that. Don't get too close to Eliza. She'll

leave you in the dust without a backward glance in her pursuit of good times and lots of money."

"You're not exactly slumming it," Eliza's mother interrupted. He was being unfairly harsh.

"In Vengeance, Texas."

Aegina drank some more, but Eliza caught the hurt in her eyes.

"You have a wife and family here."

Ryker drained his whiskey and placed it on the table next to Aegina's empty champagne glass. "I'm going to go mingle. It's my birthday party after all." He zeroed in on Eliza. "Or is that what this is all about?"

"Of course it is. What else would it be?"

"Another way for you to be the life of the party." With that, he walked off.

"If he's so damn unhappy, why the hell doesn't he divorce me and move to the East Coast like he's always complaining he would have done?"

"Because he loves you," Eliza said.

"He loves his kids, too," her mother added.

"He loves you, too, Mom."

"Oh, I know that." Her mother swatted the air with her hand.

Aegina grunted contemptuously. "He accuses you of being selfish. What does that make him?"

Eliza had never thought of it that way. Her brother always made her feel guilty for leaving him here. And he was doing the same to his own wife. She tied him to Vengeance the same as his mother. Or at least that's how he'd calculated it in his mind. "Selfish."

Aegina shook off the slight sheen in her eyes. "You aren't selfish, Eliza. You went after your dream and got it. That's admirable. Don't let anybody tell you otherwise."

"Hear, hear." Her mother lifted her wine and then sipped.

Eliza's first impulse was to agree. Something kept her from letting it carry her away. Why had she gone to Hollywood, and why had she worked so hard to be among the best event planners in the country? Moreover, why hadn't she spent more time here in Vengeance, with her mother and her brother?

The answer was standing across the room, a woman jabbering away while all he did was stare at her. For a moment, she slipped into that gaze, so full of impossible fantasies. If only…

The woman followed his gaze, and Eliza recognized Jillian. Her face tightened with jealous intimidation. Covering it before saying something to Brandon, she managed to capture his attention. He said something back that made her smile. And then he took two glasses of champagne from a passing waiter and handed her one. She beamed even more. The woman had it bad for him. The poor thing.

As she sidled closer to him, she looked across the room at Eliza, pure triumph and a dash of warning. If that wasn't a hands-off sign, Eliza didn't know what was. Brandon better be careful. If he kept leading Jillian on like that, she might do more than pound on his door and yell.

Chapter 3

The party was a hit. The whole town would be talking about it tomorrow. Eliza would probably be in the local paper. The Vengeance High School bad girl was back with a bang. Good thing his stupidity wouldn't be printed. How could he have allowed that kiss to happen? Brandon was still cursing himself, and guilt came at him in waves. How could he do that to his own brother? A brother who was missing and could be in trouble while they enjoyed a party.

Watching her direct the cleanup, Brandon knew deep down why he'd kissed her. He'd watched her all night—to make sure Jillian didn't try anything. But as the night had gone on, something else entirely drove him. The Eliza he remembered thrived on being the center of attention, and tonight she'd done it without stealing her best friend's boyfriend or dancing on the bar with a beer in her hand. She'd changed. Matured. Brandon had to commend her for turning her bad habits into a lucrative career.

Her brother had left hours ago, when people had first

begun to leave around ten. He'd practically had to drag his wife with him. She'd wanted to stay with the rest of the diehards who hadn't left until midnight. This wasn't a nightclub. It was a birthday party for a thirty-seven-year-old. One David hadn't shown up for.

Something had to be driving him away from Eliza. After witnessing her hosting this event, he wasn't as convinced she was the main cause. David hadn't come to Brandon for help, and that could only mean bad news. What kind of trouble had he gotten himself into this time? And did the note Eliza had received have something to do with it? Brandon didn't think so. Jillian might have sent it. He couldn't be sure, though. He'd been busy all day around the ranch and hadn't seen anyone drive up. It could have been anyone.

But Jillian was his first bet. She'd shown up here tonight as though nothing had happened. He'd been civil with her because they were in public. He was afraid that had encouraged her. She'd left happy, sending him bedroom eyes as she waved goodbye around eleven. Crazy woman. If he hadn't been there, would she have gone after Eliza? He wouldn't take the chance.

Checking his watch, Brandon had an idea of where he'd find David. Unless something had happened to him. Hopefully, he was all right and only drinking his troubles away for the day. Or gambling again.

When all that was left was the hotel staff, Eliza finally noticed him. Or maybe she had noticed him and hidden it by pretending to be busy until now. That kiss had to be weighing on her, too.

She approached him and stopped a few feet away, keeping her distance. "What are you still doing here?"

He'd have to make extra sure he never touched her

again. "I think I know where David is." He pushed off the bar and started for the door.

"Where?"

"The Cork. We have about an hour before they close."

"How do you know he's there?" She walked with him toward the exit.

"I don't. It's worth a try, though. He goes there every time he comes to town."

"He spends all afternoon and night there?"

"It's a favorite nightspot. I'm hoping he's there."

Outside, she walked beside him. "I'm not so sure I want to find him."

Because he'd kissed her or because David hadn't shown up tonight?

"We need to make sure he's all right." He opened his big diesel truck's door. "We'll get your car later."

Reluctantly, she climbed up into the cab and he shut the door, annoyed that he was aware of every curve in that dress of hers.

He drove away from the hotel. The tension was palpable between them. He could almost feel her thinking about that kiss, just like him, and at the same time wondering why David had disappeared all day. If something had happened to him, Brandon wasn't going to like the guilt trip that would surely follow. While he and Eliza had been groping and hot for each other, David could have been running from gangsters, gambling debt collectors

He had to get his mind off that. "I noticed you didn't drink at all tonight. Did you quit or something?"

"I never drink when I work."

"It was your brother's birthday party."

She shrugged. "I don't drink much anymore."

That was new. She hadn't drunk much the night before, so she must be telling the truth.

"What made you come to the party?" she asked.

He'd rather not tell her he came to protect her from Jillian. Even when she was in grade school he'd had the instinct to do that. Apparently that had never gone away. He was glad she was staying at his ranch so that he could keep an eye on her.

"Curiosity." What he'd intended to be a lie turned out to be partly true. That was the other reason he'd come here tonight. To see if she'd changed at all. She had, and he worried he liked it too much.

She smiled. "Did you think I'd still be dancing on bar tops?"

He chuckled, that old attraction coming back. Only now it was a lot stronger. He fought the building desire that threatened to set aside reason. Eliza may have grown up, but she was still a party girl.

Parking in front of the brick-and-white-trimmed bar, Brandon saw his work truck the same time Eliza did.

All her animation fled. "There's your truck."

She both looked and sounded so deflated, and it seemed as though more than catching David drinking had triggered it. Why was she upset? Because their moment of reuniting would come to an end? Or did finding David here instead of with her hurt her that much?

Why? She didn't actually love him, did she?

"Why did you marry him?" he asked out of annoyance.

After shooting a look at him, she didn't respond. She didn't have to. They both knew she'd married him to spite Brandon. Now David was out of control and she and Brandon were fighting this damn attraction that he had thought they were both over. Why couldn't she have married someone else? Someone who wasn't from Vengeance. An actor or something. Then she'd have her limelight that she craved so much and she wouldn't have to come for family visits.

He stepped out of the truck. When she didn't do the same, he came around to her side and opened the door. She kept staring at the front entrance to the Cork, as though dreading what she'd find inside.

He couldn't resist her. "Don't worry, I'll be with you. We'll get him and bring him home."

"It isn't that." She lowered her head and then lifted it to meet his gaze, her eyes full of sorrow.

"What's wrong, Eliza?" he asked softly.

After a brief hesitation, she began, "He's been acting strange lately."

"Drinking too much?"

Again she hesitated. Whatever troubled her, she didn't want to say. She was humiliated and would rather not go into the bar. Did she know about David's gambling problem? It didn't seem so. And there was no gambling at the Cork.

"He's probably with another woman," she said at last.

David? He'd never known his brother to be unfaithful to any woman. Was it only her insecurity, or had he really gone off the deep end?

Cheat on Eliza? She was stunning and beautiful. Who could David prefer over her?

"David wouldn't cheat on you," he said.

Her eyes disagreed with him and made his brow crease in question.

"It's not just that," she said self-consciously, not wanting to talk about it. "H-he…keeps looking over his shoulder…taking his cell phone outside to talk. Like he's afraid of something."

While that wasn't the real reason she'd rather not go into the bar, it was another thing that troubled her about

David. Alarm somersaulted through Brandon. David's gambling debts had mushroomed in the past few months, ever since he had married Eliza. Except she didn't seem to know about that.

"What's he afraid of?"

"He won't talk to me about it. I try, but..."

He was too busy screwing other women. He could swear that's what she was thinking. It was so unlike his brother, the Casanova who lured women by charming them into believing he was a gentleman. Was it all a facade? He was a little conceited....

"Do you want to wait out here?" It might be better for her.

"No. I have to face this."

When she started to step out of the truck, he helped her with his hands on her hips and she put hers on his shoulders. He lowered her, and she stood right there for a second too long. A second was all it took to feel enough of her to want more. He moved back, and Eliza marched to the entrance.

She opened the door before he could do it for her. And then she stopped short when she saw David sitting at a booth—right beside Jillian.

Brandon did the same. This he hadn't anticipated. Catching him with a woman was one thing, but Jillian...

What was she doing here with his brother? She wouldn't try to sleep with David, would she? Would David sleep with her?

There were a few other patrons in the bar. An old man who paid his tab to the bartender, talking to the young man as if he was a regular. A handful of tables were occupied. Laughter and an Elton John song playing from the jukebox filled the air. Willa Merris and another grade-school teacher sat at the booth beside David and Jillian, deep into some discussion. Willa's long strawberry-blond hair gleamed under the dim bar lights. Her father kept her in upper-class social circles and it was odd seeing her here. At this low-end bar.

Not as odd as finding his brother with Jillian. Had she deliberately arranged this? Why?

Jillian lifted her dark drink and sipped. As she lowered her glass, she caught sight of Brandon and her eyes popped open wide.

He stopped with Eliza at the booth.

"Well, look who's here," David slurred.

Eliza folded her arms indignantly, but the sexy cock of her hips in that slinky dress diffused her seriousness. "Is this why you didn't show up at my brother's party?"

"I thought you'd prefer it that way." Scorn dripped off him like the alcohol swimming in his blood. "Did you two have a good time?"

What did he mean by that? "Why haven't you been back at the ranch?" Brandon asked.

"Three's a crowd, *brother.*"

As in him, Eliza and David? Did he actually believe…?

"I don't know what's gotten into you, but there is nothing going on between me and Eliza." He had to know Brandon had no intention of pursuing her. He couldn't call her wild anymore, but she still craved the spotlight. His mind hadn't changed about her.

"I saw the way you looked at her last night." He drained his drink.

Seeing Eliza had taken him aback. He'd forgotten just how striking her beauty was. He'd rather not think about kissing her. Not knowing how to respond, he decided it was better not to.

Instead, he met Jillian's discontented eyes and wondered how long it would be before the she-snake in her struck.

"What are you doing here?" he asked her.

She passed David an uncertain glance. "I ran into him when I left the party. David was just arriving."

"She told me *you* were there." David's drunken reproach landed on Brandon.

"He drew his own conclusions," Jillian quickly added. "And then invited me to accompany him here. I agreed, but only to make sure he made it all right. He'd already had something to drink, so I drove his truck. My car is still at the hotel."

That was more explanation than he needed. She was covering her tracks. She hadn't intended for Brandon to find out she was here…with his brother. Her uncertain look earlier had him suspicious. What had they been discussing when he and Eliza had arrived?

The news relaxed Eliza. She lowered her arms. David wasn't with Jillian to sleep with her.

"Jillian's been quite a chaperone," David said. "I've been sitting here with her trying to figure out why you broke up with her. I mean, I could understand if you knew she—"

"Maybe I should drive you back to Brandon's ranch now," Jillian interrupted, turning from David to Brandon. "Then maybe you and I can talk."

They had nothing to talk about. Or did they? What had David been about to say? She was obviously hiding something. And he didn't believe she was here by coincidence.

"I'll drive him home." Brandon would like to question her, but his drunk brother was his first priority. "You take his truck, and I'll arrange to pick it up tomorrow." Eliza moved forward and extended her hand to David. "Come on, David. You and I can talk about this tomorrow…when you're sober."

"I don't need to be sober." He waved her hand away. "And I'm not going back to the ranch."

"David…" Eliza was clearly mystified. "Why?"

"I'm doing you a favor, Eliza." Pain and resentment laced his tone. "Go home with Brandon. That's what you wish for." He turned to Brandon. "It's what you both wish for." And then more somberly, "You belong together anyway."

"That's enough, little brother," Brandon said. He'd had enough of this nonsense. "Let's go."

He took hold of his brother's arm to help him up from the booth.

David yanked free. "If I go anywhere, it'll be with Jillian." He turned to her. "Right, sweetheart?"

Jillian turned a narrow-eyed, warning look to David. Was David threatening her? Why had he called a woman he barely knew sweetheart? Had he discovered something about her? Once he had David alone and sober, he'd be sure and ask.

"Brandon, come back to the ranch with us," Eliza said.

Brandon shot a look at her. David went utterly still.

"I—I mean…David," she corrected.

David smiled without humor, calculating and cruel. "You see? You're even saying his name instead of mine now."

"You drank too much," Brandon said. "You're overreacting."

"It was an accident. It doesn't mean—"

"Come on, Eliza, let's not pretend what this marriage is all about," David cut her off. "We both know it's him you've always wanted. I only married you so I could see what all the fuss was about."

Eliza drew in a sharp breath just as the jukebox went silent with the last notes of piano music. She gripped Brandon's jacket sleeve. David's insensitivity was hurting her. Why was he acting this way? It couldn't be that he truly believed his own brother fancied his wife.

"Brandon doesn't want Eliza," Jillian said to David. "She's married to you. Besides, Brandon and I are seeing each other."

The woman really grated his nerves when she did that, talking as though he hadn't broken up with her and she hadn't gone crazy on his front doorstep.

"He doesn't care about you," David said and sneered. "He doesn't care about any woman. Except maybe Eliza here. Other than her, all he cares about is himself and that ranch of his."

Eliza's face had gone pale. "That isn't true."

David got up from the booth and staggered to her, making a show of running his gaze down to her hand still gripping Brandon's sleeve and back up again. "Yes, it is."

Jillian slid out of the booth and hooked her arm with David's. She said to Brandon, "I'll drive him home."

"I don't want to go back to the ranch. Let's go to your place."

"David—"

"Now," David growled, making Jillian's head flinch ever so slightly.

This was not the brother Brandon had grown up with. This man Brandon felt like punching. The way he'd just given Jillian another order kept him from acting. It was as if David had something on her, whatever she had stopped him from saying earlier.

David rounded on Eliza, cold eyes scathing. "I want an annulment. I can't believe I was stupid enough to marry you." And then he began walking toward the door, his arm around Jillian's waist.

Jillian looked back apologetically at Brandon and mouthed, "I'll take him home."

They left through the door. David didn't want to be anywhere near him or Eliza. What bothered Brandon was that all it had taken to send his brother walking was seeing Eliza with him. The friction hadn't been there after they'd first been married. Clearly David had worried his wife still felt something for his brother. Seeing them together had confirmed his suspicion.

Beside him, Eliza silently cried.

Anger boiled up hotly in him. He had sound reasons for letting Eliza go all those years ago. She may not be as wild as she once was, but she still put her parties ahead of anything else, just as he'd predicted. David hadn't seen that about her. He was accustomed to women falling all over him. He was a good-looking man. And now he thought Brandon and Eliza wanted to be together.

When had David become so vulnerable? Since he'd started gambling and drinking and doing drugs? Or since he'd married Eliza, the one and only woman who didn't worship him? That had to be it. He must have discovered that her parties came first. She didn't care about him as much as he needed her to. It wasn't that she wanted Brandon more. In the morning, he'd make sure David understood that.

As David and Jillian left the bar, Eliza turned to him, still crying. Brandon took her into his arms, all his conviction to stay away from her vanishing. She buried her head against his chest and cried while everyone in the bar watched. In grade school some boys had bullied her and he'd comforted her after chasing them away. Now she was a grown woman with grown-woman tears pouring out of her.

Would she be this upset if she didn't love his brother? He hoped she did. How terrible would it be if David was right about them? Seeing her for the first time in years had struck him intensely. More intensely than he'd anticipated. He thought he was long over her. Seeing her stirred up too much old chemistry.

Sparing her any more of this public display, Brandon guided her outside. At his truck, he lifted her onto the seat, her legs over the side. He brushed her heavy, silky dark brown hair away from her face. It fell back down, swooping across her face. He tipped her chin up a bit.

She sniffled and those sad eyes met his. "He doesn't think our marriage is real."

Was it? Brandon would have guessed not. But Eliza obviously had believed it was. Despite her unspoken motive to make Brandon jealous or otherwise regretful for ever letting her go, she'd intended to stay with David. Maybe she really did love him.

"He's been drinking. People say things they don't really mean when they drink."

"I should have known better," she said. "I shouldn't have married him." She wiped tears from one cheek and then the other.

He wished she hadn't married him. None of this would be happening if she hadn't. "It was a little impulsive."

She wiped another tear with the back of her hand. "I didn't mean to hurt him."

Was that why she was crying? Her sweet sincerity cracked his resolve. He was tall enough to be eye level with her. He touched her damp cheek and let his hand rest on her shoulder, wanting to comfort her.

"I'll talk to him tomorrow." He'd set him straight.

With his deep murmur, Eliza's sniffling stopped and she blinked away the last of her tears. "You will?" Her gaze drifted softly over his face.

"Of course."

She was his brother's wife, and he'd do all he could not to get between them. Looking into her blue eyes, the energy shifted. He slid his hand to the base of her head. In the warmth of the moment, she leaned closer. Relentless desire made him close the distance.

Their lips melded together, slow and tender. She ran her fingers into his hair, and he both heard and felt her breath.

He wrapped his free hand around her waist and pressed her torso closer. She responded by parting her legs to make more room for him. He kissed her harder, fisting some of her hair and tugging her head back so that he could kiss her neck.

"Brandon."

He wanted her so much. Kissing her mouth again, he drank in the sound of his name.

Headlights shone as a car passed in the street.

Brandon pulled back. Eliza's beautiful eyes were droopy with desire. Her breasts were crushed against his chest. His hardness lodged against the heat between her legs.

"Damn it," he hissed, pushing back and walking to the front of his truck, where he paused to pound the hood and lean over with his hands braced there, head bent, furious with his loss of control.

How could he vow to talk sense into his brother one second and get between the same brother's wife's legs the next? This persistent attraction had to stop. And yet he felt powerless in its grasp. When he was kissing Eliza, the world retreated to an untouchable place.

He lifted his head and saw Eliza watching him, her hand over her mouth, equally appalled.

Having showered and dressed more than an hour ago, Eliza sat curled in a chair near one of the windows in the guest room. There was a beautiful view of a rolling, tree-lined pasture through the giant bedroom window. Cattle grazed beneath a partly cloudy sky. The scene of such peace clashed with the confusion singeing her on the inside.

David hadn't come back to the ranch last night. It was after lunch already. He was probably still with Jillian. Punishing his wife and brother.

And how could she fault him? Twice now she'd kissed Brandon. She hadn't been back in Vengeance three days and already she was carousing with another man. David didn't know what she'd done. He didn't have to. He accused her of being stuck on his brother. She was, in a way, but things were different now. And then not. Brandon still wouldn't want her, but Eliza wasn't an over-the-moon adolescent anymore.

While she didn't fully understand why Brandon had allowed the second kiss to happen, the way he'd looked at her through the windshield of his truck would be permanently scorched into her memory. One more to add to the fantasy that was Brandon. He desired her. Passion had never been their shortcoming. But what they'd done was wrong. David was Brandon's brother.

Would David even care? He wanted an annulment. Their marriage hadn't meant enough to him to call it a divorce, and she had no right to be angry with him.

Their marriage was going sour because of her Brandon fantasies. For years she hadn't been able to keep them away. Every once in a while they transported her to a fictional world, one where he was with her. She secretly yearned for him. Everybody wanted what they couldn't have, right? That was her only problem. Had it truly led to the poor state of her marriage? She found it difficult to accept.

There had to be more to it than just her. David had cheated on her. The disrespect he'd shown her by having sex with another woman less than six months into their marriage hinted at deeper problems. Eliza hadn't had an affair with Brandon and she wouldn't.

Even as the thought came, the truth taunted her. Both times she'd kissed Brandon, the invitation for sweet passion had ruled. David had not entered her conscience, not even the peripheries of it. And his declaration to seek an annulment hadn't pained her much. Her failure in marriage had. So had the cause of David's change of heart.

Other than an ego wound, his infidelity didn't hurt her. What hurt her was the truth behind why she'd married him. She'd entertained the possibility that doing so would get back at Brandon for rejecting her. It hadn't seemed so big back then, just an innocent triumph, one only she would enjoy. Now it rocked her, how shallow she'd become. That she would minimize marriage so much. Six months ago, she'd rationalized that it was better than loving someone who didn't love her back. And David had the added bonus of being Brandon's brother, the next best thing to perfection. Except he'd turned out to be far less.

That pained her. She truly hadn't meant to hurt him. She hadn't really believed her feelings for him mattered that much. As long as he loved her it would be enough.

She'd been mistaken. Kissing Brandon proved it. The deep, raw feelings he stirred were so much more powerful than they had been years ago. That frightened her like nothing else could. Love had to be reciprocated, and

Brandon would never feel the way she did for him, now or ever. He wouldn't allow it.

She was in a loveless marriage, still yearning for a man she could never have. It was disheartening, not having the ability to lock him out of her heart, move on without him, forget him forever. Be happy. As always, happiness eluded her. Her company filled that void. Her success. Her popularity. Marrying David was supposed to be fun, like running her company was. What a fool she'd been.

Despondent, she got up from the chair. She had to do something. She couldn't keep waiting for David to return so that she could face the pitiful demise of her faux marriage.

Outside, she headed for the stable. She'd been gazing at this beautiful land all morning. It was time to explore.

The stable was empty, but there were horses in separated corrals. A pretty palomino whinnied and bobbed her head, white-streaked mane flowing. Eliza brought the communicative mare into the stable to saddle her. When her father had been alive, they had lived on a farm. Eliza missed those hardworking days when nothing plagued her, when the world was full of optimism and death was something that happened to other people.

As she climbed atop the big horse, it dawned on her that she hadn't been riding since her father had died. Reining the well-trained palomino out of the stable, she headed for the emerald hills of Brandon's ranch.

When the ranch buildings disappeared from view and she topped another hill, she stopped the palomino. In the valley below, Brandon finished closing a pasture gate; the cattle he'd just herded with two of his ranch hands were inside. The clouds overhead were gathering into what might develop into a thunderstorm. Eliza considered turning back.

Brandon saw her just before he mounted his big red horse. Saying something to the two other men, he reined his horse in her direction. The two other men rode away in another direction. It was probably too early to quit for the day, so he was probably going to catch up with them after he talked to her.

Eliza wasn't sure how he'd feel about her taking the liberty of riding one of his horses without asking. She was too impulsive to wait for permission.

Watching him send his horse into a gallop as he approached, Eliza felt a surge of anxiety. It wasn't wise to be alone with him in any setting. As he drew nearer she saw his flat-lined mouth. Was he annoyed? Had he approached her out of courtesy?

His horse blew out a long breath of air as he stopped beside Eliza and her horse. The way his gaze wandered all over her wasn't deliberate. It seemed involuntary.

"I forgot you grew up on a farm," he said.

He'd forgotten *her,* so that didn't surprise her. "I'll take care of her when we get back." And had he said that to cover up his unwanted interest?

"Willow is one of my best horses. She loves to get out and run."

Eliza smiled. "I can tell." She patted the mare's neck and received an answering bob of her head along with a nicker.

He watched her, fondness for her practiced ease on a horse smoothing out his mouth into an ever-so-slight curve of amusement. "You look good on her."

"Minus riding pants." She extended her leg a little to show him her fashionably holey jeans and expensive loafers.

He chuckled, at home on his land and at peace. She

didn't think she'd ever seen him this relaxed before. Riding in nature did that for her, too. It had been too long.

"As long as you're out, I might as well show you around." He turned his horse.

Ignoring the nagging voice in her head that warned of the temptation driving them both to do something they'd regret, Eliza prodded Willow forward to walk beside Brandon. "What's there to see other than a bunch of cows?"

He feigned insult. "Those are prime-grade Wagyu and Angus cattle."

"I'll remember that the next time I eat steak at the Prime House." The restaurant was the kind that would meticulously age the meat bought from ranchers like Brandon.

Nothing but the sounds of the horses walking leisurely along, the squeak of leather saddles and chirping birds passed for a few strides.

"Where's David?" Brandon finally asked. "I didn't want to wake him this morning."

"He isn't back yet." She was careful not to look at him, instead trying hard to stay immersed in the beauty that surrounded her.

"He's not?" Worry laced his tone.

Maybe she should be, too. "He must still be with Jillian."

Brandon took some time to think. "I've never known him to cheat on a woman."

Only now had he taken up that pastime. With her. "That's nice. He cheats on me and no one else."

"He's never been married before."

"Oh, well there you go.... That explains it." She let her hand slap gently down onto her thigh, the motion triggering Willow into a trot. "Whoa." She pulled on the reins, slowing the frisky palomino into a walk.

"You both rushed into it."

A blunt explanation and an accurate one. She almost thanked him for including David. "It would have worked if he'd have stayed faithful."

"Maybe."

"I was committed."

He glanced at her, doubtful and then not. Uncertain. Because of their kisses. She hadn't been committed then, had she? If she could kiss Brandon the way she had, how could she say she was committed to a marriage with his brother? Is that what he'd concluded after last night?

"He would have stayed closer to home if he had a wife who wanted the same," Brandon said.

"I did."

He didn't believe her.

"Everything would have been fine if we hadn't come here," she told his frowning profile.

"Stay away from his family? That's no marriage."

That made her mad. She wasn't the only one to blame for this. "I didn't ask for a cheating husband, and I wasn't the only one involved in our kissing."

"No, but you didn't want commitment, either."

Her jaw dropped down. "You're not being very nice."

"You didn't. You never did."

"Commitment? Of course I did." He had gall saying that, the king of isolation.

She listened to the horses' hooves crunching over a dry, rocky patch. Anything to keep her cool.

"You're committed to event planning. A husband is only a prop to you."

She couldn't believe this. "Not everyone finds true love. You of all people should know that."

He turned his head toward her, more of a pounce with that direct gaze. "Your events are a surrogate to true love. You never give it a chance."

"I gave you a chance," she shot back. And look at the reward she got for that.

"I didn't have a chance in hell with you."

Taken aback, she stared at him, unable to zero in on just one comeback. What was he saying? That he'd have loved her if she hadn't put so much energy into event planning? That was ridiculous.

"If I hadn't walked away, you would have," he said.

Once again, his words rang true. At the time he'd walked, their relationship had reached a feverish pitch. Overwhelming, powerful emotion had gripped them. She could never get enough of him and could sense him struggling with the same. It had frightened her as much as it had frightened him. They were young and didn't know what to do with so much feeling.

But he attributed her partying to their demise. "What was I supposed to do? Not make a living?"

"I'm not saying it didn't work well for you. It did."

Work well for her?

"I just wish you would have chosen someone other than my brother to fill the void in your personal life, what there is of it."

The way he said it came across as harmless, the sound of his casual voice, the way he looked out across the land, a satisfied man on a ride. All the while his meaning hit hard. She was about to lay into him, then stopped herself. That note had been painfully accurate. So had David when he'd said he wanted an annulment. They'd both made a mistake getting married.

"You don't know anything about my personal life before I married David," she said quietly.

"I don't mean to judge you. I just call it the way I see it."

And for the most part he was right. The irrational side of her unwilling to agree, she faced forward. He termed it wrong. Filling a void wasn't what anyone aspired for when seeking a life partner. Some found love with less trouble than others, stumbled into it. Some searched doggedly and found it. No matter how, they found it. Eliza hadn't been so lucky. She'd thought she'd found her true love the first time Brandon had kissed her. To discover Brandon hadn't felt the same had been the shock of her life. She'd been so sure. And he'd turned on her. He'd abandoned her.

She had no animosity toward him. He'd been totally honest back then. He'd told her the truth. She'd dated many men after him. It was the ones who lied to escape a relationship that were the worst experiences, the ones she wished she could erase from memory. Men like that were too conceited. They treated her as if the truth would hurt more, as if losing them was so terrible. What was wrong with just saying they weren't interested? It happened. She'd had no interest in some of the men she'd dated, too. That's why men and women dated. To find the perfect match.

Maybe that was why she could never get over Brandon. He had a true, pure heart. He had honor and integrity. Even when he was fooling himself into solitude, he was a man to respect.

She looked over at him, her gaze drifting down his trim and muscular shoulders and arms, to flat abs and thick thighs straddling the horse. The candy that was always out of reach, denied her. She was denied her perfect match. All the men she'd wanted hadn't wanted her. Brandon had been one of those men, one who didn't want her. That was why she'd agreed to marry David. Didn't he see that?

"I was ready to share my life with a man when David came along," she finally said. She'd given up on finding her perfect match.

"Were you?" In her peripheral vision she was aware of him turning his head, waiting patiently for her to respond.

"Yes."

"You married my brother." Disbelief dripped from his tone.

She'd married David to fill a void and to spite Brandon. Because she wasn't over him. She'd never be over him. So, yes, parties were a surrogate to love. If he couldn't see the real and true reason for that, then she wasn't going to explain it to him.

Lightning flashed and thunder followed not long after.

"I think you're running from it," Brandon said, briefly noticing the lightning.

From love? She returned her gaze to him. "That's priceless coming from you."

"I'm not confused over what I want."

"Yeah, well, love isn't what you want."

"I'll take love—if it's right."

"What's right for you, Brandon? Someone who doesn't challenge you? Someone who won't pry you off this land, even for a night out?"

"I go out."

"You're so quick to ridicule me for making a career out of party planning—look at you. You've made a career out of being a loner. There's no bridge over the moat around your cold heart. No wonder Jillian turned to your brother. I bet she wasn't the first one!"

"Jillian didn't turn to him."

"Why was she with him then?" She was probably still

with him. "She doesn't have to sleep with him, or even love him, to use him to get to you."

"Sounds just like you, except you slept with David."

Eliza stopped arguing, stunned that he'd voiced his jealousy.

"Yeah, it bothered me that you married him."

"Why?"

He scowled at her as though she should know.

She didn't. How could she? Unless he still had feelings for her. And Eliza could not allow herself one crumb of hope that he did. She could not endure another heartbreak over him. The original one was still wreaking havoc on her life.

An outbuilding came into view. It was a yurt, and not just any yurt. It was designed much like a cottage, a warm and welcoming refuge in bad weather. With a quick check on the sky, she wondered if they were going to need it. There was even a small barn for horses. The charm went against her perception of Brandon. To her he was a hard worker with a great capacity for love that he shut himself off to. Why did he shy away from love so much? There had to be a reason.

She dismounted near the stream and let Willow drink. Brandon did the same.

"How come you never got married, anyway?" Willow's ears twitched with the sound of her voice and her whiskers moved as she drank.

"I haven't met the right one."

Such a simple answer, one that stung but also didn't dig deep enough into the truth. "Have you ever thought you were close?"

"Why do you ask?" he sounded wary.

Thunder rolled in the sky again. Willow lifted her head and perked her ears.

"You accuse me of using parties as a surrogate. I'm just curious as to what your excuse is."

"I have none."

When he didn't meet her eyes and instead scanned the land ahead, Eliza was sure she was onto something. Something about love scared him. It made her think of the day her dad had died.

She'd been a sophomore in high school. Ryker had come to her classroom and interrupted the teacher, telling her it was an emergency. Several possibilities sprang to mind, none of them involving her father in a tractor accident. Their dog had died. A horse had been seriously injured. One of her grandparents had fallen to old age. Never had it crossed her mind that either of her parents had died.

She'd gone with Ryker to the hospital, only to find their mother hysterical and in tears. She'd had to be sedated. The next week had been surreal. The funeral. Her mother's grief-stricken lethargy. Her sorrow had been all-encompassing. Eliza and Ryker had talked about their concern. Would she die, too?

Ryker had stepped in and taken care of her from the start. He'd taken care of his little sister, too. She could imagine the burden that had caused. She also had seen how the deepest love could destroy a person. Seeing the destruction of her mother's heart and soul, Eliza had feared falling in love. After Brandon had rejected her, she'd sworn off it altogether.

Had Brandon experienced something similar in his past? Remembering his mother had committed suicide when he and David were young boys, she wondered if that had played any kind of role in influencing him as a man. He'd grown up with only a father, one who'd gone to prison. What had his mother's life been like in those early years?

"Why did your mother kill herself?" she asked.

He swung his head to look at her, no doubt wondering where that question had come from. That brooding look that was his trademark descended. "Any woman who was married to my father probably would have killed herself."

She felt raindrops on her skin. "She did it because of him?" Talk around town had painted Brandon and David's father as a 24/7 drunk. The hit-and-run that had sent him to prison had confirmed it. "Because he drank?"

He mounted his horse. "Come on. Let's go into the yurt until this passes."

Scowling up at the sky for the interruption, she climbed up onto Willow and followed Brandon across the stream. At the yurt, they put the horses in the barn. The anticipation of being alone with Brandon kept her edgy and a little too excited. If her cavorting with him had ended badly in her teens, it was sure to end worse now if she allowed anything to happen. As easy as that kiss in the driveway had been, waiting out a thunderstorm in a remote yurt was pure folly...and enticement.

Chapter 4

Thunder accompanied lightning, and rain poured from the sky, splattering the dry ground. Brandon took Eliza's hand and ran with her to the yurt door, which had been left unlocked. Slamming the door, Eliza caught sight of a rough kitchen that took up one side and two cots on the other. Above and ahead, a loft provided cramped but extra sleeping space. A woodstove in the middle guaranteed warmth if it was ever needed.

She went to one of two front windows and watched the torrent outside.

"What was your dad like?" she asked idly. "You never talked much about him."

"With good reason."

Only then did she realize he stood right behind her. He moved to another window, removing his hat and putting it on the cot.

"Was he abusive?"

Something dark and forbidding emanated from him as he turned only his head to look at her. She'd received a similar reaction from David every time she tried to get him to talk about their father. Except David had always relied on distractions and his sense of humor to get her off the topic. Brandon relied on menace. Silent menace.

Eliza faced the window again.

So, their father *had* been abusive. She'd guessed as much a long time ago. Their mother had committed suicide, and now David was a cheating drunk and his brother was a surly recluse. The aftereffects of their miserable childhood? Losing their mother that way had to have been terrible for both of them. Things like that split families apart. But would it keep Brandon from finding love? From finding happiness?

She looked over at him watching the rain. Had he ever been happy?

The time he'd dared her to dance in her underwear in the city park came over her. They'd just started seeing each other. It was after one of her Friday parties. Brandon had always teased her about her wildness. She couldn't walk away from any of his dares.

She'd stripped to her bra and underwear, tossing her clothes at him. Very aware of him standing there holding her clothes and looking at her, she'd danced for him. Slow and sultry around the stop sign. She was a good dancer, party girl that she'd been, and he'd been entranced with her. His own personal pole dance. It wasn't long before her English teacher had strolled by with her husband.

"Eliza Harvey?" she'd called from across the street.

Brandon had taken her hand and run with her deep into the park, laughing as she dressed behind some bushes. She hadn't heard him laugh that hard since. She hadn't been around to.

Growing aware that she was still watching him, she saw that he was now watching her back.

"What were you just thinking about?" he asked, moving toward her.

He must have picked up on something or he wouldn't have approached her. "That time you dared me to dance in my underwear."

Stopping before her, he chuckled. "You did everything I dared you to do."

"Why wouldn't I?"

Her wildness had been what had driven him away. Why had he dared her and taken such pleasure in doing so if he didn't like it? Her wildness. Her daring. It was as if he'd needed a safe place. Safe from violence or anything resembling it.

Peace. Everything that surrounded him here.

The rain was beginning to abate.

"You mooned an old man, stole a neglected dog and took pictures of your brother's best friend with another girl."

She turned and leaned against the window frame. "And you loved it."

A happy light touched his eyes and remained, memories filling him whether he accepted them or not. For now he did because they made him feel good.

"My mother took care of that dog until the day it died, warm and safe and dry in her house." The old man who'd beaten him couldn't hurt him anymore.

The light in his eyes warmed her.

"Booger." That's what her mother had named the poor creature. Eliza laughed.

"I heard that old fart was kicked out of his house when they foreclosed on his mortgage."

"Moved to Kansas and died in a tornado," she finished. "I kept track of him, mainly to make sure he didn't buy any more dogs."

"Karma exists."

Her smile matched his as she met his eyes. His shaggy hair stuck out in all the right places. His broad shoulders loomed over her. Working on his ranch had sculpted his muscles over the years.

The joviality eased into another kind of warmth. Eliza was stuck back in time when all their cares and concerns were easily forgotten when they were together. They had good memories from back then. Eliza had focused on the negative ones until now, and she guessed Brandon had done the same.

"Do you remember the first time you kissed me?"

"I drove you home from school."

"About thirty times before you actually tried."

"Your dad saw us."

Her dad had died shortly after that. She'd started her Friday Party Club and Brandon had begun daring her.

With his index finger, he coaxed her head back to him. "I know how much you miss him."

If it hadn't been for Brandon, she might have been worse off than she already had been.

"He came out onto the porch to stop us."

"He liked me."

Eliza laughed. "He did not. You were too old for me."

"Senior. You were a sophomore."

"I was his baby girl."

"And then you were my girl."

She nearly blushed with the memory of the first time they'd had sex. He'd been her first. She'd never told anyone that, not even David. She'd lied and said a boy who was a junior had been the first, when she hadn't had sex with anyone else until she was twenty.

While she grieved for her father, Brandon was careful not to take advantage. It had been months later, the summer after her sophomore year. The same summer he'd broken her heart. By then her Friday Party Club had really taken off. By the time she had graduated from high school, the police were onto her and she'd had to stop.

As Brandon's hand slid to the back of her neck and his thumb caressed her jaw, Eliza knew he was traveling down the same path in history as her. She melted in his eyes, so much passion there. Rewind to yesterday when he'd kissed her in the driveway and the truck, and the dynamics changed.

If he kissed her now, again, it would be as a man, not the eighteen-year-old who'd taken her virginity and her heart. First loves were always unforgettable, but he was more than that to her. Somewhere in their youth, their souls had met and melded. There was no denying that. Even during those darkest months following his rejection, the truth remained doggedly in place. Theirs had been a rare joining.

Eliza waited with bated breath, lifting her head a bit to encourage him. She couldn't stop the desire racing through her.

He did kiss her.

Her breath whooshed through her nose, and she welcomed him deeper. His soft mouth moved over hers, so different from her memory. The foundation that had formed back then caught fire now. She looped her arms around him, her body pressing close to his. He slid his strong arm around her, bringing her firmly against him.

Eliza raked her fingers through his hair, loving the soft thickness, urging him for more. He gave her more, his tongue seeking hers. She'd dreamed of this.

Planting fevered kisses down her neck, he moved his hand from her head to her breast. She let her head fall back and moaned.

Breathing raggedly, Brandon lifted his head and stared down at her. Uncertainty made him hesitate.

Eliza couldn't bear for reality to intrude. Not yet. She moved her head to put her face under his ear, breathing him in. She kissed his skin.

An instant later, he lifted her and carried her to one of the cots. She reveled in all the masculine desire coming down on top of her, kissing her, ravaging her. She could feel his hardness through their jeans.

When he began to unfasten her blouse, a horse's snorting broke them apart. The sound hadn't come from the small stable.

Hissing a curse, Brandon got up off her and hauled her up after him.

She expected it to be David, out looking for her and Brandon, and wished she could hop on Willow and gallop away before he saw her. She wondered if he'd had that much decency this morning when he'd woken up in another woman's bed.

Brandon opened the yurt door.

The rain had stopped and the sun was peeking out, brushing the rolling landscape in vibrant shades of green and gold. One of his ranch hands guided his horse up from the stream.

He drew his horse to a halt. "Saw the lightning and came back to make sure you were okay. I didn't see you follow like you said you were going to do." His gaze passed over Eliza before returning to Brandon. "I didn't mean to interrupt."

Now Eliza's skin did flame to red. He thought they'd—

"It started to rain," Brandon said.

The cowboy nodded once, an awkward movement and a poor attempt to cover what must be obvious to him. "See you back at the house then."

The cowboy turned his horse back for the stream.

Brandon glanced at her, brooding as though this were all her fault. Sparked to annoyance, she pivoted and went to the small barn. If kissing her made him upset, then he should stop doing it!

Back at the ranch stable, Brandon suffered Eliza's help with the horses despite his insistence that he could do it without her. Ever since they were interrupted at the yurt, he felt like punching a hole in the wall. What was it about her that kept melting his self-control? She was his brother's wife.

"You shouldn't be here with me right now." Why didn't she just leave him alone?

She paused in brushing down Willow. "Why?"

"Because I feel like hitting something right now."

"Why do you feel like hitting something?"

"You have to ask?"

After a more lengthy pause, she faced him. "We keep kissing. Your ranch hand caught us. Why does that make you so mad?"

He stopped working on his horse and stood toe-to-toe with her. "Do you even care that David is missing?"

"He isn't missing. He's screwing another woman!"

He could understand her anger over that, but she had to be dealing with guilt of her own. "That makes it okay to sleep with me?"

"We didn't sleep together."

She needed more pushing. "David is my brother. Nothing is going to change that."

"And that's what makes you want to hit something?" She scrutinized him, disbelieving, fishing for information, for the real root cause of his turmoil.

"Go inside, Eliza."

"No. Go ahead and push me away because I'm getting too close. I care about David, but that isn't the only reason that has you so mad."

Stubborn woman. He resumed brushing his horse. That was better than acknowledging what she said. Any minute she'd have him kissing her again. Yes, that made him mad. Mad at himself. It hadn't been this hard to resist her when he was eighteen; why was it so different now?

His opinion hadn't changed about her. He didn't want her life. He wanted this life. Alone. With no danger of falling into the same patterns his father had fallen into. What he'd learned about raising a family terrified him. He never, ever would allow even the slightest chance of that occurring. That's why he was so careful about the women he dated. Only the one who struck the right chords, who fit into his life, would last. And so far he hadn't met her.

She had to be calm and quiet. Not extroverted, bold and outspoken. He and David had both been out of control growing up, especially after their mother died. His father had turned to violence to force control on them. Violence was never the answer to controlling your kids. Brandon preferred no family to one he had to control with force. He needed a woman who balanced him, one who'd keep him calm, not bring out every gene he'd inherited from his kid-beating father.

At last the horses were ready for their stalls and some dinner. Eliza knew exactly what to do, and when that impressed him, he grew even angrier with himself.

He walked toward the house, Eliza right beside him. He wondered if she did it on purpose. To see if he'd actually hit something. Damn her. She was tenacious and bold. Two qualities he avoided in women. He'd been controlled enough as a kid by his father.

A tan car parked on top of the hill on the road leading

to the yurt made him stop. He couldn't tell from here if it was a man or a woman inside.

"I saw that car when David and I first arrived," Eliza said.

She'd seen it? "Where?"

"Right there, at the top of the hill. He followed us here."

"The driver of the car was a man?"

"I'm not sure. The person was large enough to be, but the car was far away."

Brandon looked toward the hill. It was far away. Too far to identify the driver.

"At least we know it wasn't Jillian," she said.

Jillian had been inside with him. Was someone following David? How far would they go to get what they were after? And was that why his brother was nowhere to be found? Was he running? Hiding?

"Wait here." As soon as Brandon headed for his truck, the car moved, turning around and disappearing unhurriedly over the hill.

"That's what he did last time."

Foreboding thickened in him. Should he go after the car? By the time he caught up it would be too late. The driver had seen him head for the truck. He was racing away by now.

Brandon decided talking to David first would be best. If he ever found him. What if something serious had happened to him after he'd left with Jillian? She wasn't very stable emotionally. Except David wouldn't have rejected her. He was either staying away because he'd been followed or he suspected something was happening between Brandon and Eliza. Had he seen them this afternoon?

Brandon felt sick with the idea. He'd endured several

waves of sickness over his weakness for Eliza. Sick anger. Again he'd kissed her. His brother's wife.

Hell, he'd have done a lot more than that if his ranch hand hadn't come back for him. Too much history plagued him. He had to find David. Fast.

Inside, Brandon found his housekeeper in the kitchen. A tall, plump sixty-one-year-old widow who was quiet and kept to herself most of the time. He liked that about her.

"Have you seen David?"

She straightened from the dishwasher. "No."

"At all? Has he come back at all today?"

"I've been here since eight. No. He hasn't."

Something was wrong, more wrong than David sleeping around. Where was his brother? If he was having an affair, he wouldn't have stayed with the woman this long. Trouble or not, he would have come back for his things at the very least.

He found Jillian's number in his cell and called her. Leaving the kitchen, he almost ran into Eliza, whose eyes were round with matching worry. She must have heard him talking to the housekeeper.

"Brandon." Jillian sounded surprised.

"Is David still with you?"

"How are you? Is something the matter?"

"I'm looking for David. The last time I saw him, he was with you."

"He isn't with me. He drove me to my car after we left the Cork. He was upset that I wouldn't let him drive me home."

Damn. Where the hell was his brother? Real, strong worry swarmed him. David was in trouble again, and this time it was serious. "Where did he go?"

"He didn't tell me and I didn't ask. I didn't take him home, Brandon."

It was important to her that he believed her. He didn't doubt she hadn't slept with David. Given her reaction to their breakup, why would she do anything to jeopardize getting him back?

He almost asked her what David had been about to tell her and interrogate her about why David had been so upper-handed with her but decided now wasn't the time. He'd find David first.

"Will you please call me if you hear from him?"

"Of course. I promise I will."

He disconnected, real apprehension racking his nerves. Not much ruffled him, but this sure did. Someone was following David. He was afraid. Exactly what Brandon had feared could be coming true. David was in over his head, and now even his brother couldn't help him. That must be why he hadn't confided in him. Brandon had tried to talk him into stopping. No more gambling.

If only he would have listened....

Aegina kept mentioning that he should invite his sister over for a barbecue. Ryker ignored her this time, too. He wouldn't care if she never came back to Vengeance. He didn't know why she bothered. She'd planned his birthday party as a way to smooth things over with him, but the damage was done. She left him here in Vengeance and didn't lift a finger to help him with their mother.

Part of him argued their mother didn't need taking care of, only a roof over her head. But the roof was in Vengeance. Their mom wouldn't leave the town where she'd met and married their dad. It was all she had left of him.

It had been good seeing Eliza. He had to admit. She looked good. She seemed different now, too. Softer. Not as wild. And she still had it going for Brandon. He was surprised to see Brandon reciprocating. What a mess that would turn out to be. Eliza was married to his brother.

"Have you talked to Evan yet?" Aegina asked.

"No, why?"

She tucked her thick red hair behind her ear. "There's a boy bullying him at school."

"What's he doing?"

"He won't say. I was hoping he'd tell you." Her green eyes were distant, as though talking to him was a chore.

"I'll talk to him." This was the most they'd spoken to each other in more than a week. Aegina was drifting apart from him, and he didn't understand why. He'd asked her once and she'd given him a short answer that wasn't an answer at all. He was starting to think their marriage was in trouble.

That's all he needed. Add a failed marriage to his miserable life in this crappy town.

Ryker headed up the stairs and opened the first door in the hall. Evan sat on his red race-car bed, baseball glove on, catching a ball as he looked up.

"Got a minute, buddy?"

His son nodded. His green eyes that matched his were sad now.

Going to sit next to him, he caught the ball Evan tossed up again and rolled it in his hand. "Mom says somebody's giving you a hard time at school."

Evan averted his head without responding.

"Why don't you tell me about it."

"It's nothing."

"Tell me about it anyway."

"It's no big deal."

"I can see that by that happy face you're wearing."

Evan laughed at that.

"What did you do?" he coaxed.

"I didn't do anything!" Evan reported as Ryker had expected him to. "Bobby was picking on a girl, and I got between them. He wouldn't leave her alone!"

"You defended a girl? That's my boy." He smiled proudly. "What was Bobby doing?"

"He always calls her peppercorn and she doesn't like it. Her name is Judy Pepper. He makes her cry all the time."

"Why does she get upset when he calls her peppercorn?"

"She yells back at him so he thinks she has a bad temper. But she doesn't."

"You didn't do anything wrong. Why is he giving you a hard time?"

"He says I'm a girl. He always calls me a girl. In front of everybody!"

"What do you do when he calls you a girl?"

"Nothing. He's a lot bigger than me."

"Do you want me or your mom to talk to the principal?"

"No way!"

"Maybe you should just go punch him then."

"He's bigger than me."

Ryker wasn't sure how to handle this. He'd let it go for now. "If it keeps up, I'm going to have to call the principal. You know that, right?"

"Yeah."

"Handle it yourself or I will, okay?"

"Yeah." He sounded so down. But Ryker saw no other way.

After a bit, Evan looked up at him. "Are you and Mommy going to get a divorce?"

Did he know what a divorce was? "No. Why do you ask?"

"She always yells at you, and when you're not around, she says you love your job more than her."

Aegina didn't think he loved her? Where had that come from? No doubt about it. He had to do something. If it wasn't already too late.

Chapter 5

Exhausted from lack of sleep and worry, Eliza walked beside Brandon down Main Street the next morning. They'd searched most of last night for David. They hadn't found the ranch truck. They'd asked for him at hotels and restaurants. It was as if he'd vanished, left town. Eliza almost hoped that was the case, although her gut kept warning her that it was far more serious than that.

Their last stop had been the police station. He hadn't been arrested, and there had been no incidents reported the night before. It was too soon to report him missing.

Eliza no longer thought David had been with another woman all this time. Jillian might be telling the truth. He hadn't gone home with her. He'd gone somewhere else. But where?

"Maybe he went gambling," Brandon commented, his long strides gobbling up twice as much ground as hers.

Gambling? What was he thinking? "David gambles?" He was a professional sports journalist. He ran in the same elite circle as her. Until more recently, he didn't have any hang-ups. He wasn't addicted to anything. And he'd have to be to go gambling in the middle of the night.

Brandon turned to give her a funny look, like he wasn't surprised she didn't know but was testing her. "You didn't know he gambled?"

"No." He'd gambled in Vegas when they'd gotten married, but that was normal. This new side of him didn't mesh. Or maybe it did. She hadn't really known David all that well. Theirs wasn't exactly a close marriage.

"He's asked me to bail him out more than once," Brandon said. "He's asked me a lot since he married you."

There was that hint of blame again. "Are you saying I drove him to his reckless ways?"

"Haven't you noticed him gone a lot?"

"I thought he was out drinking." He had, but he'd also been gambling. If he lost more than he won, she could see how he'd accumulate some bad debt. The worst kind of debt. It wasn't as though he couldn't pay his credit cards. He couldn't pay gangsters. That explained his fear when they'd first arrived at Brandon's ranch, the way he'd looked over his shoulder, the car at the top of the hill.

Brandon met her eyes, and they shared the gravity of David's situation. She felt so helpless. What could they do? They'd done all they could until some sign of David, or David himself, showed up.

The waiting was killing her. David was missing, and she couldn't control her desire for his brother.

Brandon put his hand on her lower back and guided her to the other side of the street at a crosswalk. The turreted entrance of a café faced the corner, its doors open.

"What are we doing?" she asked.

"We have to eat something," he said as they reached the café.

Her stomach was empty, and she was lethargic from

lack of food. And worry about David. But she wasn't sure she could eat.

He told the hostess there'd be two for breakfast and she followed him to a table. A woman with her husband and two kids watched them. One of the waitresses did, too, leaning over to another worker to say something. That one's eyes rounded as she carried pitchers of tea and water into the kitchen.

Sitting across from Brandon, Eliza dismissed the unwanted attention and looked at him over a vase of dainty white carnations. "You said David went to you when he needed money."

"He did. But not this time."

"Why do you suppose he didn't? And don't say it was because of me." She wasn't going to put up with that anymore.

"Maybe he found someone else to turn to."

Someone else to bail him out? Why would he do that? Because of her relationship with Brandon?

Eliza turned her head, only vaguely aware of the semibusy café's polished wood floors and white crown molding. She had no relationship with Brandon. He'd made it clear he didn't want one, years ago and even now. If she went running from love after that, then he was the reason.

Unless she and Brandon were both letting too much of their past influence what was happening with David.

"Maybe it wasn't gambling that made him run," she said to Brandon.

"What else could it be?"

"Maybe he thinks you can't help him." If he was in that much danger…

"I can help him. No matter what kind of trouble he's in. He just didn't feel like he could because he married you."

"That wouldn't have stopped him." Even as she said it

she wasn't sure it was true. She and Brandon had dated in high school. If it had ended there, then she'd be more confident. Kissing him and feeling it all the way to her toes sort of negated any argument.

Still, she couldn't give up the possibility that David was in deeper than either of them had estimated so far. "Have you been after him to stop gambling? You helped him financially, but have you ever urged him to stop?"

"Of course."

And he hadn't. A waitress came to their table, and Brandon ordered coffee and breakfast. Eliza waved her off with a shake of her head.

"She'll have oatmeal."

She targeted him with her eyes as the waitress left.

"It's the best thing for an upset stomach. Nice and bland. And you have to eat something."

Eliza saw the worker whose eyes had widened pointing toward them. The woman beside her started toward them. Her short, straight and graying hair was mannish, and her black-rimmed glasses magnified bright blue eyes. She wore a red apron like the other staff members, her apple frame stretching the material tight around her middle.

"Good morning, Brandon," she greeted as she reached the table.

"Morning, Candace."

Brandon knew her? He smiled up at the woman with a familiarity that proved he did. Eliza wouldn't have thought he had any kind of popularity in town.

"It's not often we see you here this time of day. Leaving the ranch to your manager today?"

"Trevor is the best worker I've ever hired."

"You saved him by giving him that job. His divorce just about ruined him. That dragon he married took everything. Poison, that woman is."

"He's seeing a girl from town now."

Eliza could only gape at Brandon. This was not the Brandon of her teenage years. He was socializing as though he enjoyed it.

"No." Candace breathed her delight, eating up the gossip. "Who?"

"Ted's oldest girl. Charlene."

"Oh, she's a pretty one. Saving herself for the right one, too."

Brandon didn't cover his wince.

"Had her heart broken by a real rake." Candace nodded. "She and Trevor will be good together."

Did two people have to get their hearts broken to be good for each other?

"He's going to ask her to marry him this fall."

Candace beamed. "I was hoping he'd come around. You're a good man, Mr. Reed. Trevor wouldn't be where he is right now without you."

He chuckled while Eliza gaped at him some more. "You're exaggerating, but thanks." He registered Eliza's fascination and he noticed her surprise. She could tell.

"I hear you've been looking for your brother."

Eliza looked at Candace with Brandon. "Have you seen him?"

"Not since yesterday morning." To Brandon she said, "He was with a woman. A college girl named Naomi Peterson. She's getting her master's over at Darby."

David had found another woman to spend his time with. Eliza had to take a few seconds to recover from the blow. Not just one woman, but two. When Jillian refused him, he'd gone out in the middle of the night and found another. He refused to be at the ranch with her and Brandon. At least she and Brandon didn't have to go to the police. David was fine. Just fine.

"Where did you see him?" she asked Candace, concealing her anger.

Candace kept her eyes on Brandon as though nervous over Eliza's reaction to what she was about to say. "They came in for breakfast. They were…you know…real cozy. And it was late morning, like about this time."

"Did they leave together?" Brandon asked.

"They left the restaurant together. I don't know where they went from here. I didn't think to ask, either." She glanced warily at Eliza.

Funny how Eliza didn't care that David was with yet another woman. "Do you know where Naomi lives?"

"No, sorry."

The woman was genuine enough. Eliza wasn't going to calm her by explaining the state of her marriage, though.

On one of the televisions hanging from the walls of the café, a news program switched to Melinda Grayson's kidnapping. The anchorwoman announced a video had been released from her captor, and the screen showed a brief clip of her pleading for her life.

All three of them stopped to watch.

Melinda was disheveled, hair a mess, bruised and scared.

"Please, let me go," she sobbed one final time. And then whoever filmed her ended the clip. No demands had been made. It was as though her captor were taunting authorities. Maybe whoever it was got a thrill over doing so. Eliza felt ill imagining what horrors the woman was suffering. Minutes must seem like hours and days like months.

"That poor woman," Candace said. "Did you hear she was kidnapped?"

"Who would film her that way?" Eliza asked.

"A sicko."

"Has there been a demand for ransom?" Brandon asked.

"Not yet." A woman two tables away waved to get Candace's attention. "Duty calls. Good luck on finding your brother, Mr. Reed."

"Thanks."

With that she went to the other table, glancing frequently at the television. A news anchor reported there were still no leads to Melinda's whereabouts.

"Why do you think she was kidnapped?" Eliza asked.

"Hard to say. She's a popular professor. Who would be against her?"

Jillian's harsh words came to mind. "Didn't Jillian go to Darby?"

Brandon shot a look her way. "She disagreed with Melinda's thinking, but is that enough to kidnap her?"

And film her being miserable? "Maybe she wants to make a public statement."

"By turning to violence?"

"She yelled and pounded on your door after you broke up with her."

"She wasn't expecting it, that's all. I should have waited until the next day to do that."

"When it's time to run, it's time to run, right?"

"You would know more about that than me."

Did he really believe that? Seeing the passion in his eyes, she knew he did.

"You could make any girl run, Brandon."

Stormy anger flared in the radiance of his dark eyes, shadowed by a tensing brow. "Some of them should."

Did he mean her? She should run from him? She'd already done that, to save her heart. But why did she get the feeling he was referring to something else entirely?

* * *

Against Eliza's wishes, Brandon took her with him to track down Naomi and, hopefully, David. It seemed like his brother was all right, but Branson needed to be sure. He couldn't shake the nagging instinct that told him something was wrong.

Near the Darby campus, they waited in the parking lot of a plain, square brick apartment building with metal-framed windows. It was old and in need of a face-lift. The lines of the parking spaces were badly faded, and weeds grew from cracks in the lesser-traveled areas. Brandon had found Naomi through her Facebook page. One of her posts mentioned this apartment building. She should be more careful.

He spotted her get out of a car and head for the building as he walked beside Eliza. Her words still bothered him. He could make any girl run. She couldn't have stabbed closer to what he held inside if she tried. He hadn't made any woman run. Eliza held the only record for that one. He did try very hard not to, however. Priority number one with women was not making them feel like running. The first red flag was when he felt cornered, as he had with Jillian.

He'd felt the same with Eliza back when he was eighteen. She'd been his first lesson. The woman he married would complement him so perfectly, there'd be no conflict, no waters disturbed in the relationship. No stubbornness. No arguments. No insecurities whatsoever.

He glanced over at Eliza in her capri jeans and silky soft green top that brought out the green in her eyes. And no need to be the center of attention instead of the object of a man's love.

Gaining ground on the woman as she reached a narrow, uneven sidewalk leading to the front entrance, he called, "Naomi Peterson?"

The woman slowed long enough to look back but didn't stop walking.

"I'm Brandon Reed, and this is Eliza Reed."

"I'm David's wife," Eliza informed the woman.

That made her stop and turn. Brandon watched how she visibly stiffened and stared in fear at Eliza. Then she pivoted. "I'm running late." She walked faster up the sidewalk.

Brandon went after her. "Wait."

"I don't have time." She half walked, half jogged to the apartment entrance.

"We know you were with David yesterday morning," Eliza said from behind him. "We just need to know where he is now."

With her hand on the door handle, the woman hesitated and glanced over her shoulder.

"He hasn't contacted us," Brandon said. "We're concerned."

After hesitating a bit longer, Naomi said, "He dropped me off here after we had breakfast. I haven't seen him since." Her gaze shifted to Eliza. If it was after breakfast, then she must have spent the night before with him. From a little after 1:00 a.m. onward.

"What time did you have breakfast?" Brandon asked.

"Late. Around ten."

"Do you know where he was going?" Eliza asked.

"No. It was just one of those nights. I didn't care if I ever saw him again. We had fun, and that was it. He went his way and I went mine." She spoke to Brandon, giving Eliza only a brief glance, nervous about what she might do after discovering another woman had slept with her husband.

"Where did you meet him?" Brandon could see it was easier for her to talk to him than Eliza.

"At the Vengeance Hotel. I attended a wedding reception there. He was getting a room. I went with him for a drink. The bar was closing, so we took a couple more to his room." Again she sent Eliza an uncomfortable glance. "Do you think something happened to him?" she asked.

"We're not sure." He put his hand on Eliza's back and guided her to turn around. They weren't going to get any more information out of her. "Thank you for talking to us."

Eliza looked back at the woman, who stood there for a few seconds longer watching them, no doubt wondering what that was all about and why Eliza hadn't gone after her for sleeping with her husband. She was holding up rather well, more interested in David's whereabouts than his infidelity. David had been with Jillian when they'd found him and then had taken another woman to bed. He'd been on a quest. Determined to find someone to cheat on her with. And aside from crying last night, it didn't bother her all that much. His lack of respect had hurt her more than anything. Or was it her mistake in marrying him that had upset her?

Brandon avoided analyzing that any further as he walked beside her toward his truck. Her arm brushed against his and almost directed his attention to a more scandalous place.

"Why do you think Jillian was with David last night?" she asked.

David might have slept with her if she'd let him, but Jillian had gone with him for other reasons. Eliza had picked up on the undercurrents, too.

"Not to spend the night with him," he answered.

"She said David was on his way into the party. What happened to change his mind?"

"Maybe Jillian told the truth. He might have asked if I was there with you."

Her profile turned down with a disgruntled pinch at the corner of her mouth. She disliked their undeniable physical attraction as much as he did. And she didn't want to believe that was why David hadn't come inside.

"David must know something about her that she doesn't want anyone to find out," he said.

She lifted her head to look at him. "Or something she doesn't want you to know."

Jillian did seem desperate to have him. Any negative detail getting out about her might be horrifying. "Then maybe it's nothing. Whatever she stopped him from saying was probably nothing." Insignificant gossip.

At his truck, Eliza faced him. He hadn't expected her to do that, and now he stood too close to her. The mood changed in an instant. Her eyes drank in his upper torso and then his face.

"She seemed really tense," she said, sounding mechanical, as though she forced herself to say it to keep from doing something naughty.

"She didn't want to go with David." Putting on his sunglasses, he looked down her body and back up again, envisioning her legs where they didn't belong right now. Around him. Long and slender. Firm. Just the way he remembered.

"But felt she had no other choice." Her breathy reply wasn't in response to his perusal. His sunglasses had hidden that, but she still picked up on it.

"No," he managed to say. How would her butt feel in his hands with her legs anchored to his hips?

"She scares me."

Luckily that snapped him back to attention. He opened the door for her. "She won't try anything."

And if she did, he'd be ready.

Eliza tried calling David's cell phone again, more to dull her awareness of Brandon than anything else. The call went straight to voice mail. It was after eleven. She'd changed into her pajamas, a pair of silky white pants and a short-sleeved shirt that Brandon had spent several agonizing seconds taking in with a hungry look.

Now he reclined on the sofa, his bare feet up on the big coffee table, jeans cupping his crotch and black T-shirt tucked in. Feet had never been sexy to her, but his sure were. There wasn't an inch of him that wouldn't turn her on. She was convinced.

Giving up on the phone, she dropped it onto the coffee table. "He isn't coming back."

He must have left her here. She'd tried calling their home number and looked up their credit cards to see if he'd charged an airline ticket. If he had bought a ticket, he hadn't used credit. Was he with another woman? The college girl? Or was he in trouble, as she had originally thought?

Brandon had called Jillian earlier. She didn't answer at first but later that night she did. She still hadn't seen David, and he hadn't called her.

Brandon stood up. "You should try and get some rest."

His brown eyes were shadowed and grim, and his mouth was in a flat line. It had been a stressful day for both of them.

She wouldn't be able to sleep, but she nodded. She'd go to the guest room and turn on the television. Maybe that would settle her mind enough.

As she started toward the hall, a sound stopped her. Something outside. Some scraping and then a crash. Something, or someone, was on the patio.

Brandon went to the back double doors and peered through the glass. He had no blinds on them. Why bother with so much remote isolation surrounding him? He flipped on the light.

Eliza moved around the kitchen table and stood close behind him. A squirrel was chewing on the edge of the wood railing. It had knocked a flowerpot onto the patio floor. She breathed her relief. All her thoughts of gangsters and David had her edgy.

As she turned to go to bed, her bare foot slipped on the cool tile floor. Brandon caught her around the waist. Her hand came against one of the chairs, and it tipped over with her unsteady weight. Brandon tried to keep her from falling but she tripped over the legs of the fallen chair.

She brought him down with her. He let go of her waist as he tried to avoid crashing on top of her. She landed painfully on the toppled chair. Holding her side where the seat had dug into her flesh, she grimaced.

Above her, Brandon straddled her with a chuckle. "Are you all right?" He stood up.

She rose to her knees, which put her face right in front of his crotch.

Brandon took hold of her arms and lifted her. She put her hands on his forearms, unable to answer. Being so close to his man parts had flustered her.

"Are you okay?" he repeated.

She could only stare up at him.

Still smiling, the first levity of the day, he lifted her pajama top and inspected her ribs. They were a little red but otherwise unscathed. Eliza watched his hands on her, one curved around her bare waist and the other caressing the reddened skin with his thumb. Instant heat washed any and all negative tension away. If he moved his hand up he'd find her bare breasts.

It was unreasonable how much she craved him to do it. Her nipples hardened with the thought.

His hands stilled.

She lifted her head. He was staring down at the very thing that ached for him. Her top button had come free in her fall and gave him a great view. All that was left to the imagination were her nipples, and their jutting only made that more erotic.

She watched his impassioned face. Then his eyes met hers and a moment of question passed between them. Something beyond control took over. She saw it in him and felt it inside her. There was no stopping this.

He moved his hands up.

Her skin tingled, and drugging passion intensified. When his hands cupped her, she thought she'd erupt with sensation. How could something so wrong feel so right? She didn't understand it and didn't have the wherewithal to try now. She only knew that Brandon had been her one and only true love. He hadn't reciprocated when they were teenagers, but he was now. That's all that mattered to her in this moment, this moment that could vanish any second. She held on to it.

She ran her hands down his arms and then under the hem of his shirt, racing further out of control with the feel of his six-pack abs. This was nothing like what she remembered. This was new. He was all man to her touch. His chest. His shoulders. Back down to his abs and around to his lower back.

He unbuttoned her pajama top. Thumbed her nipples. And then she met his eyes. The wrongness of this remained just far enough away. She tipped her chin up as he lowered his mouth to hers. Gentle. Maybe hesitant. Wrong but, oh, so right.

When she moved her arms up over his shoulders, he lifted her and she wrapped her legs around his waist. He carried her up the stairs. She had never been up here and didn't pay much attention. Instead, she kissed his mouth and jaw and cheeks, loving how his eyes watched where he was going and how his gruff breathing revealed his passion.

In his large bedroom, he put her gently onto the mattress. She removed her pajamas while he undressed. He had his boxers off before she had her underwear off and came down onto the mattress to slide them down her legs himself.

On his hands and knees, he looked down at her, from her legs to her hips to her breasts and at last her face, where he hesitated. She vibrated with yearning, felt him doing the same. And yet…

David was gone. Her marriage was over. Soon it would be nonexistent. But David was Brandon's brother.

Brandon lowered himself down onto her, his breath sighing out of him as he put his head beside hers.

He couldn't do it. She couldn't do it.

"Why does this keep happening?" she asked.

He lifted his head without replying. He didn't understand it, either. His hand was beside her face and he caressed her cheek.

"I thought you didn't like party girls," she teased. Best to lean toward humor.

"You're not a party girl anymore."

When had he drawn that conclusion? The heat lingering between them stirred in her. His voice was low and deep. His body warm and hard. Eyes windows to the struggle he shared with her.

David would always be his brother, so even if she were no longer married to him, there would be a barrier between them. He'd never be able to be with her like this. Make love to her. Over and over. Daily. Maybe that wouldn't even be enough.

Eliza ached for him. No other man could make her ache the way Brandon did.

David would be hurt if anything happened between them now. He was already hurt.

Bittersweet regret made the ache deeper. She saw a mirror image of it in Brandon's eyes. They couldn't have each other. And beyond the physical, they lived completely different lives. Eliza couldn't picture herself tucked away on his ranch any more than he could picture himself traveling to all her events, thrown into the throng of social frivolity. And yet they hungered for each other. The tastiest steak, the most succulent crab, the richest chocolate, none compared to the delicacy of having Brandon.

This was the last time she'd feel him against her. His caressing fingers, his legs entwined with hers, his stomach, his erection.

Eliza lifted her head to kiss him. One last kiss.

He kissed her back. She arched upward for more, a rush of desire numbing her thoughts. He kissed her harder. She sought a deeper mating with her tongue. He accommodated, holding her head for the devouring.

She parted her knees, so hot for him she couldn't stop it. She couldn't stop the inevitable.

"Eliza," he rasped, caution flying away.

"Just do it, Brandon. Please." She squeezed his rear, urging him to satisfy this gnawing hunger.

His hips moved in answer.

She moaned in unbearable pleasure as he probed

into her soft, warm opening. Slid deliciously inside. He groaned with her and pulled back for another incredible stroke.

Eliza arched her body, electrified with mindless sensation. She came apart from the most powerful, instantaneous orgasm she'd ever experienced, pulsing deep and endlessly. Sensations didn't abate as he continued to move, nowhere near finished.

Carried away in the aftermath, Eliza was powerless against the swell of adoration and love that consumed her. His face, strong jaw and impassioned eyes, breathing with her, his mouth coming down for a searching kiss.

It restarted her. Having not come completely down from her pleasure, she was urged onto a new wave. She kissed him back, meeting his tongue and taking each of his slow and tortuous penetrations in rhythm.

The next slide was harder. And the next after that. Her flames reignited into a roar. One hard slide after another fueled the inferno to white-hot intensity.

"Brandon." She was out of her mind with lust.

He began pumping faster, gruff sounds coming from him.

"Brandon," she rasped again, raising her arms above her head.

He took one of her nipples into his mouth and then kissed her sternum. The side of one breast received his loving next and then the other. One more sweet caress of her other nipple and then he resumed his hard thrusts. Her breasts jiggled with each impact. Her thighs were high and wide. And he saw it all.

Watching him enjoy her body sent her over the edge. Closing her eyes, she peaked with an incredible explosion.

Her release brought on his own. She was his instrument, and he'd just played her beautifully. Groaning, he finished and collapsed onto her.

She caught her breath with him, still throbbing from him. Had anything ever felt this good? Eliza stayed on the soft billowy cloud of ecstasy for a while.

Brandon's fingers were in her hair. She reached to run hers through his. He turned his head and planted a kiss on her neck. She smiled with the sweet gesture.

Then the throbbing eased, and her breathing became normal. She opened her eyes and looked up at the ceiling. Brandon's bedroom ceiling.

She felt Brandon's body tense about the same time.

As quickly as the animalistic quenching of pure physical lust had overtaken them, shame took its place.

Brandon's head lifted. She caught a quick glimpse of his eyes before she had to look away and he moved off her. Rolling to the edge of the bed, he stood. While he dressed, her need to be gone from there burgeoned. As soon as he went to the bathroom and closed the door, she rose, dressed and went down to the guest room.

Once there, she showered and donned a different pair of pajamas and lay in bed with the television on, hoping the distraction would ease her into sleep. Instead, guilt burdened her. What David would think. How hurt he'd be. And even that didn't cover her emotions. It was the total disregard for another person that got to her most. Didn't she care about anyone but herself? Was sex more important that David's feelings?

Then the kindling of rightness began a slow blossoming. Guilt faded. It didn't go completely away, but the truth emerged. Making love with Brandon had been the product of rightness, of what they'd shared in their youth. That was why it had been so explosive. Disconcerting it was so explosive. She couldn't even wrap her brain around it.

She and David had married on impulse. He didn't love her any more than she loved him. Even without the history between her and Brandon, their marriage would have ended anyway. It may have lasted awhile longer, maybe even years. But the truth wouldn't change. They hadn't loved each other. They'd married out of convenience. He was thinking he could continue his wild ways; she would have at least the semblance of love.

Eliza was a one-love woman. She would never love anyone the way she loved Brandon. So why not marry a close second? Was she supposed to live her life single? Waiting for another love like that to come along? What if it never did? The thought of growing old alone saddened her. It always had, ever since she'd left Vengeance.

Being alone didn't scare Brandon. He preferred being alone. She was glad there'd be no chance for them to make something of what had happened tonight.

He hadn't changed. He'd keep running until someday it would dawn on him that he was an old man and he was still alone. Needlessly.

What had made him so dogged? So afraid of love?

Chapter 6

September 9th

The next morning, Eliza woke to soft knocking. Blinking her tired eyes open, she stretched, utterly rested, basking in—

She sprang up on the bed. Brandon's guest room bed. Not his bed.

Had she dreamed it?

The bedroom door opened. She lifted the sheets over her pajama-covered breasts. Was David home?

Seeing Brandon's tense face, she almost relaxed. They were going to have to face what they did sooner or later.

"The police are here."

Shock cauterized her. "What?"

"It's…" He lowered his head, obviously struggling with heavy emotion. Grief.

Alarmed, Eliza threw off the sheet and stood from the bed. "What is it? What happened?"

He lifted his head, his mouth tight and eyes a portal to great pain. "David."

"What about David? Is he here? Did he see us?" Panic made her grip her pajamas at her neck.

"He's dead."

Going still, sucking in her breath, she covered her mouth with her free hand.

"The police are here to question you. You better get dressed."

Frozen inside, she lowered both of her hands. "Me?"

He entered the room and closed the door. "There were a lot of witnesses at the bar the other night."

Witnesses had told of David's unhappiness and how upset she'd become. Did that give her motive to kill him?

Numbly, she found some clothes and went into the bathroom to dress. The slight soreness between her legs was an ugly reminder of the scandalous act that put it there. David was dead. While he was dying or already dead, she'd been screwing his brother.

Back in the bedroom, Brandon leaned against the wall next to the door, his head back and eyes closed. He opened them and lifted his head when he saw her.

His brother was dead.

"Did they tell you what happened?"

"He was murdered. Strangled. Some geology students found him with two other bodies near Darby College yesterday afternoon."

Darby College. Yesterday afternoon…

Three bodies…

"David was one of them."

She shared a lengthy gaze with him, overwhelmed. Confused. Sad and guilt-ridden. Scared.

"They think I…?"

"They asked to speak with you. That's all." He opened

the door and waited for her to precede him down the hall and into the living room. To possible doom.

"When was he killed?" she asked.

"His body was found yesterday, and the time of death is estimated twenty-four hours before that."

Dear God. While she'd kissed Brandon in the yurt, he'd been dead. And last night…

She stepped into the living room to a throng of police officers and detectives, sick to her stomach.

"Mrs. Reed?"

She turned to see a six-foot-tall detective with salt-and-pepper hair. His pale blue eyes had faint lines around them, and the dark shade underneath hinted at sleepless nights.

"I'm Detective Zimmerman. I'm helping out with the murder investigation on your husband and the others. Why don't we have a seat and talk for a while?"

A very nice way of saying he wanted to question her.

She sat on the sofa, and he sat on the chair adjacent to her.

Another man approached, standing in front of her on the other side of Brandon's big, bulky wood coffee table. This man was bigger. Blond hair thinning. He flashed a toothy smile that didn't reach his eyes.

"Detective Kelly here will be taking some notes," Zimmerman said.

Eliza merely nodded. Politely saying it was nice to meet them seemed pointless.

"We're very sorry for your loss," Zimmerman said. He sounded very practiced and neutral, as though he'd done this more times than he could count.

Eliza felt awkward. Did she have the right to call it a loss? "Thank you." And did he even mean it? He probably only said it because he had to.

"Why don't we start with the last time you saw him?"

Eliza rubbed her hands in her lap, a gesture that the detective didn't miss. "Two nights ago."

Detective Kelly began writing on his small notebook. "Where did you see him? What were you doing?"

He must already know. "He didn't show up at my brother's birthday party." She looked up at Brandon, who stood with his hands in his front pockets, watching her with that same tense set to his mouth and eyes. Then she met the detective's patient regard. "Afterward, I… Brandon and I went looking for him and found him at the Cork. He was with another woman."

"Who was the woman?"

Again, that was something he already must know. "Jillian Marks."

"Did he leave with her?"

"Yes." She explained the entire exchange. "Our marriage isn't doing so well right now."

"How did you feel when he told you he wanted an annulment?"

"I was hurt."

"Hurt enough to do something about it?"

Anger shot through her. "Like kill him? No. Maybe you should be questioning her."

"We're questioning everyone," he said without inflection. "Is this the first time you've caught him with another woman?"

"No." She lowered her head and moved her eyes to see Brandon, who still watched her. Did he wonder if she'd killed his brother?

"How many times before now?"

"Just once." As far as she knew. He could have been sleeping with many more than one. "He had an affair with someone before we came here on vacation. And after he was with Jillian, he took another woman to a hotel room."

The detective studied her as he digested that. Then he asked for the woman's name, and Brandon was the one who gave it to him.

"How long have you been married?" Zimmerman asked.

"Six months. We married quickly in Vegas."

"Did you love him?"

The deceptively personal question was anything but.

"I…thought I did." She looked up at Brandon again and added, "I thought I felt enough to make it work."

Now it was obvious that she hadn't. Brandon was the man she loved, the man she'd never stopped loving.

Brandon's eyes blinked and softened briefly.

But being with him was detrimental. Destructive. The cost to her heart too great. She should remember that the next time they were in bed together. If that ever happened again.

"You're well acquainted with Senator Merris and Sheriff Burris, aren't you?"

Turning back to the detective, she answered, "Yes. I grew up in Vengeance. They're friends of mine."

"Friends or business associates?"

"Friends. I've planned parties for them both from time to time, especially John. Why?"

"David used your services before, too, didn't he?"

That gave her pause. "I planned a party for an athlete he knew. That's how we met…or how we reconnected. He found out I was in Hollywood and called. We arranged everything over the phone, and I saw him in person at the party."

Detective Kelly hadn't stopped jotting things down in his notebook since the interrogation had started.

"The senator and the sheriff were also murdered."

Eliza gasped. The sheriff and the senator were dead? Questions slammed her. How had David ended up with the senator and the sheriff? How did he know them? Through her parties?

Did the detective think her event planning was somehow related?

"I—I don't understand. How? Why?"

"You've had no contact with your husband since the night of your brother's birthday party?" He didn't answer her question.

"No."

"Were you concerned about his whereabouts?"

"Of course. We tried to find him."

"Yes, and dropped by the police station to see if he'd somehow ended up there."

He knew. "At first I assumed he was with Jillian."

"You say he was on his way into the party when he ran into Jillian Marks?"

"Yes."

"And met up with this other woman after he left Ms. Marks."

"Yes."

"At a hotel."

"That's correct."

"That will be easy to corroborate."

Did he doubt her? "Naomi said he got a room."

Zimmerman glanced at the other detective, who nodded. Silent communication for checking into what she said.

Eliza was beginning to dislike Zimmerman. He was clearly a detective who'd formed his own assumptions about her. And they had guilt plastered all over them.

"Did Jillian mention anything to you about what she and David discussed at the Cork?" she asked.

"Let's stick with you for now." He evaded her.

"Jillian Marks is hiding something," Eliza said. "She wants Brandon all to herself."

Zimmerman looked up at Brandon. "She claims to be seeing you, Mr. Reed. Is that true?"

Brandon remained rigid. "We broke up the night before the party."

"The two of you were together the night of the party?"

"No. Well, not really. She came to the party and we talked."

"When she left the party, did she have any reason to believe the two of you might be together?"

Brandon hesitated. "Possibly. She took the breakup hard. I didn't want her to cause a scene at the party. She may have gotten the idea that I'd changed my mind. I haven't."

"So you were nice to her."

"Yes."

"She told us she ran into David on the way out of the party," Eliza said.

"She told us the same."

"Did she say why she left with him?"

"She said he didn't like it that Brandon was there."

So, Jillian was sticking to her story. "Don't you find it strange that she went with him when it's Brandon she wants?"

"A few drinks as friends is fairly harmless." Zimmerman's hand went out, palm-up, adding to the condescension Eliza was detecting. "And she didn't let him go home with her. Even you agree that's what happened, correct?"

Now she really didn't like him. "David knew something about her that she didn't want Brandon to know."

"Something that would give her motive to kill him?"

Eliza said nothing. He was goading her.

Detective Kelly still scribbled away.

"What motive would she have for killing the sheriff and senator?" Zimmerman asked.

"What motive would I have?" she countered.

Zimmerman stood. He had no motive to implicate her in all three murders. He wished he did, but he didn't.

"Are you planning to stay in Vengeance awhile, Mrs. Reed?"

He said her title and name sneeringly.

"Yes, until David's killer is captured."

"Good. We'll contact you if we need anything else."

"I'll do the same."

He met her belligerence dead-on. "One more thing. There were three greeting cards found on each body. Each had a word written on it. Liar. Cheater. Thief. Do you know why anyone would do that?"

She wasn't about to give him the satisfaction of answering that directly. "Let me guess. The one found on my husband's body was Cheater."

"Good day, Mrs. Reed." He nodded at Brandon. "Mr. Reed."

His sarcasm was barely masked. Eliza trailed him to the door and slammed it after he left.

"The nerve of that man!" She turned to Brandon, who now stood in the living room. "Can you believe that?"

He just looked at her.

"What?"

"Did you go anywhere the day David was killed?"

Stunned, she took a second or two to reply. Why was he asking? "No. I was here." When he said nothing, she snapped, "I didn't kill David, Brandon. Don't piss me off."

"If you went somewhere, the police might be able to put you close to the crime scene."

"I didn't go anywhere. Ask your housekeeper."

"She didn't see you."

He'd already checked? "Then ask someone else. My rental stayed in the driveway. All day."

After studying her, his speculation cleared and he sighed. "Sorry. It's just such a shock."

Shock.

Yes. It was also bizarre. And terrible.

And infinitely sad.

David died believing she wanted Brandon more than him.

Ryker was about to leave his auto repair shop in the hands of his manager. That morning his wife had told him she was going to spend the night at her mother's. It was a girl thing, she'd said, her sister was going to be there, too. He didn't believe her. He was afraid she was seeing someone else.

"Going home early?"

Distracted, Ryker hadn't seen Jillian Marks enter the shop. He'd repaired her car a few days ago, and they'd had a friendly talk. He'd seen her around town before that. She'd moved here not very long ago, and it fascinated him that she'd chosen Vengeance.

I like the name, she'd said. *Dallas is too big.*

He'd give anything to live in a big city. Why was she here?

"Hey, Jillian. What brings you here? Is your car acting up again?"

"Are you busy? Can we talk?"

Talk? They weren't close friends. What could she possibly need to talk to him about if it had nothing to do with her car?

"Sure."

She glanced around. "How about we go over to the coffee shop across the street?"

Whoa. She really wanted to have a talk. What could it be about? "I don't really have time." He needed to know where his wife was.

"Please. It won't take long. I just need to ask you some questions about your sister."

His sister? One of his mechanics had come in this morning and told him about her husband. He'd thought about talking to her, but he didn't know what to say. Besides, he hadn't felt like picking up the phone to talk to Eliza in years. She wasn't picking up the phone to ask for his help or advice anyway.

Even as conflicting feelings nudged him, he said, "All right."

The Corner Newsstand was an older coffee shop that sold used books. He walked with her over there.

"I'm sure you've heard what's happened," she said on the way.

"Yeah. You holding up okay?" He opened the door for her, wondering if she'd told the truth about David merely dropping her off and that she'd spent the night alone.

"Sort of." She entered and found a table. "Have you talked to Eliza?"

"No."

She searched his face as though surprised and wondering why.

"What would you like?"

"Vanilla latte."

He hurried to get the coffees and returned, sitting across from her at a small table.

She sipped first before starting. "David was upset about his brother and your sister."

"Really?" Eliza and Brandon had dated in high school, but that was ancient history. He had noticed how Brandon had watched her the night of his birthday party, though.

"I ran into him after I left your party. He invited me for drinks. He wanted to know why Brandon broke up with me. Brandon didn't say it outright, but I know it was because of Eliza. She came back, and all the old feelings started returning. David said he didn't think she was still hung up on him until he started talking about coming home to spend time with his brother. Eliza didn't want to go. He kept asking her why, and she never told him. Then it dawned on him that she was still in love with his brother. He was angry that she married him without telling him that. He said he had an affair and would keep having them to hurt her the way she hurt him."

"Why not divorce her if he's that unhappy?"

"He loved her." Jillian looked down at her cup. "Why does that always happen to me? Every man I meet and have feelings for is in love with someone else. Not that I want David."

"You love Brandon."

She nodded unhappily.

"Eliza wouldn't have married David if she thought there was any chance of having Brandon. I remember the crush she had on him. She was heartbroken when it ended between them. Why do you think she hightailed it out of Vengeance?"

"David thought his brother was going to sleep with her."

Picturing his wife with another man, anxiety pushed him to hurry and find her. "They wouldn't do that."

He checked his cell phone for the time, thinking about

Eliza. She had been wild in high school. Stealing other girls' boyfriends. The social butterfly of Vengeance High. It's what had driven Brandon away. The rancher was the antithesis of Eliza. Plus he had some shadows in his past. A mother who'd committed suicide. A father who was a drunk. That kind of childhood had to be hard on a kid. Ryker had always thought it peculiar that he'd sent his own father to prison. He'd witnessed him in a hit-and-run accident that killed the other driver. Then he'd testified without any emotion. He hadn't had any trouble at all slam-dunking a prison sentence on his father.

Ryker had always wondered what had happened to make him such a hard man. Whatever had driven him to put his own father in prison would answer that question. Ryker might be angry with Eliza for not holding up her share of the responsibility in caring for their mother, but he didn't wish her ill. Maybe leaving Vengeance—and Brandon—behind had been the best thing for her.

"Is she going back to Hollywood?" Jillian asked, sounding so small and insecure that he took pity on her.

He laughed. "Now there's something you never have to worry about. Eliza would never live here. She couldn't get out of here fast enough. Hollywood is her gig. She's got a thriving business there. I'm sure as soon as David's murder is solved she'll head back."

"What if she doesn't?"

"You mean, what if Brandon gets her to stay?"

Jillian nodded.

"Eliza told me Brandon isn't the marrying kind. If she stays, it'll only be until he's had his fill of her." He searched Jillian's sad face. "You're a beautiful woman, Jillian. Go find a man who makes you feel like you're the only woman in the world. Brandon Reed won't give you that. He won't give any woman that."

The smile that shaped Jillian's mouth was warm, but there was something else there. Desperation. "Thank you for telling me that."

"I'm sure I'm not the only man who's told you you're beautiful." What did she see when she looked in the mirror? No ogre.

"Not many have."

"Well, you are. Don't settle for less than you deserve." Meaning, a man like Brandon, who was capable of loving no woman.

"If you weren't married, Ryker Harvey, I'd be calling you all the time."

The way she said it had an odd ring to it. Starved for male attention. Clingy. How could a woman who looked like her be so desperate?

Aegina wasn't at her mother's. Ryker had just come from there, and now he was sick with foreboding. Her mother didn't have a clue where her daughter was. They hadn't spoken all day. Her sister didn't know where she was, either.

Aegina had lied. Pain sliced through him. She'd lied to him. Why? He wanted to deny it. But he couldn't. Aegina was having an affair. This town was rampant with them. It bore too much similarity to his sister's predicament. He wasn't embroiled in a murder investigation, but his spouse might be cheating on him. He'd suspected something was wrong, but this was worse than he'd imagined. Aegina. His Aegina. How could she?

He drove by the second hotel in town and saw her car. An unmanly lump formed in his throat. He hadn't cried since he was a boy, but he felt the urge to do so now.

He sat in his truck for a few minutes, trying to grasp the reality that his wife was in there with another man. No wonder she'd been so distant lately. He thought she was just tired of his complaining about living in Vengeance. Maybe that was part of what had driven her into the arms of another man. Maybe she never loved him to begin with.

No…it couldn't be. He couldn't have lost her.

He loved her.

The realization assaulted him in a rush. He loved Aegina so much. His sweet, beautiful Aegina. Mother of his kids. His lover. His best friend. He'd loved her from the second he saw her at the library. He'd been looking up colleges on the computer, and she'd been looking for books to read. She read nonfiction. Biographies were her favorite.

He wiped a traitorous tear off his face and climbed out of his truck. Everyone in town had envied them. Their love had been that perfect. Ryker and Aegina, a match made in Vengeance.

In the hotel, he spotted Ben Richardson behind the counter, the hotel manager.

Ben's eyes popped open wide when he saw him. Standing frozen, he said, "Ryker."

"Tell me which room she's in, Ben."

"I can't do that."

Ryker leaned over the counter and grabbed Ben's uniform, hauling him forward. "What room."

"Two-ten."

"Give me a card key."

"Ryker, I can't do that."

"Give it to me." He shoved Ben. "My wife is up there screwing another man. You think they're going to open the door for me?"

Ben hesitated, sympathy in his eyes.

"As a friend…" He and Ben had gone to school together. "Please."

Ben blinked in resignation and silently worked on the computer. Then he handed him a card key.

In the elevator, he put his head back against the wall, pain twisting his insides. Why? Why did she have to do it?

The doors opened and he walked with shaky legs to room two-ten.

Did he really want to do this?

If he didn't, he might overlook it just to keep her. Swiping the card key, he pushed the door open.

Aegina sat at the table in the room, a man next to her. They both stopped eating to look at him.

"Ryker!" Aegina sprang to her feet.

At least she was still dressed. Then he recognized the man. One of his mechanics.

"You're fired," he said.

"What are…how…?"

Ryker walked into the room, letting the door swing shut. He tossed the card key onto the TV stand.

"Hiding in the room for dinner?" he indicated the room service they'd ordered. Steak. Wine. Not very romantic with the TV playing. Apparently Aegina didn't need romantic. She only needed another man to screw.

His mechanic backed away, glancing fearfully from Aegina to him. "How did you get in here?"

"Leave. Now. Before I kill you."

The man grabbed his keys and left.

Aegina stood there gaping at him. Her shoulder-length red hair was thick and shiny, her eyes not as lively as they usually were. She was still slender and beautiful. Baby fat didn't stay on her. The thought of another man sampling that body killed him inside.

"Did you sleep with him?" Maybe he'd gotten there in time.

She lowered her head, unable to meet his eyes. That

answered his question well enough. His heart was imploding.

"How many times have you been with him?"

She shrugged, defeated. "Four. Five. I wasn't counting."

"When?"

She lifted her head, tears forming in her eyes. "I didn't think you'd care."

She didn't think he'd care? Rage consumed him. "You're my wife."

"A wife who chained you to Vengeance."

"You're going to cop that attitude again?"

"It's true. You settled for me because your sister left and you felt obligated to care for your mother."

"I didn't settle for you."

"You wanted to be a doctor."

He had. But after facing this lost dream over the years, he no longer felt so strongly about it.

"I love you," he said. "Don't you know that?"

She started crying. "Now you tell me."

He was at a loss for what to do. His wife had slept with another man, believing her husband didn't love her.

Aegina used a napkin to blow her nose. Still sniffling, she looked up at him.

"If I'd have asked you to move with me to another state, would you have?" he asked.

"Vengeance is my home. It's yours, too, Ryker."

"You didn't answer my question."

"When we were first married, yes. Now? No. I wouldn't go anywhere with you."

How had it gotten to this point? How had their marriage been destroyed so easily? One minute he was happily married; the next he wasn't.

"Why?"

"You have to ask?"

Because he hated living here. "Vengeance has nothing to do with the way I feel for you." Felt. He wasn't sure how he felt about her now. She'd let another man where only he belonged.

What about their kids? The thought of visitation made him ill. Would Aegina fight him in court? How far out of love had she fallen?

"It has everything to do with it. You can't stand it here. I love it here. You want to leave. I want to stay. You blame me and your sister for being trapped here."

"I don't blame you."

"Yes, you do, and I can't live with it anymore. You're a bitter man who's never taken charge of his own destiny."

"I've made a good living for us. I support you. You never had to work raising the kids."

"I might as well work for you then. I married you because I loved you, not because you could take care of me. I don't need anyone to take care of me. What I do need is a husband who loves me."

"I do love you."

"I don't believe you."

It was the same argument over and over again. "That's why you threw our marriage away?"

"You threw it away long before I did. Stop looking outside yourself when you look for someone to blame for your unhappiness. You've done it to yourself."

And he'd driven her away. His unhappiness over living in Vengeance. Being stuck here. This was all Eliza's fault.

Chapter 7

September 10th

Eliza left the stable after a long horseback ride, careful to stay away from the pastures where Brandon worked. Being stuck in the house had driven her mad. Once, she'd caught him in his office with his head in his hands, a picture of grief. And then he'd lifted his head and the grief had morphed into a dark sort of desire and then anger. He'd gotten up from the chair and left the room through doors leading to the back patio.

She didn't dare go into town right now, not with suspicion flying around that she may have murdered her husband. The only thing saving her reputation was the lack of motive to kill the senator and the sheriff. She planned parties for the senator. They were friends. Why would she kill him?

In riding pants and boots with a tucked-in short-sleeved shirt, Eliza stopped short when she spotted Ryker's impeccably refinished 1970 Charger. Her brother rose out of the muscle car and approached.

As they closed the distance, she could tell right away that something was terribly wrong. "Ryker? Are you okay?"

"I just caught Aegina with another man," he blurted.

Her brother never came to her for comfort. She felt his need erupting now. Careful not to get too close too soon, she reached out to touch his arm.

"Oh, Ryker. Let's go inside and talk." She guided him easily into the house.

"Where's Brandon?"

"Out with the cattle." He'd avoided her since that morning.

Eliza had considered getting a room in town until David's killer was captured. She stayed because Brandon was his brother, and she couldn't stop worrying about the car she'd seen twice on the road leading here.

As she sat beside him at the kitchen table, Eliza began to surmise a few things. First, it wasn't surprising that Aegina had done it; second, Ryker would no doubt blame her, even though it wouldn't make sense. Was that why he'd come here today?

Ryker put his head in his hands. Eliza had never seen him this way. "I don't want to go home."

"You can stay here. Brandon won't mind." Maybe they'd have a chance to mend their differences.

He didn't move.

"You don't have to go back there. I'll drive to your house and pack a few things for you. And I'll go get your kids whenever you can arrange to see them. I'll bring them here."

He lifted his head. "You'd do that for me?"

"I'd do anything for you. You're my brother."

After a while he put his head back into his hands. "This isn't your ranch, Eliza. You can't invite me here."

"I'll talk to him. He wouldn't turn you away."

His head rose again, and this time he put his hands on the table. "I have to go home for the boys."

Of course, she should have thought of that.

"Evan's having trouble at school. He's being bullied for defending a girl when the bully teased her."

"You're raising him right." She smiled.

"He asked me if his mommy and I are going to get a divorce."

She reached over and put her hand over his. "I'm so sorry, Ryker. I'm here for you whenever you need me. If there's anything I can do, all you have to do is call. Okay?"

He nodded. "Thanks."

"And if you need a place to stay, even if it's just for tonight, you're welcome here." She regretted what she'd said. She sounded as though this were her house, too. Why did it feel as though it could be?

After studying her while he registered that, he said, "You seem to be getting close to him again."

Closer than she had to her husband, he left unspoken. Eliza averted her gaze to the big window. Rolling hills. Trees. Blue sky.

"You feel comfortable enough to invite guests into his house?"

"I've known Brandon since I was a kid." She tried to minimize it, but it was obvious that there was more going on.

"You've been in Hollywood for years. When is the last time you saw him?"

Disconcerted under the weight of his pointed grilling, she couldn't answer.

"You still love him."

"No."

"Oh, come on, Eliza. Admit it."

"No," she said quieter, still raw and remorseful over last night.

"Poor David."

"Ryker, don't." It was cruel of him to throw that in her face now.

He seemed to realize the same and softened. "Do you know what happened to him?"

She shook her head. "The police came to question me."

"They suspect you did it?"

"Maybe."

He swore. "You didn't, right?"

Gaping at him with an audible gasp, she didn't have to answer.

"Sorry."

"I didn't kill David. It's bad enough that I married him."

That drew a chuckle out of him. "At least you're being honest now."

She smiled a little at him, glad for this glimmer of connection they were having, but David's death bereaved her, especially with the weight of her and Brandon sleeping together.

"I'm sorry I didn't call you," he said

When? After he'd learned David was killed? "You have a lot on your mind."

"Yeah."

"I'm glad you came here today, Ryker."

Resistance to what she said crossed his eyes. He stiffened. "I don't know why I did, to tell you the truth. I just drove and this is where I ended up. All I can think about is Aegina with another man. The way only we should be." His eyes glistened as he fought against tears. "I can't stand it."

Eliza squeezed his hand where she still covered it on the table.

"She thinks I don't love her."

"You never wanted to live here. She did, Ryker. That had to have taken a toll on her."

"I know. I know that now."

Leaning back, she met his misty eyes. He loved his wife, and he may have lost her because of his wish to leave Vengeance. "Do you want to stay married?" *He might do it for his kids,* she thought, *but what about his wife?*

His hesitation revealed his doubt. Infidelity was a big hurdle to overcome. Some people couldn't do it.

But Ryker and Aegina had real love. It would be a shame to see it go to waste.

"I wish I was more like you."

What did he mean by that?

"It's easy for you to walk away."

His honesty stung. "I didn't walk away from you."

"You walked away from everyone."

"No—"

"Ever since Dad died, you've walked away. When you married David, I wondered if you did it because he was Brandon's brother, or if you did it because he was another person you could walk away from without feeling too much. Look at you now. You haven't even cried yet, have you?"

The sting of truth burned in her chest. "You make it seem as though I'm a terrible person."

"You're a selfish person, Eliza. So is Brandon. The two of you make a perfect pair. You both don't feel a thing."

Letting go of his hand, Eliza leaned back against her chair and tipped her head back with a long breath. When she regained control, she looked over at him. "You're hurting. You just caught your wife with someone else."

"That doesn't mean I'm blind to the truth."

"Why did you come here, then?"

Abruptly, he stood from the chair. "I must have needed to. Looking at you, I can see what I have in Aegina. For a while I wondered why both of us had spouses who cheated on us. Maybe I did have trouble letting go of my dream. Maybe that did make my wife feel unloved. But I do love her. And I know she loves me, or she did. If I can make her love me like that again, I will. And I'm not going to waste any more time resenting you for stealing my dream from me."

"I didn't steal it from you, Ryker. You never went after it."

"Because I couldn't!" His voice was raised.

"You still blame me."

"You went after your dream no matter the cost to anyone else. Now you have your dream. What you don't have is love."

"That's not because I walked away from you."

Ryker laughed cynically. "You're still walking away, Eliza. From everybody!" He stormed out of the house.

Laden with dejection, Eliza followed him to the door and watched him go, restraining herself from calling him back. Nothing had changed between them.

Then why did she feel so different?

As she contemplated that, she lowered her head and caught sight of an envelope lying on the stone porch. Her name was written on it. Shock cauterized her for a second. She quickly searched the property and the road, where she saw Ryker's Charger vanish over the hill.

She didn't see anyone else. Crouching, she picked up the envelope and opened the unsealed top. Slipping out another card that was blank on the inside, she read, "Go back to Hollywood while you still can."

"Something wrong?"

She jumped and spun around to see Brandon standing there. She was startled that she hadn't heard him approach. Wordlessly, she handed him the card. He read it and lifted his head grimly.

"Ryker was just here," he said.

Did he suspect her brother had left the card? "Yes, but he wouldn't have—"

He took her hand and pulled her inside, closing and locking the door.

"He resents you for leaving him here."

"Were you listening to us?"

"I only caught the last part."

He must have come in from the pasture and she hadn't heard him.

"He didn't leave the note. My brother may resent me, but he would never do something like that." Besides, Ryker wouldn't write a note encouraging her to go back to Hollywood, would he?

"He's having marital problems that he blames you for."

Was he suggesting her brother had killed David? "A card was left on all the bodies. Whoever wrote this note and the one before this could be David's killer. Do you really think Ryker would kill three people over his animosity toward me?"

Brandon tapped the card against his hand, thinking. "No."

Who could it be? And were the notes connected to the murders? They had no way of knowing. Not without more leads in the case.

* * *

The next morning, Eliza drove to her brother's house. She wanted to talk to him about his issue with her leaving Vengeance. After that, she was going to stop by the police station to give Zimmerman the cards she'd received. When she parked, she noticed another car park behind her. Had it been following her and she hadn't noticed? It wasn't tan in color and there were two men inside.

As fear reared up and sent her pulse racing faster, she got out of her car and recognized the detectives who'd questioned her before. Zimmerman and Kelly.

What were they doing here?

Ryker appeared outside his front door, looking curiously at the two men as he approached her car.

"Mrs. Reed?" Zimmerman said, stopping in front of her, Kelly beside him.

"Everything okay?" Ryker asked.

"I'm not sure." She waited for Zimmerman to explain himself.

"Would you mind coming with us? We'd like to ask you a few questions."

"Then ask me." She'd answer any questions they had.

"We'd like an official statement from you."

An official statement…

Ryker glanced at her with surprise and alarm.

"Am I being arrested?"

"Right now, we'd just like to talk to you."

He had that funny, bored way about him again. He must have been trying to hide what he really thought and ended up looking that way. He thought she was his number one suspect and was trying to avoid antagonizing her with his opinion.

"You don't have to go with him," Ryker said.

"If you'd like a lawyer present you may," Zimmerman said.

Could she refuse to go with him? Then she berated herself for being so paranoid. She had nothing to hide! Besides, she didn't want to make matters worse by being uncooperative.

"It will be all right. I was going to stop by the station after I talked to you anyway," she said to Ryker.

"What's going on, Eliza?"

"They think I may have killed David."

He smothered a few guffawing laughs. "Seriously?"

Zimmerman didn't crack a smile.

Ryker sobered. "Call a lawyer, Eliza."

"No. It's all right. I didn't kill David." She started for Zimmerman's car. "Will you call Brandon for me?"

Brandon was wedged between two reporters shoving microphones at him. After Ryker had called him, he'd felt a shot of alarm and then worry for Eliza that transcended that for a sister-in-law.

"The whole town is going crazy with this," Ryker had said.

No kidding. Now he wished he would have accepted Ryker's offer to go get Eliza. Instead, his protectiveness overruled.

"Did Eliza Harvey kill her husband?" a reporter shouted.

"Is it true she slept with both you and your brother?"

How the hell did they know that? It had to be speculation. Rumor that had traveled around town after the murders were broadcast.

"What was her relationship with Senator Merris?"

"No comment." He pushed by the last of them and entered the police station.

Eliza had called him, breathless with fear even though she probably thought she was in control of it. The police had brought her to the station for formal questioning.

Inside, he gave his name to the woman behind the counter and told her he was there to pick up Eliza. The police had driven her here.

To make matters worse, Melinda Grayson's kidnapping and a triple homicide had attracted national attention. The media had flocked to Vengeance, Texas. He wished he could go back to his ranch and stay there until all of this blew over. Dealing with David's death was bad enough.

Eliza emerged. The police were letting her go. He had suspected that's what would happen. David had affairs and that might give her motive to kill him, but where was the motive to kill the sheriff or the senator? Eliza didn't have the makings of a killer. She did, however, have what it took to drive his brother to his grave.

Her skin was pale, and her blue eyes were stark and weary. When she saw him, relief washed away her strain.

"Thank you for coming."

"Ryker called." He'd rather not analyze why she preferred him over her brother. Taking her arm, he guided her to the door. "There's a throng outside."

"Mrs. Reed?"

He and Eliza turned as Zimmerman called to her.

"Don't make any plans to leave town."

In other words, they still hadn't eliminated her as a suspect. They didn't have enough evidence to hold her, but she was still a person of interest.

Brandon glanced down at Eliza, who met the look nervously. He'd talk to her later.

"Let's get out of here. Don't answer any of the reporters' questions."

"They were here when I arrived."

Outside, reporters shouted questions in the late-afternoon sun. Brandon shoved a microphone away from Eliza's face. He'd parked his car in a handicap space to stay close. At the passenger door, he pushed an overzealous reporter.

"Hey!" He stumbled backward.

Eliza climbed into the cab of the truck, and he shut the door, herding another reporter out of his way on the other side. His height and size helped to deter the others. He shoved another reporter away from his truck so he could get in. Then he backed from the parking space slowly, not stopping as reporters knocked on Eliza's window, still yelling questions.

Brandon tapped the gas to scatter the roaches.

"Brandon, be careful."

"They'll get out of the way or get run over."

"You don't mean that."

He didn't, but the reporters were getting out of the way.

As they left the police station, he heard a sigh of tense breath leave her and she leaned her head back against the headrest.

"Why did they bring you in?" he asked.

"They found some unexplained deposits to Peter Burris's account, and some pictures of Senator Merris with an arms dealer who was caught trading with an embargoed country. The pictures came from the sheriff's safe-deposit box."

The sheriff was blackmailing the senator? "Where's the connection to David?"

"That's why they needed to question me. They think the senator may have been funding his gambling habit."

What about the sheriff? "I still don't see the connection."

"I introduced David to the senator. I did parties for

all three of them. They kept asking about my relationship with the sheriff. Did I ever talk to him about David's gambling problem? Did I know the senator was involved with arms dealers? Things like that."

"They think the sheriff may have been working with you?" Why? To get money from the senator? Money David had lost and couldn't pay back?

"I guess so."

"It's weak."

"Tell Zimmerman that."

"I hear he's not even the lead on the murder investigation."

"I hope I never meet the lead. Isn't the FBI working the case now?"

"Yes. Did you give Zimmerman the cards you received?" She'd told him she would after she'd talked to Ryker.

"Yes. And he treated me as though I wrote them to take suspicion off me. Add confusion to the investigation. He doesn't think they're related to the cards left on the bodies because the ones I received are threatening. The ones on the bodies are more like a piece to a puzzle."

"If he thought you were the killer, he'd have arrested you by now."

"That's encouraging. Why do I still feel so violated?"

He smiled. "He might be a little crusty around the edges, but once he's sure he's got the right suspect you'll see a new side to him."

"You know him?"

"Not personally." He stopped at a stoplight, and a man knocked on his window.

"Damn reporters are everywhere. Can't even go into town anymore." He blew the light and drove out of town.

"My car is still at Ryker's."

"I'll send a couple of ranch hands to go get it."

He hated the spotlight, especially when it was exaggerated. Like gossip and Eliza's Friday Parties. It was all about sensationalism and the attention that brought.

"What was David doing with the sheriff and the senator? And who would want them dead?"

Brandon didn't know, but there sure was a lot of hype going on in a town that otherwise never had it. Melinda had been kidnapped and now this. Two serious crimes all at once.

"If I'd never introduced David to the senator, he'd probably still be alive."

He noticed how her head had bowed, torn with guilt. "His gambling did get worse after he married you."

"Do we have to do that again? Kick me while I'm down, why don't you."

She was the one who'd brought it up. Did she think he'd disagree with her? "I could have saved him if he hadn't married you." May as well get it all out in the open.

"That's just plain cruel."

It was how he felt. It's what he'd thought from the day he had discovered they'd married. David's wild ways, perpetuated by Eliza's, had driven him to the end.

"I didn't enable his gambling," she argued. "Just because I plan parties for a living doesn't mean I enabled him."

She might have a point. Eliza had changed. She'd matured. He could no longer deny that. Her parties were elegant, and she didn't dance on bars and get drunk anymore. She was professional. A good influence for someone who did drink and had a gambling problem.

Something in him resisted. Thinking that way would get him in trouble again. No more flirting with a disaster in the making.

Reaching the ranch entrance, Brandon drove up the driveway and stopped. Eliza hopped out. He followed her inside.

When she went for the big-screen television, he said, "Don't turn that on."

She did anyway, flipping to the news. The film of Melinda played, followed by all the drama of the triple homicide. An FBI agent was questioned and gave vague responses.

David had been upset when he'd heard of Melinda's kidnapping. How was he acquainted with the professor? Personally or had her popularity reached him? Maybe his reaction to the news hadn't been significant. Even if it had and Melinda was a friend, Brandon didn't see how that would be related to the murders.

A car appeared on the winding dirt road leading to his ranch. He spotted it through one of the big front windows. It wasn't the same car as the one he and Eliza had seen. He'd still be cautious, though.

Going to the entry table, he opened its single drawer and retrieved the pistol he'd put there after David and Eliza had arrived. Eliza stopped at the threshold of the hallway leading to the guest room.

"Since when do you own a gun?"

He decided no response was better than explaining he felt the danger justifiable. Not only had David been murdered, but Jillian was unpredictable. Had he been alone, he may not have dug it out of his gun case, but Eliza was here, and hadn't she always brought out the defender in him?

He pulled the slide, familiar with the weapon after consistent practice, then moved to the door beneath Eliza's raised brow. He didn't shoot guns when he was eighteen. He'd learned how to use them when he bought the ranch.

As the vehicle came to a halt in his circular driveway, he recognized the driver. While that surprise took some grappling with, he stepped out onto the front porch as Derek Jenson started toward him.

The prosecutor smiled and pointed toward the gun Brandon held at his side. "Expecting company?"

"Not you." Brandon stopped before him.

Derek scrutinized his face as he'd done to the witnesses during Jack Reed's trial. "So, you haven't heard."

"Heard what?" He had a hunch, though, and foreboding expanded. There was only one reason Derek would go out of his way for a personal visit.

"Your dad escaped from prison a few days ago."

Brandon stiffened even though he'd expected as much, glancing back to see Eliza nearly beside him. He wished she wasn't here to listen to this.

"He took a guard hostage and made it to the gate, where a car was waiting for him. We traced the car, and it's been reported stolen. I got a call this morning from a friend who's working the homicide case. He says the federal marshal leading the search is on his way here. He thinks Jack is here in Vengeance."

Unbelievable. Brandon cursed. His father had promised he'd escape. He'd probably spent every waking moment locked in his cell dreaming of the day he'd break out and come after his sons.

"What makes the marshal think he's here?"

"The stolen car was reported at a gas station just outside of town. They're checking hotels in the area now."

"Why would he risk coming back here?" Eliza said.

Ordinarily that would be a stupid move on a fugitive's part, unless that fugitive had a compelling reason to come back, and Jack Reed certainly did. He hated his two sons. Hated Brandon the most. He'd threatened more than once to come back and kill him. In the courtroom just after sentencing, he'd spat his threats to Brandon.

"I'll get out," he'd hissed. "I'll get out and when I do, I'm going to do what I should have done when you were a worthless little boy…."

Nothing like unconditional love from a father. Brandon often wondered what it would be like to have a normal father.

"You should keep your eye out for him, testifying the way you did at his trial," Derek said.

Brandon nodded. "Thanks for coming out to warn me."

"I told you I would."

Derek was a family man and a good prosecutor. Bad guys didn't get away from him, and he'd always been sensitive to the price of a son testifying against a father. What he didn't get was that Brandon had taken great pleasure in sending his father to prison.

Brandon had been nineteen when he'd testified. Derek had been the closest thing to a father figure to him. Looking back, that was so sad. A prosecutor he hadn't known a year had been more of a father to him than his own had.

"When did he escape?" Eliza asked.

"Last week."

Before David's murder. Brandon shared a look with Eliza before turning to Derek. "Are the police looking into whether he had anything to do with the murders?"

"Actually, that's another reason my friend called. They don't have anything to go on, but they aren't discounting the possibility he went after David."

He'd told Derek all about Jack's abuse. He was a predator who was capable of killing his young. Just another dinner.

"If you see anything, be sure and call Detective Zimmerman. He's been briefed on the matter."

Eliza didn't appear happy to hear that bit of news. But Zimmerman knew about the car that had followed David here and that someone had been following him. Had it been Jack Reed or someone else?

"Will do. Thanks again for coming out," Brandon said.

Derek went back to his car. As Brandon watched him drive away, he braced himself for Eliza.

"That man thinks your dad will come after you, doesn't he?"

Brandon moved by her and went inside to put his gun away. He wasn't in the mood to talk about his father.

"Is he that dangerous?"

"He killed someone after drinking too much and trying to drive home."

"And you helped lock him up."

Was this her way of manipulating him into talking? She'd attempted to broach this subject before.

"What was it like after your mother died?"

At least she hadn't phrased it the other way…suicide. The wall he'd erected to block attacks like this rose up. The promise he and his brother had made still stood strong. Never talk about what happened after their mother died. Their father's alcoholism and their mother's suicide were unavoidable. Both were common knowledge around town.

He strode into the kitchen and opened the refrigerator to find something for dinner.

Eliza entered the kitchen, taking a seat at the island.

Selecting some thawed chicken breasts, he retrieved a pan and put some oil into it, flipping on the gas burner. Then he went about chopping up the chicken to make a stir-fry. Cooking would give him something to do with Eliza so close. And inquisitive.

"Was he abusive?" she asked him again.

He stopped cutting the chicken to look at her. She'd asked the question, but she sounded as though she already knew the answer.

"He was, wasn't he?"

"Leave it alone, Eliza."

"It's me, Brandon. I've known you a long time. I remember all the days you missed in school. You wouldn't talk about it. You still won't. I didn't piece it together then, but now…"

Now she was a grown woman and she could see things much clearer. There was a reason for his bad-boy persona during school. "Some things are better left unsaid."

"Not something like that."

Her eyes misted. David had died with his secret. Brandon still had a chance to free himself of his. He could feel her thinking that. She was backing him into a corner.

"Leave it be, Eliza," he said more sternly.

"Did he beat you before your mother died?"

No. Her death had spawned the hell he and his brother had lived through until Brandon was able to send their father where he belonged. The change in their father had been startling. He'd always been a drunk, but not an abusive one. A week of surreal grief had passed after Brandon's mother died. He and David had helped their dad plan the funeral. They'd received condolences from everyone in town. And then they'd gone home to the emptiness.

One night when his father was well into his bottle of whiskey, he'd flown into a rage and gone after David first.

"You did this!" he'd roared. "You drove her to her grave, you sniveling brats!"

The quicksilver violence had stunned Brandon. He'd watched in terror as his father beat David. After the third or fourth blow, he'd regained his senses and stepped between them. He'd tried to stop his father, and when he'd become the next punching bag, he'd struck back. At nine, he was hardly a match.

He and David had missed a week of school that time.

Eliza moved the burning chicken from the stove and turned it off. She put her hand on his shoulder, eyes soft and warm, ready to comfort.

That was what he always hated. Women who thought they could make it better. While no other woman had guessed the abuse he and David had suffered, some of them had tried.

"You need to talk about it, Brandon. If not with me, then someone."

That was awfully selfless of her. If only she understood all of it.

After that night, Brandon had protected David as much as he could. There were times when their father's unpredictable temper had been unleashed on David. It had been enough to push his little brother into a vulnerable shell, one some kids at school picked up on. David had been teased a lot. The wimpy kid of Vengeance High. More than once, Brandon had beaten the lunch out of boys who had dared to taunt him. He'd gained a bad-boy reputation. David had become a shadow of his older brother. He didn't have many friends. But it had soon been established that anyone who touched him would have Brandon to deal with. And Brandon had no qualms about doing some damage to any boy's face who tried to hurt his brother.

It had led to the use of the same method with his father. At sixteen, Brandon had grown into a big kid with a crackling voice. He'd honed his fighting skills. On one rainy night, his father was working on his usual indulgence of whiskey and in a particularly foul mood. Brandon had gotten good at flying below that radar and had trained his brother to do the same. Stay in Brandon's shadow.

Except that night David hadn't listened. He'd yelled back at their father's insidious remarks, the blame for their mother's death, the hatred he harbored for his own sons—all of it David had rebuked.

His father had attacked him in a vicious rage. It had spurred one in Brandon. Such a fast reaction. One second he'd been calm, the next a mad animal. He'd beaten his own father. Even to this day he couldn't recall every detail. So blinded by fury, he'd let go of every fiber of control. Let anger take over.

That time it had been his father who couldn't leave the house. The next two years were a new form of torture. Brandon had to constantly look over his shoulder. And every chance he got, his father beat David. He couldn't beat Brandon anymore, but he could beat the life out of David. Brandon couldn't be there every time to save him. But he retaliated every time David's face was battered and bruised. He made sure his father's face looked the same. But that had only made the beatings worse. Brandon worried he'd kill David. That's when he began looking for ways to send his dad to prison. Luck went his way. Or maybe luck had nothing to do with it. Jack Reed was a felon who'd managed to avoid arrest. All it took was someone to watch him. Brandon had watched for only a few months before the hit-and-run.

But the damage was already done. David was a shell of a man, and Brandon had grown up learning how to fight. Using violence to right a wrong. He wasn't proud of that.

"Brandon?"

Eliza still stood close to him, her hand on his arm.

"David never escaped it," he said without thinking.

"The abuse?"

"He suffered the most." The words kept coming. "My father wasn't a pedophile. His was a crime of hate. He beat us repeatedly because he blamed us for our mother's suicide."

"Oh, Brandon."

Her sympathy made him nearly cringe. He couldn't stand sympathy.

As though sensing that, she lowered her arm. "I always knew there was something he wasn't telling me. And he looked up to you so much. And then…not."

Living in his shadow…

"He was jealous of you."

That was painful to hear. He leaned both hands on the stove's edge and bent his head. Although the truth had always been there, having it voiced made it undeniable.

"You were always taking care of him. And people didn't see him when you were in the room," she said, making it worse.

That's because they were afraid of him. He turned his head to see her. "I had a reputation."

"You protected him. You weren't a bully. I was there, remember? Don't make it something it wasn't."

His heart lightened unexpectedly. Had she really seen it that way? Had everyone else? He straightened from the stove and faced her.

"You were a superhero."

He breathed a derisive laugh. "That's a little much."

"Most kids revered you. They cheered you on when you beat up a bully."

Brandon hadn't noticed any of that. He'd been too wrapped up in anger that anyone would try to harm his brother.

"If you hadn't been such a loner, you'd have been the most popular boy in your class," Eliza said.

What about David? She was missing that piece. David had been the helpless kid who always needed his big brother. "You said it yourself—no one saw David when I was in the room." Including her.

He saw her remember. She'd been just as guilty of not seeing David.

"That's what I mean when I say David never escaped. My father beat him and bullies beat him, but only when I wasn't around. His only existence back then was as a weak kid." One who'd grown into a handsome man who hid behind his looks and bad habits.

And then he'd come to Brandon's ranch for a visit, only to discover Eliza had only married him to spite his older brother.

"Brandon, David wasn't helpless. He went to college and became a very successful journalist. He was smart and kind and loving. He just had some demons in his past that he never dealt with. That's why he made bad choices, and that's why he isn't here now. He isn't here because of anything you did. If anything, he made it as *far* as he did *because* of you."

All flattering and whimsically optimistic. "He's dead because he had a drinking and gambling problem. He had a drinking and gambling problem because he hated living in my shadow."

"He was abused by his father. Not you."

Their father had made David prey to bullies. That's what she was saying.

"What would have happened to David if you hadn't been there?" Eliza persisted.

He would have been beaten far worse by their dad and the bullies. Maybe their dad would have killed him. Because Brandon was certain he was capable.

"You see?" She moved a step closer to him, once again

putting her hand on him, this time on his chest, and this time her other hand joined in.

There was so much more that she didn't understand. Taking a hold of her hands, he removed them from his chest. "Talking about it isn't going to make it go away. Or change what is."

"No, but it will heal you. Why do you think you're such a recluse? You haven't stopped running from the abuse you suffered. Don't make the same mistake David made. Don't keep it all bottled up tight and secure from the world until it eats you alive."

"I'm not running." He'd never run from it. "I'm the one who sent my father to prison, remember?"

"You may think you have it all resolved in your head, but you don't."

"Yeah? Well, you may think you understand, but you don't. I'll ask you again, leave it *be*."

Just when Eliza thought she had Brandon figured out, he surprised her yet again. There was more, still more to what made him the solitary man he was today. The abuse he'd suffered was one piece. His brother's jealousy another.

She let him leave the kitchen, abandoning dinner to turn on the television in the other room.

Eliza resumed his task, salvaging the chicken and making a quick stir-fry, guessing that's why he'd chopped the chicken. As she finished, her cell phone rang.

Going to her purse in the living room, she passed Brandon. The caller was Ryker.

Was he going to apologize for the way he'd left her the last time they'd spoken? "Hi, Ryker."

"Eliza. I need you to come and get me."
"Where are you?"
"I've been arrested."

Chapter 8

Brandon wouldn't let her go alone, so Eliza brought him with her despite his grumbling over being dragged into more drama. He'd gotten mad when she'd reminded him that he didn't have to go with her. He was being protective. He'd protected his brother and protected her when they were growing up, and he was still doing it.

If only this didn't stem from his abusive father. She was afraid of how much more he had to hide about that. How much worse could it get? He and David were beaten as children, blamed for their mother's death. What more could there be?

The police released Ryker on bail and he emerged into the front area of the police station, where she and Brandon had been told to wait.

Ryker was a mess, his brown hair uncombed, dark circles under his green eyes.

"What happened, Ryker?" Eliza asked as they walked toward Brandon's truck.

"Aegina moved out." He raked his fingers through his hair, mouth an upset line.

First the affair and now this. "Did she move in with that man?"

"No. She went to stay with her mother. She said she needed time to think." Ryker punched the side of Brandon's truck.

Brandon grabbed his wrist, his eyes an unmistakable message to cool it.

"She won't even talk to me."

"Then you should give her what she wants. Time to think about it."

"Don't you mean time to convince herself she's better off with my mechanic?"

"Ex-mechanic."

He smirked at her.

"Stalking her at her mother's house will convince her faster than anything," Brandon said.

"Who asked you?"

Brandon put up his hands. "Just saying."

Ryker wilted. His shoulders slumped and his head lowered.

Eliza rubbed his back a little.

"I can't believe she moved out."

Eliza met Brandon's gaze, at a loss for what to say. If she said too much it would make patching things up with her brother that much harder. But the truth was he'd driven his wife away.

"Do you want to come out to the ranch for a few days?"

Ryker lifted his head, a lost man in love. "No. I want to be home in case she changes her mind."

"What did you do to get arrested?" Eliza gently asked.

Her brother sighed and opened the back door of Brandon's truck. She climbed into the front passenger seat.

When Brandon began driving, Ryker finally spoke. "I came home from work to a note. Her clothes are gone. All her cosmetics. Even her shampoo." He pinched the bridge of his nose. "I went crazy."

"Did you hurt her?"

"No!" he shouted. "I would never hurt Aegina. I love her. I didn't realize how much until now."

Until she was gone.

"I went there, and her mother said Aegina didn't want to talk to me. She said to give her time to think.

"I forced my way inside and found her in the kitchen at the table. I pulled her up by her arms and pleaded with her to come back home. When she refused, I started yelling. I wanted her to come back home."

"Her mother called the police?" Eliza asked, and Ryker nodded, head low again.

"Stay away from her," Brandon said.

And Eliza wondered over the hint of passion in his voice.

"I can't," Ryker said meekly. "I have to convince her that I love her and I always have."

Eliza was glad to hear that he was finally coming to terms with his bitterness over being stuck in Vengeance. He'd never been stuck.

"You've had what I always dreamed of having, Ryker."

She said it without thinking. Brandon's sharp glance made her realize that.

"You have what you want," Ryker said.

"My event planning company? Yeah, I have that. But I don't have a family. I don't have two beautiful children and a husband who loves me."

"You did have that. A husband, I mean."

Until David died.

Turning toward the window, she said, "No, I didn't."

Silence in the backseat told her Ryker was thinking about that. "You and Brandon should have stuck it out."

"We were just kids," Brandon spoke up.

"None of this would be happening if you had."

Brandon's eyes shifted to look into the rearview mirror.

David wouldn't be dead and Aegina wouldn't have left Ryker. Ryker wouldn't have resented Eliza and she wouldn't have married David.

"You can't be certain of that," Eliza argued. "I would have left Vengeance with or without Brandon."

"Another reason why you and I would have never worked."

Not back then. Now...? Eliza would be better off never having that question answered.

When she and Brandon returned to Reed Ranch, someone was waiting for them. Jillian. She was returning to her car just as Brandon drove over the hill on his long driveway. Going on nine at night, it was late for a social visit.

Eliza approached behind Brandon and caught Jillian's unwelcoming glance. She was in tight jeans and a deep V-neck tank top, her dark hair silky and falling onto the bare skin of her chest. But it was her beautiful blue eyes that chilled her, so full of animosity, leashed but ready to break loose.

"I tried calling," Jillian said. "I came by to tell you how sorry I am to hear about David."

"Thanks, Jillian."

"If there's anything I can do..."

"I appreciate the thought, but there really isn't anything anyone can do. Eliza and I will handle it."

Jillian's gaze slid briefly to Eliza. "When is the funeral?"

"We're waiting for the body to be released for burial."

"Will you tell me when it is? I'd like to help in any way I can."

"Sure. I'll make sure someone lets you know."

Instantly, Eliza saw how that remark chafed her. Jillian's back jerked ever so slightly, stiffening. She stared at Brandon. Then she glanced furtively at Eliza.

Brandon strode toward the door, clearly ready to leave Jillian standing there.

Eliza looked at Jillian, whose dangerous eyes held a clear threat.

Brandon slammed the front door shut behind him.

Damn him for leaving her to get rid of Jillian on her own. "I—I'm sorry. Brandon's dealing with a lot right now."

Jillian's brow lifted higher on one side. "Is he now?"

This was a woman who'd hollered and pounded on the door after Brandon had broken up with her. Something warned Eliza to tread lightly. "Aside from his brother's death, yes."

"And he talked to you about this?"

The image of Brandon talking freely was funny in her mind. "Brandon doesn't talk to anyone about his problems."

"And yet he talks to you."

Eliza smiled with an ironic laugh. "Not willingly."

The other woman put her hand on her hip. "But you know him so well that you get him to…open up to you, is that it?"

"Well, I have known him since I was in grade school." A cool breeze made her rub her arm. She'd like to go inside now—and yell at Brandon for doing this to her.

"Yes, I heard all about that. Didn't he dump you in high school or something?"

Dump her… "He broke up with me, yes."

"So, what is all this about?" She swung her arm toward the house. "What's going on between the two of you?"

"Nothing." Eliza felt her face begin to heat.

"Yeah…it looks like nothing."

"No. Nothing is going on between us. David was just murdered—"

"Ever since you came here he's been different."

Different?

"That night…when you and David arrived. Brandon and I were getting on just fine. We were in the middle of a romantic evening. And then you showed up and his whole demeanor changed. He couldn't take his eyes off you. You couldn't take your eyes off him, either. It was like you hadn't seen each other in years."

They hadn't.

"David noticed, too, did you know that?"

Now Eliza bowed her head. That fact would always hurt her. She hadn't meant to make David feel jealous or worry that she'd leave him for Brandon, or that she loved Brandon more…which she did. What David died never knowing was that there would never be another man she'd love more than Brandon. If only she'd have thought of that before she agreed to marry his brother. It wasn't fair to David.

"You should leave Vengeance."

Eliza's head snapped up. It sounded so much like the note she'd received. The second note.

"You're taking the man I love away from me."

"No. I'm not. And I can't leave until David's killer is caught. Look, Jillian, you have nothing to worry about. Brandon doesn't love me. He never did."

"Then stop trying to make him!"

With that Jillian stormed to her car, got in and raced out of the driveway, spraying up dirt under the exterior lights until all Eliza could see were car lights disappearing over the hill.

When she headed for the house, Brandon stood in the open doorway, gun at his side.

"You would have shot her?"

Inside, Brandon closed the door and returned the weapon to its trusty place in the entryway table drawer. "You didn't think I'd leave you out there alone with her, did you?"

Jillian was a chameleon with her emotions. One moment she was normal and the next she was lashing out.

"What if she lied about the night we caught her with David?"

"David was last with Naomi, remember."

Eliza was still bothered. There was something not quite right about Jillian Marks.

"The police will find David's killer. Come on." He reached for her. "Let's go heat up dinner. I'm starving."

"I am, too." She walked in front of his arm and he touched her briefly, getting her going in the direction he wanted.

While the instinct nagged that this friendly ground they were on was dangerous, she did need to eat.

Not having David around and being with Brandon after so long had a strange but not unappealing mystique. The fact that David was dead did play its part and plagued her with guilt, but it hovered in the recesses of consciousness. The raw connection she had with Brandon couldn't be denied.

She watched him move around the kitchen with smooth agility, manly hands giving her some water and then a plate. Then he came around and sat at the island beside her, digging in.

"You're a good cook," Brandon said after he had half his plate devoured.

"A party girl doesn't always have others do all the work." She deliberately didn't say event planner and eyed him askance to see if he caught that.

He chuckled.

"I like cooking. It's a celebration all on its own."

"You would say that."

"Only because you expected me to say something like that."

"Then it's not a celebration?"

"I love to cook. It's soothing." She tipped her head up dreamily. "Satisfying. I have some recipes I came up with. I have a collection. I was thinking about doing a cookbook someday." She hadn't had the time yet. Upon reflection, she should have made time.

Why had she kept so busy? Why had her event planning company been so important? She had to make a living.

Surrogate for love.

Of course it was that if she truly believed she couldn't fall in love with anyone other than Brandon. That seemed so…shallow. Like there had to be more depth to it. She could have waited for another man to love.

"You should."

She turned to Brandon in surprise. "Should what?"

"Do a cookbook."

Figures he'd say that. "Why, so I stay at home more?"

He scooped the last bite from his plate and ate it. After drinking some water, he said, "Don't go there, Eliza."

She couldn't get past the passion that had led to sex. There had to be something that had survived between them. How could Brandon have ended them so easily back then and want her so much now?

"If I'd stayed at home more, would we have lasted longer?" she had to ask.

Pushing his plate away, Brandon turned to her. "If Ryker would have moved his wife out of Vengeance, would they be having the problems they're having?"

Why was he asking that? Was he avoiding her question? "Probably."

"I disagree. You and your brother have that in common. You both run from love."

That again? "I don't run. Ryker doesn't, either. He loves Aegina."

"And only now realizes it."

Now that Aegina is gone. Eliza pushed her food around with her fork. "I wouldn't have run if you'd loved me in high school."

"You ran because of me?"

Didn't he know that? She looked at him incredulously.

His eyes took in the answer on her face. "We were kids."

"I loved you."

"How could you possibly have loved me at sixteen?"

"Seventeen. I did love you." She'd known it then, and she knew it now.

His head withdrew, jerked back as though the impact of her reply hit him. And then blankness came over him. A trapped kind of blankness. This is what most women probably saw when he began to shy away from them, retreat into the safety of his solitude.

"You're doing it again."

Confusion put a furrow between his eyebrows. "Doing what?"

She'd use his word. *"Running."*

He scoffed. "I am not. I just never knew you felt that strongly back then."

"You must have."

"No. You were young and I didn't want to hold you back."

Convenient. She didn't say the word out loud. There was no point. He'd have ended them no matter what he felt in return. Standing from the stool, she took her plate to the double-sided sink and rinsed it. As she placed it in the other side, Brandon came up behind her, putting his plate in the sink with the still-running water and, in true boy fashion, not rinsing it.

His hands touched her biceps, gentle yet packing instant flame.

"I'm sorry. If I'd have known…"

He'd have what? Not broken up with her? No. He would have been a little more sensitive than simply stopping his calls. The end would have been the same. Destiny had called him in the direction he'd gone, opposite the party girl. And though she'd ached for him, she'd have been the one to leave if he hadn't done it. They were getting too close. Her father had just died. She'd been so lost. He must have sensed her need for escape.

She looked up at him, tipping her head up to see over her shoulder. "We both did what we needed to do."

Why did it feel as though everything had changed?

He seemed to be feeling the same. The way his gaze moved from her eyes to her mouth ignited the fire that had drawn them together the night of David's disappearance.

David.

Eliza stiffened and Brandon's hands dropped as he stepped back. She turned and leaned against the counter. He stood there, hands at his sides, tall, windblown and handsome…debating.

That's when the degree to which she was falling for him crashed down upon her. This was far more involved than it had been when she was seventeen. The adolescent first love paled in comparison to what she'd feel for him if she allowed this to continue.

And she could not forget David. She could not allow her marriage to him to fade as though it had never existed. Though David had been a lying, cheating trouble-seeker, he didn't deserve her disrespect. No man did. No person did. In the name of humanity, she had to back away.

Brandon would thank her when the time came for her to go home to Hollywood.

Chapter 9

Eliza knocked on Aegina's parents' front door and waited. It was a clear, sunny day, and the neighborhood was alive with activity. People worked in their yards, washed cars, walked or biked. Kids laughed and shouted from somewhere a block away. No cars drove by. A typical small-town neighborhood where families thrived, something she'd missed out on ever since she'd left Vengeance. It gave her a nostalgic feeling, one that came with a sting of regret.

The front door opened and Aegina's plump, gray-haired mother appeared. "Eliza." She sounded wary.

"Is Aegina here?"

"Yeah," Aegina said from behind her mother's bulk. "Let her in, Mom."

The woman stepped aside, still wary.

"Thanks." Eliza hugged Aegina. "I'm so sorry for what my brother did."

After glancing over Eliza's shoulder at her mother, Aegina took her hand and led her through a kitchen that was still messy from lunch. Outside on the back patio, Aegina sat at a table with a bright red umbrella and flowers blooming all around them. A pitcher of sun tea was on the table with a stack of disposable cups.

"Are you having a barbecue?" Eliza asked.

"No. Mom just felt like having tea for the day. She thought it would cheer me up." She dug into the ice bucket beside the pitcher and filled two cups.

Eliza waited while she poured the tea, and then she accepted one of the glasses and took a sip.

"Where's Brandon?" Aegina asked.

"I left him at the ranch." It hadn't been hard to elude him once he'd started work for the day. Although he'd instructed her to come and get him if she needed to go into town for anything, this was one trip he didn't belong on. This was girl-talk time.

"Any news on David?"

Eliza shook her head.

"Sorry. It must be so hard for you."

Losing a husband and over the moon for his brother. Yeah, that was pretty hard.

"I went out to breakfast this morning with some friends. I heard some things that were kind of surprising."

"About David?"

"No…about you. Is anything going on between you and Brandon?"

"People are talking about me and Brandon?"

"He was with you the night you and David fought at the Cork."

"Yes, but—"

"One of my friends said David freaked because he found out about the two of you."

"That isn't true!"

"And the affair is still going on. You and Brandon are

glad David is gone. They even speculated you're about to get away with murder, that maybe you killed David to be with Brandon."

And two other people? Eliza had been away for a long time. Most people in town didn't know her very well. They may have heard about her strained relationship with her brother and her high school love affair with Brandon. The party girl who left town to plan parties in Hollywood. On the surface she had the résumé for scandal. But murder? Killing one man would require a lot of insensitivity and motive. Killing three, one who was a good friend to her, was too much of a stretch.

"That's ridiculous." Who was spreading those nasty rumors?

"I set my friends straight, don't worry, but I thought you'd want to know what's blowing through town today."

"Who told your friend that?"

"Her sister, who said Jillian Marks told her. Who knows where it started though."

"It started right there. Jillian is doing that on purpose."

"Really?"

"She wants Brandon."

"That's right. I heard they were seeing each other."

Until Eliza had come to town.

"Well, it'll be over by morning, you wait and see. End of the week tops."

Eliza sighed her exasperation. "Will that woman never give up? Brandon broke up with her. I'm hardly stealing him from anyone."

"You have to admit, the timing is pretty bad. You show up, Brandon breaks up with Jillian and then your husband is murdered."

"I didn't kill David."

Aegina put her hand over hers. "I know."

Eliza smiled with warm appreciation. It was time to get to what she came here to say. "You've always been a good friend to me."

"You've been a good friend to me, too." Her tone was tense, preparatory for what was to come.

"What Ryker did..."

"I really don't want to talk about it."

"Just hear me out, okay?"

Aegina sipped her tea. "He kicked open the door and said ugly things to me."

"I know. And he deserved to be arrested. But, Aegina, that isn't my brother. He's a good man. He's just confused. And then finding out you're seeing someone else...he broke down."

"He's not as confused as you think. He's just upset that I was with another man. Men can't handle that. Their egos are weak that way. He's upset, nothing else."

"You're wrong. Ryker loves you."

"He'll love me more after we're divorced and nothing is stopping him from going anywhere but Vengeance."

"You don't think your kids will stop him?"

Aegina looked away. "They might, but I won't."

"What about our mother? Ryker is always throwing her in my face. Would he leave her here?"

Her sister-in-law turned back to her. "It doesn't matter. It's over. I'm finished. I can't do this anymore. I can't be with a man who doesn't love me enough to have a strong enough reason to want to stay in Vengeance."

"But you are enough reason for him. Every bit as much as your kids."

"I appreciate you trying, Eliza, but this has been a long time in the making. Ryker and I haven't had a real marriage for years now. We haven't had sex in months. We fight all the time."

"That's because Ryker was confused. He isn't anymore. He loves you, Aegina. You have to believe me."

Shaking her head, Aegina looked away again. "No, he doesn't. He never did."

"You're wrong. He thought leaving Vengeance was what he wanted. It isn't. Your affair made him see that."

Aegina kept her head averted.

"He'll forgive you for the affair."

"That's what you don't get. Ryker will never forgive me for that. It'll be his convenient excuse for agreeing for a divorce."

"No—"

Aegina stood, the chair scraping on the stone patio. "Thanks for coming by, Eliza. But I think you should go now. We can be friends if you're able to respect my wishes. I want to divorce Ryker. If he's had a change of heart, then I'm sorry, it's too late."

It was futile to keep trying to convince her. In time maybe she'd relax her stance. Reluctantly, Eliza stood with her and led the way to the door. Once there, she paused.

"All I ask is you consider what I've said. I know my brother. He wasn't happy about being stuck with our mother here in Vengeance. What he didn't realize until now is that has nothing to do with you. I should have helped him more."

"Oh, Eliza, stop being such a saint. Your mother has nothing to do with what's going on between me and Ryker, and you have nothing to do with it, either. We've managed to mess that up all on our own."

Eliza smiled for lack of anything else to say or do. "I hope you change your mind about him."

Aegina said nothing, only hugged her before waving goodbye when Eliza turned on the front walk to do the same.

On the way to her car, her thoughts turned from her brother to what had lain beneath the surface ever since Aegina told her. David believed she and Brandon were having an affair. If the rumors were true, even partially, he'd died thinking such a horrible thing. That bothered her, festered in her conscience. The wrongness. The scandal. The lack of respect for another human being. Her husband.

She shut the car door a little harder than necessary, and the glove box bounced open. Leaning over, she saw a cell phone and froze. David's cell phone. She picked it up and stared at it. She turned it on. The battery was low, but she was able to navigate to his recent call list.

There was a number she didn't recognize, and the call was received the night before he was killed. She called the number.

A man answered. "Who is this?"

"Who is this? Why was David Reed receiving calls from you?"

"Are you his wife?"

Eliza ended the call and started the engine. The man knew David was married. Did he also know he was dead? Had she just talked to his killer? Why would he answer if he killed David?

She began driving. As the busy town center gave way to a rural landscape, she noticed a car following her. It was the car she'd seen parked on the hill at the ranch. Swallowing a sudden flash of anxiety, she pressed for more gas. The car stayed far enough behind that she couldn't see the person driving. The bulky shirt suggested it was a man.

The turnoff for the ranch appeared ahead on the road.

Eliza drove onto Brandon's gravel driveway and watched the car pass along the highway. She breathed a sigh of relief.

Brandon ran out of people to call to find out where Eliza had gone. Damn her. His father could be anywhere. The thought of his dad harming her made him want to punch the wall. He'd suffered enough of his father's cruelty. No more. Eliza had to stay with him so he could keep an eye on her.

The sound of tires over gravel spared him. He went out onto the front porch. Seeing her drive up in the rental eased his tension. He waited for her to climb the steps.

She held up her hand. "Before you say anything, I went to see Aegina. Men weren't welcome for that talk." She entered the house.

"I told you not to go anywhere without me."

She swept her hands in front of her body, palms out. "As you can see, I'm fine."

More than fine. She looked great in white shorts and a black-and-white summery top. Except she seemed tired and preoccupied with something. And she glanced back at the road, which caught his attention. "You were gone a long time."

"I had to stop at the police station."

Had something happened? "Why?"

"I found David's cell phone in the glove box of the rental. A strange man tried calling him the night before he was killed. The police are looking into it."

"What was the man's name?"

"I only had a number. He wasn't in David's address book." She looked back, searching the road again.

Brandon didn't miss it. "Did someone follow you? Do you think it was him?"

Her head spun back to him and her lack of response answered for him. He had to quell angry frustration. She'd sneaked away without him and then, just as he'd feared, she'd run into trouble. She'd made it back here, but what if something had gone wrong? Why did he care so much anyway? She was a grown woman. She could take care of herself, and she hadn't been alone. And she was obviously fine.

"Who followed you?" he demanded anyway.

"It was that car."

"The one that was parked on the hill?"

"He passed the turnoff to the ranch, though."

Someone was watching Eliza. Did it have something to do with David's murder? The notes? Or was it his dad? Was his dad responsible for all three incidences?

"Was it a man?"

"He was too far behind to tell. It looked like a man, though."

His dad. Jack Reed had the personality of someone who could kill his own sons, like what he saw on the news every once in a while. The man who killed his wife and kids and then himself. No rhyme or reason. Just a lethal dose of mental instability. Maybe he'd gotten to David. Maybe the senator and sheriff were involved somehow. But why would he send the notes to Eliza? To make Brandon afraid for her welfare? It was working.

No matter where his concern came from, he had to protect her. He had to keep it platonic, however. His heart could not be involved.

"Don't go anywhere without me anymore, Eliza."

"All right. I won't." She walked around him and entered the house.

She was acting strange. As though she was uncomfortable with him. After putting her things down, she veered a wide arch around him on her way to the kitchen. Curious over her seemingly exaggerated distance, he went there with her.

She opened his refrigerator and took out the milk, then found a glass.

"One of those nights?"

"I have a lot on my mind. I just need to let go. Unwind."

He chuckled because he'd teased her and she hadn't caught it. She looked at him, lowering the glass of milk and eyeing him quizzically.

"I have something stronger for that."

"Milk relaxes me."

"Wine would, too." Especially if she wanted to let go and unwind.

Frowning in reproach, finally catching on, she took her milk to the living room and turned on the television. Avoiding him again.

He followed, sitting on the chair next to the couch where she switched channels until *Entertainment Now* played. Milk and celebrity news. It was so like her…and then…not.

Unable to stave his adoration, he watched her for a while. As the entertainment program led into the latest Hollywood breakup, she leaned back with a sigh and sipped her milk. When her gaze wandered away from the television, he wondered what had made her so tense. She was distracted, and something was keeping her from acknowledging his presence. He should leave her to her quiet mood. He was glad she was home. Before she'd arrived, he was so worried. Now he needed to know why she was stressed, even melancholic.

"What did you and Aegina talk about? Why did you go there?"

Her brother, but that didn't answer all of his questions.

"Ryker."

"She must be upset." Ryker had been arrested because he'd threatened her.

"She is," she answered without taking her eyes off the television.

Another noncommittal answer. Was it her brother who made her that way or something else? Had she and Aegina talked about something other than Ryker?

"What did Aegina say?"

"She doesn't believe Ryker loves her."

There had to be more. "What else did she say?"

That snapped her head toward him.

So, she did say something. "Did she tell you something that upset you?"

She turned away again. "It's nothing."

Now he was certain there was something. "What did she say, Eliza?"

With another sigh, this one not so relaxed, Eliza turned off the television and moved so that her body faced him more, her legs angled along the couch. "People are saying we're having an affair."

"Us?" Had his ranch hand said something? Or someone else? Jillian? Why would she do that if she was so hell-bent on having him that she'd stalk him?

"They're also saying that David knew."

He was beginning to understand her melancholy. That didn't settle well with him, either. He'd slept with his brother's wife. If he could change that, he would. But murder wasn't something that had been on his radar.

"And that I could have killed him to be with you."

The last delivery of information caused his mood to plummet down with hers. The David from his childhood, the one not burdened with physical abuse, had been kind and fun-loving. He didn't deserve to die the way he had, much less believing his own brother was in love with his wife.

"It could be just rumor," he said.

"It's not."

"But it could still be a rumor. No one saw us…." He couldn't say it.

"They saw us together."

"We aren't having an affair." But they had.

Now it was his turn to want distance. He bent his head, wondering if it was too late to go find something else to do. Why had he followed her in here, anyway? Did he mean to seduce her again? Could he do that to his brother, even in death? A deeper part of him argued he and Eliza had more history than she and David did. David should have talked to him before he ran off to Vegas to marry her.

"We did, Brandon," she made it worse by saying. "And it may have killed David."

"How could that have killed David?"

"I didn't love him. If he thought I did when he married me, he may have been driven to extremes."

"Did he love you?" Brandon suddenly doubted that he had.

"I don't know. I made a mistake marrying him. That mistake led to his decisions to sleep with other women and gamble more. It's what kept him away from your ranch. If not for that, maybe he would have been here instead of walking into his death." Eliza lowered her head as her voice quivered and she struggled with a few rogue sobs.

The guilt was hard on him, too.

She wiped her eyes as tears spilled.

Not going to her didn't seem like an option. He got up and went to her, sitting beside her and wrapping his arm around her. She leaned against him and cried softly, the tears of real remorse.

He wished he could do that. Cry. But crying had become something he was incapable of doing. His father had seen him cry once, and he'd vowed it would be the last. His father had taunted him, calling him a crybaby and then hitting him and yelling that no amount of crying would bring his mother back. Crying wouldn't absolve him, either. The beatings had grown worse and worse, beating the guilt into his sons.

Until Eliza had shown up and he'd slept with her the day his brother was killed, Brandon had sworn off guilt the same as he'd sworn off crying. Could he swear off guilt where his brother was concerned? His brother had been a victim just like Brandon when they were kids. Victims of their father's warped abuse. His blame.

Back then, he was innocent. Now he wasn't. He'd taken his brother's wife. And if his brother had known that before his death, Brandon deserved to feel guilty.

And then, maybe he didn't. Maybe he shouldn't feel guilty at all.

Eliza's tears eased and she lifted her head, red eyes needy and blotchy, puffy skin wet. "Do you think he would have blamed me if he hadn't been drunk or in trouble with gambling?"

It was uncanny that she used that word. "Blamed you for what?"

She quieted another sob. "Loving you."

Eliza's sincere plea for a reassuring answer kept him from withdrawing from those words. She was a sophomore again. Needing him.

If his brother had been thinking clearly when he ran into her at the athlete's party, he wouldn't have been so reckless. David had confronted Brandon after he broke up with Eliza and told him he thought he was making a mistake, that he and Eliza belonged together. That had puzzled Brandon when David had called to brag about marrying her, something he would have never done when they were teenagers. He and David had always been a team. Something had changed that. Something had pushed David too far. And now that he was dead, Brandon was certain that something went beyond drinking and gambling. His addictions may have triggered what had led to his murder, but David hadn't meant to alienate his own brother. Brandon was sure of that.

"I think he would have never married you."

Eliza tensed and pushed away from him. He removed his arm from around her, letting her go. Distance was better right now. She'd already told him she loved him when they were teenagers. That had been a guided missile. To hear her talk like that now…

"I didn't mean that I love you now." She stood, hugging herself and moving away from the couch and coffee table. "I was only talking about when we were teenagers. I thought I loved you."

Backpedaling.

Gladness that she'd clarified, regret that she didn't mean it and doubt that she didn't all clashed in him. He didn't dare get up, lest he try and convince her she should love him.

"I'm going to get a room in town tomorrow."

That got him to his feet. "No."

"Yes, Brandon. People are talking about us."

He went to stand before her. "I don't give a damn what anyone says. You're not going anywhere."

His father had escaped prison. David's murderer could be anywhere or anyone. Jillian…

And something deeper motivated him, something he was reluctant to identify.

"I can't stay here."

Brandon noticed how she'd picked up on whatever undercurrents were in operation between them. "Yes, you can. And you will."

"I'm going to stay in town." She headed for the hallway. It was much too early for bed, but she was eluding him. He had to let her go.

But he'd protect her. Even if he had to get his own room wherever she was staying.

Something woke her.

Eliza sat up on the bed, listening. Her cell phone. Its distinctive chime was muffled inside her purse. She got up and retrieved it, checking the caller ID to see who it was. She didn't recognize the number. It was after two in the morning.

She answered.

"Eliza Harvey?" a man's voice said. His voice was deep and a little crackly, like he was talking through an apparatus. A little muffled.

"Who is this?" And why was he calling her Harvey?

"That's not important. I need to talk to you. It's about David."

Eliza breathed through her alarm. His voice frightened her, so calm, deep and slow. Sinister. "Tell me who you are."

"I can't. Please. If anyone discovers I've called you, I could be in serious danger. Can you come outside to meet me?"

"Outside?"

"I'm here, at the ranch. I've taken a risk coming here." The voice was slow and careful. "I'm sorry for the hour. I didn't know any other way. Whenever I see you in town, you're always with Brandon."

Someone was trying to reach her. In secret. What did this man know?

"Brandon could help you."

"No." The voice sounded panicked. "I'll leave if you bring him."

"What do you want me to do?" Who was this? They were afraid.

"Come to the stable. Alone."

"What do you know about David? Who are you?"

"If you want to find David's killer, come to the stable. Alone." The caller disconnected.

Eliza would either go out there alone or the man would leave. What should she do? Wake Brandon? If the caller saw him, would he run? What if this was a ploy? What if the man wanted to get her alone to harm her?

But what if it wasn't a ploy? What if the caller was truly afraid? If he knew something about David…

She moved to the window and looked out. She couldn't see anything through the darkness and nothing moved in the lights near the stable or driveway.

Still undecided, she went into the entry and opened the drawer of the table where Brandon kept his pistol. She lifted it out. She had a cursory knowledge of guns and had seen him handle it. Copying his moves, she readied the weapon and went outside, leaving the door open just in case.

It was a quiet night. Clear sky. Stars speckled the blackness. Seeing an ATV parked alongside the stable, she wondered if one of Brandon's workers had left it there. At the stable, she saw that one of the doors was open. Stepping inside, she saw no one there. Willow nickered softly.

Then something hard hit her on the back of her head.

Chapter 10

A high-pitched whinny brought Eliza back to consciousness. She coughed. Smoke filled her nose and throat. Where was it coming from? She lifted her head. Flames engulfed the loft of the stable, right above Willow's stall.

The mare wasn't the only one neighing wildly. All four horses skittered frantically in their confinement.

Coughing and blinking against the sting of smoke and heat, Eliza crawled unsteadily to her feet. Her head throbbed, and she was dizzy. Willow crowded toward one side of her stall, pushing at the gate, eyes flashing white in fear, screaming for help.

The horse in the stall opposite reared in terror, pummeling the stall door. Flames engulfed the far wall. Eliza had to go there first. She fumbled with the latch before swinging the door open. The horse ran free, charging out of the stable.

Balls of flame dropped down into the stall beside that. Eliza unlatched the handle. The fire seemed to have been started in the loft, where a lot of hay was stored. The entire stable would go up in an inferno in no time.

Swinging the stall gate open, she glanced back at Willow. The horse reared and pounded at the gate to her stall. The fire had crept down one of the vertical beams. Soon the hay on the floor would catch.

The horse in the stall she'd just opened bolted through, pushing the gate and slamming Eliza. She fell to her knees. The smoke was getting thick. She coughed. She crawled toward Willow's stall. The horse in the one next to it neighed in panic, bucking its hind legs and kicking the stall wall. She had to hurry. Fire dropped from above. Creaking and snapping joined the increasing roar. Smoke and fire began to surround her. It was spreading fast. Almost to Willow's stall, she managed to get to her feet, coughing, unable to see through heavy smoke and burning eyes. Then a loud crash preceded something falling on her. A flaming beam crushed her.

Brandon heard the horses neighing through his open bedroom window and saw the stable on fire. He hurried into a pair of jeans before rushing downstairs. The front door was open. Had Eliza gone without him?

Swearing, he grabbed his cell phone and ran. He dialed 911 and told the operator there was a fire and where. Then he dropped the phone before passing through the open gate of the corral. He entered the burning stable, putting an arm across his face to ward off the heat and smoke. He couldn't see. Coughing, he opened the first stall and let that horse free. Fire was spreading rapidly over the floor, gathering fuel as it devoured hay. Beams lay crossed on one side.

That's when he saw Eliza, lying under one of the beams, flames beginning to lick at her legs. Brandon hefted the beam off her and threw it aside. Sparks flew, and the fire heightened.

Willow neighed in frenzied panic, kicking the stall door. He lifted Eliza and ran with her out of the stable; the sounds of Willow's screaming haunted each stride.

Placing Eliza gently on the ground outside the corral, he bent to check for breathing. Worry swallowed every thought and emotion in him. The beam that had fallen on her was big. Had it hit her head or had she been knocked out when she struck the ground? He couldn't lose her now. He'd already lost her once.

Warm breath assured him that she was alive.

Willow's screams propelled him back to the stable. The flames had grown. The heat was unbearable as he entered the structure. Another beam fell, missing him by inches. Reaching the mare's stall, he opened the door and jumped out of the way as she ran through, neighing in that frightened way.

Brandon followed her. She galloped through the corral and didn't stop running for the pasture.

Back at Eliza's side, he knelt beside her, sagging with relief when he saw her eyes open. She tried to sit up, but he stopped her. She saw the stable. It would surely burn to the ground.

"Willow." She searched around for the horse. She stared up at him with wide, horrified eyes. "Is Willow dead?"

Flashing lights appeared over the hill. He hadn't heard the siren until then. The roar of the fire was intense. His eyes still stung, and his throat was sore.

"Brandon." She gripped his biceps to sit up, wincing as she did. He hadn't put on a shirt.

Realizing he was tormenting her by not telling her where Willow was, he said, "I let them run."

"Willow's okay?"

"She's fine. Scared but fine. Are you all right?"

While she closed her eyes in relief, she nodded. Lifting her hand, she felt the back of her head. "Someone knocked me out."

Brandon helped her to her feet as the first fire truck stopped in the driveway. "What?" Had she gone to the stable because of the fire or some other reason?

"A man called me. He said he had some information on David and told me to meet him in the stable."

"Who was it?"

"I don't know."

He searched her face, absorbing the implications of that. "And you went there alone?"

"He demanded it. He said he'd leave if I brought anyone with me."

She'd wanted information. He'd have been desperate for that, too. And he could think of only one man who'd use that tactic to draw her out. "It was my father."

"His voice was strange. Like he was talking through something."

"Disguising his voice?"

"Yes."

His father had lured Eliza out to the stable and then he'd set it on fire.

"Why would he try to kill me?"

That's exactly what Brandon would like to know. A fireman approached while others went to work on the stable. Local police weren't far behind.

He looked toward his destroyed stable and then back to Eliza. A paramedic worked with her. She wasn't hurt badly enough to be taken to the hospital, thankfully. But Brandon would be damned if he'd let his father get another chance at her. He'd kill him first.

* * *

The next evening, Eliza sat in Brandon's library that also served as his office. It was a bright and cheery room with very little clutter. The white bookshelves and simple gray chairs promised hours of comfortable reading time. The desk with only a computer faced the window and a view of the back patio, dark now that the sun had set.

She'd come in here to think. And to get away from Brandon. With his father still on the run, he was on heightened alert and wouldn't stop stressing that she not go anywhere without him.

"There you are."

She plopped her head back against the gray-and-white fainting couch. "Can't I go into another room without you?"

"I didn't know if you'd left."

"I won't leave without you." She'd told him that more than once. Didn't he believe her? The man sure had trust issues.

Leaving would, however, be the smartest decision for both of them.

He sat in one of two solid gray chairs in front of a white corner bookshelf with a wry smirk shaping his mouth and eyes. "You keep running away from me."

Now it was her turn to smirk. His use of the word *running* had been deliberate. "Maybe you should learn by example." They both should run from each other, lest they end up in bed together again.

No longer taunting, he said, "My father hasn't been captured yet."

Would he come after her again? She'd be much more careful now. "I still can't believe he'd try to burn me alive in the stable."

"Believe it."

"What if it wasn't him?"

"It was him. It was him in the tan car. He's been watching me and David. And he's—"

He stopped abruptly.

"He's what?"

He met her eyes with reluctance. "He's seen us together."

Where? In town? Here at the ranch? Had he seen them horseback riding? If he'd noticed the chemistry between them, maybe he'd drawn his own conclusion that Brandon felt something for her and decided to take her away from him as a form of punishment. For doing nothing wrong. For crimes his father had invented against him. His father had killed someone while driving drunk. Brandon had not killed his mother. But Jack Reed was determined to have his imagined revenge.

"Do you think he could have killed David?"

"Yes." There was no inflection of doubt in his answer. His father was capable of murder. He was an evil man. "But would he kill the sheriff and senator?"

The sheriff was blackmailing the senator, not David, and David was probably taking money from one or both of them and not paying them back. Where was the connection? She didn't see a connection to Jack Reed other than through David. It must be what had the authorities stumped. Who would have a reason to kill all three? A liar, a cheater and a thief.

"I wish David would have talked to me before he died," Eliza said. And she wished they could have talked about more than his trouble. Before he was strangled to death. Strangulation seemed like such a passionate method to kill someone. A lot of hatred would have to go into that effort. And strength. Or the element of surprise.

"I wish I could have talked to him, too."

The quiet way Brandon said it veered her focus to him. What he was really saying was he wished he could have saved his brother. Again. Brandon had spent most of his life protecting people. The only time he protected himself was when he sent his father to prison. And whenever women got too close to him.

If only they'd had closure with David before he had died. If they had, maybe it wouldn't feel so awful to think of the night she'd slept with Brandon. And so good. Naughty pleasure. Remove David's murder and her marriage to him and she'd be falling in love with Brandon all over again.

"What would we have said to David?" If they'd had the chance. What would they have said? Sorry, we slept together? David may have gone through with an annulment, but the betrayal would have hurt nonetheless.

"Made him tell us what kind of trouble he was in."

Brandon was still stuck on that side of the tragedy. "Yes, of course. But what would we have said to him about..."

She didn't have to finish.

"Nothing." His brow sank low.

He would have denied it? Hidden it from his brother?

"That feels just as cheap as letting it happen in the first place."

Brandon stood up. "I didn't mean for it to happen."

"Neither did I. That doesn't change the fact that it did."

"You would have told him?"

She turned her head, trying to imagine how David would have reacted. She'd always been an honest person. Secrets didn't travel well with her. The truth was always better than the lie.

"Yes. I would have told him."

"Why?"

"I would have apologized. I never dreamed I'd be one of those women. You know, the kind who sleeps with another man when there is a marriage at stake. I don't care how bad my marriage was. David was still a good person. He deserved more respect than that."

The shadows under Brandon's brow deepened. He was growing more and more angry. "How do you think it makes me feel? If there is a way to make it right, we will."

"But how? We can't change what happened. We can't take it back." And yet, even though he was dead, she still wanted to give David respect. How else could she live with herself?

"By never making that mistake again. For David."

It was where she'd been heading, but now that Brandon had voiced it, she felt a sort of impossibility. Why did it feel so impossible to give David respect by not sleeping with his brother again? It should feel right. Integrity should rule. Instead, it seemed the scandal did.

"Do you think we'll be able to?"

His hesitation revealed he felt the same as her. "I'll make sure we do."

He would make sure. Watching how torn he was over this, she began to realize more than guilt over sleeping with his brother's wife ripped him apart. Fear played a role. This powerful attraction had mushroomed into something uncontrollable. He'd push her away again if she got too close.

She'd be a fool to let her heart get wrapped around him again. Best to follow his lead and cling to the integrity in avoiding him in David's memory.

Discontented, Eliza rose from the couch and walked to the big window. Darkness blanketed the glass. All she saw was her own reflection. Sad blue-green eyes. Flat mouth. Her long brown hair was a mess. She ran her fingers through it to smooth it a little. Distraction in its smallest form.

The figure of a tall man appeared on the other side of the glass, mixing with her reflection. Shock paralyzed her. He wore black pants and a black long-sleeved shirt, and his dark eyes bore through the window at her, menacing and purposeful.

Before Eliza could scream, the man lifted a gun.

She dove out of the way of the window as he fired, shattering glass. She landed on her side. Hearing Brandon's gun go off several times in rapid answer, she rolled as he came to her.

"Are you all right?"

She nodded quickly. "Who was that?"

"I'm going to kill him!" He straightened, his words chilling. Watching him pick up a chair and hurl it through the cracked window alarmed her. Then he jumped over jagged edges of glass and ran after the man who'd appeared in the window. It had to be his father, Jack Reed. Jumping to her feet, she followed.

"Brandon, no!" He was going to kill his father. While it seemed justified, he should leave it to the FBI.

Brandon crossed the darkness of the minimally landscaped backyard and disappeared into the trees bordering the property. Going after him, she could barely make out his form. Moving slower than him, she listened to him thrashing through the underbrush.

The sounds ceased. A few steps deeper into the woods, she spotted him. He stood with his gun raised, turning in circles in a small clearing. Eliza heard no other sounds. Jack must have either gotten away or gone still somewhere in the trees.

She was just about to go to him when Jack emerged from the trees behind Brandon.

"Brandon!" she yelled.

But he was already in motion. As he turned, Jack knocked the gun from his grasp. Then he had his gun on Brandon.

"You think you can come after me?" Jack hissed.

Brandon didn't answer.

"You think you can follow me into these woods and shoot me?"

Eliza stayed by a tree trunk, helplessly watching.

"That's okay. You don't have to say anything. All I need you to do is see this." He turned his aim to Eliza. "It's time for you to learn your lesson, boy."

Eliza ducked behind the tree trunk just as Brandon knocked his father's wrist and the gun fired. The bullet caught some bark to the left of her.

The man was delusional! He'd stop at nothing to kill her.

"Bastard!" Brandon roared, punching Jack in the face. His head bounced backward with the force. He grunted in pain and looked at Brandon in surprise. He hadn't expected his son to be so strong. He may have crept up behind him, but he couldn't overpower Brandon, who was at least four inches taller and thicker in the arms and shoulders.

Brandon grabbed Jack's wrist and squeezed. Jack winced and held firm to the gun. Brandon pushed his wrist so the gun whacked Jack on the temple. Jack resisted, but Brandon was stronger, hitting him like he was a rag doll or a puppet on a string.

The gun was loosened from Jack's grasp, and Brandon threw it in Eliza's direction. Then he swung his fist. Jack ducked and plowed into him. The two went down. Rolling on the ground, Brandon wrestled his way on top and began hitting Jack in the face.

"I'm not a kid anymore," Brandon said between slugs.

Jack swatted his arm and grabbed Brandon by the throat. Brandon stopped hitting him and tried to pry his hand away. Jack twisted his body and threw Brandon off. He punched Brandon and managed to crawl to his feet.

Brandon stood and moved toward Jack, a predator with clear and fearless intent. Jack backed away, wary of Brandon's rage and agility.

"I'm going to kill you," Brandon said, his voice low and full of dark menace.

Eliza didn't doubt he meant it. She walked toward him. There was enough murder going on in town. She slid her hand over his biceps.

He kept advancing on Jack, who kept stepping backward.

Brandon bent and came up with his gun, never having moved his gaze off Jack.

"Brandon, no." Eliza gripped his biceps again, harder this time. "Let the FBI do that."

He didn't glance at her, but she saw a softening in his eyes. She'd made contact with his reasoning.

Jack continued to back away.

"Go call the police, Eliza." He took a step toward Jack.

Jack pivoted and bolted into the trees. Brandon fired his gun several times and then ran after him.

Picking up Jack's gun, she waited for Brandon to return. A few minutes later, she hurried back to the house to call the police. Shortly thereafter, Brandon appeared in the clearing from the trees. As he neared, she saw his fury.

"What happened?"

"He got away." He began pacing along the edge of the patio on the grass, looking toward the trees, gun gripped tightly in his hand.

"The police will catch him. Let's go inside." She moved

toward him, putting her hand on his biceps. "Zimmerman will be here soon."

He stopped pacing and looked down at her, nearly trembling with anger. "I let him get away."

"It's all right. He got away. He'll be caught eventually and be sent back to prison."

The dark menace of his eyes told her prison wasn't enough. Brandon wanted to kill his father. Really wanted to kill him. The desire consumed him. His jaw was rock-hard and his eyes were a passage to the darkest part of his soul. She began to worry about him. "Brandon."

"Go inside, Eliza." He shrugged away from her touch and stepped back.

"Let's both go inside." Why did he want to stay out here? To stand guard? Or would he try to find his father? She'd never seen him like this. "It's okay, Brandon. No one was hurt tonight." She reached for his hand and eased the gun from his grasp.

The killing drive didn't lessen in his eyes. He looked at her, boiling on the inside, years of abuse swarming over him. Instinct compelled him to fight back.

He moved his gaze off her, across the patio to the table. Barely restrained, he moved to one of the chairs and picked it up, lifting it high over his head. Turning, he hurled it with a growl, sending it sailing far across the lawn.

After it tumbled and went still, he faced her again, his eyes flashed fiery brown rage. "You shouldn't be with me right now."

Sympathy poured through her. His temper was well justified. "Come inside, Brandon." She backed farther into the house to give him plenty of room.

After a brief hesitance, he did. Was he wondering if his show of temper would frighten her?

"I need to be alone right now," he said.

"No, you need to be with me right now."

"Eliza, it isn't safe for you to be with me."

Because he threw a patio chair? "You wouldn't hurt me."

He went into the living room and stood there, tipping his head back and breathing as though trying to find his chi.

She walked up to him, putting her hand on the back of his shoulder. He turned.

"It's okay." She tried to calm him.

He slid his hand along the side of her face. "I don't know what I would have done if he hurt you."

"He didn't. You stopped him."

Unable to refute that, his temper began to cool. His thumb caressed her cheek. Heat soothed the angry energy in his eyes. He kissed her, the need to finish venting his frustration compelling him. She gave him all he asked. Deep, gnashing. Until passion forged a burning path through anger and the kiss turned sweeter. Softer.

Eliza moved her hands up his chest, wrapping her arms around him. He put his hand over her rear and pulled her closer.

Careful not to let the kiss get carried away, Eliza moved back. He released her.

"You see?" she said, lightening the mood. "You don't have to be alone."

The marshal showed up with Zimmerman this time. Eliza experienced a bit of déjà vu sitting on the sofa in Brandon's living room with the detective on the same chair as the first time she'd been questioned. Last night she'd been questioned outside, and the time before that she'd been taken to the station. This should feel like old hat by now. The only difference was the austere marshal standing on the other side of the coffee table, no notebook in hand, no change in his expression as Zimmerman introduced him as Marshal Dodge. Tall and lean and wearing a cowboy hat, the marshal listened without interrupting as she explained what happened. Brandon stood beside him, facing Zimmerman and closest to Eliza.

"Your father tried to shoot Eliza?" Zimmerman directed his question to Brandon.

"Yes."

"Are you sure he wasn't trying to shoot you?"

The detective doubted even Brandon. Eliza found that very curious.

"I'm sure. He aimed the gun at her, not me."

Zimmerman leaned back on the chair, arms comfortably resting on the armrests. "Isn't it true you and Eliza are having an affair?"

Eliza felt her head move back with the impact of that. She shouldn't be surprised. She'd heard about the rumors.

"No, that isn't true," Brandon said.

"Both Jillian Marks and your brother—" Zimmerman turned to her "—Ryker Harvey, think you are."

"Ryker?" Her face went white-cold. Why had he said that?

"He told us about the history of your relationship and how close the two of you are becoming."

Eliza was too astonished and hurt that her brother would do such a thing to say anything. She couldn't think about anything other than the maliciousness of it.

"He doesn't know. He's speculating."

"It isn't only him. Jillian saw the two of you together, kissing. Ryker has seen you together, as well. Not kissing, but he's seen you and noticed something in the way you are together. *They can't take their eyes off each other* were his exact words."

Eliza couldn't stop her face from flaming. Neither she nor Brandon could deny the claim. The rumor was based on assumptions and Jillian's lie. That woman hadn't seen them kissing. She was doing everything she could to split them apart.

They weren't even together.

But who would believe that? Zimmerman didn't. He thought Brandon was protecting Eliza.

Brandon's jaw clenched with Zimmerman's skepticism. She wondered which it had more to do with, the rumor or the danger his father presented.

"Jack Reed is trying to kill me," Eliza insisted. She'd rather avoid the rumor herself.

"Why would he do that? I see plenty of motive to go after Brandon," the detective said, "but none for you."

"He was going to shoot her in the woods," Brandon said, explaining what Jack had said.

Jack blamed his sons for his wife's death and would have killed Eliza for it. But there was more to it than that.

"What about the cards?" Zimmerman finally asked.

"What about them?"

"Are you suggesting Jack Reed sent them? That his wanting to kill you is somehow related to the triple homicide?"

"What if they are?"

"I need more evidence to support the theory."

He was so aggravating! "They support the fact that someone has a motive to kill me."

"What motive?"

Eliza let her frustration out with a long sigh. "I didn't write the damn notes!"

"I'm not saying you killed your husband, Mrs. Reed."

He wasn't saying she didn't, either. "Whoever wrote the notes has a lot of animosity toward me. You can't disagree with that. What if I'm telling the truth?"

"I haven't discounted that. But if someone is trying to kill you, then who murdered your husband?"

He didn't believe the same person had committed the triple homicide. He didn't believe Jack Reed was the killer.

"My father could have killed David," Brandon said. "If the senator and the sheriff were in the way, he'd have killed them, too. Jack Reed is a man full of hate. There is no reason to his hatred. He acts on it. He drove away from an accident that killed someone. He's capable of murder."

Zimmerman contemplated him with a margin of sympathy. "You said Jack tried to kill Eliza. Why would he want to kill David and not you?"

"Maybe he thought I'd suffer more if he killed Eliza."

Eliza stared at him. Did he mean that?

"All right." Zimmerman turned to Eliza. "You said someone followed you to the ranch."

"Yes."

"How do you know they were following you and not your husband?"

"David is dead, and I'm still being followed."

She couldn't tell what the detective was thinking about that.

"I received the first note before he was killed," she continued. "And now someone is trying to kill me." Didn't that convince him the same person could be behind this? Brandon's father could have sent her the note referencing her mistake before killing David and then proceeded to go after her…to make Brandon suffer. Her mistake could be loving Brandon.

She looked up at him. He was watching her, deep in thought like her. Loving him was a mistake.

With his elbow still on the armrest, Zimmerman lifted his hand and rubbed his chin between his index finger and thumb. "One of the notes threatened you, said to go back to Hollywood."

"Yes."

"If Brandon's father intends to kill you, why would he send you threats to leave town?"

Yet again, his logic for not believing Jack was David's killer or had written the notes rang true.

"Are you sure you have no enemies here in Vengeance?" This question came from the marshal. Eliza had forgotten he was there. He was so silent. Observant.

"None that I'm aware." Her brother, but she couldn't believe he'd do something so violent.

"Reed meant to kill you because you're someone Brandon cares about," the agent went on. "That explains the attempts with the stable fire and the shooting. The cards may or may not be related."

"David's murder may not be related," Zimmerman corrected, again revealing his disconnect. Eliza had a motive to kill her husband. He cheated and lost money buying drugs and on gambling. She knew the senator and sheriff. Jack Reed's escape from prison may just be pure coincidence.

Like Melinda Grayson's kidnapping? Eliza wasn't buying it. All of this had to be linked somehow. Jack Reed had tried to kill her. Jack Reed had written the notes.

"The second note said go back to Hollywood before it's too late. That could be construed as a threat to my life," she said.

Zimmerman, for once, couldn't argue.

"It's possible that Jack wrote them, and it's possible he knew the sheriff and the senator," she continued.

"Possible but not likely that he killed all three."

"You mean just like me?" She had no motive to kill the sheriff or the senator.

Zimmerman angled his head in acquiescence. "I'll concede whoever wrote the notes could be your husband's murderer. But I need proof."

Naturally. He wouldn't be a detective if he didn't wait for proof. "What about Jillian? If you don't believe Jack could have done it, then what if she did?"

"This is murder, Eliza," Brandon said. "My brother was killed and now you were almost killed. This is more than a jealous woman who might be bipolar. And what connection does she have to the triple homicide?"

Maybe he was right. Killing someone required coldness that even Jillian may not possess. Her only crime was loving Brandon. And didn't Eliza know all about that?

"Then it has to be Jack." He was the killer.

"I agree," Brandon said. "He's capable of murder, no matter who it is. And as long as he's free, Eliza is in danger. You can't ignore that."

"I'll find your father," the marshal said to Brandon. "You can count on that."

Brandon nodded once, willing the marshal to do exactly that.

Zimmerman stood. "Let me know if you get any more notes."

He said it sarcastically.

"Let me know if you find a motive for Jack to kill the senator and sheriff."

"I always keep an open mind."

Begrudgingly, she had to agree. He was working with a team of highly trained people, from local law enforcement to the FBI. Eliza had every faith that they'd find David's killer. She just hoped she wasn't wrongfully accused along the way.

Chapter 11

Ryker waited for Aegina to leave her mother's house. One of the kids had a doctor's appointment, and he was hoping she would not only keep it, but would also go without her mother. He checked the neighborhood for anyone who would notice him. He'd rented a car so he wouldn't be recognized that way. No one stood in windows that he could see. No one was out in their yards. A cyclist passed a few minutes ago, and someone walked a dog. There were no police cars on the street.

Aegina had filed a restraining order against him. While that was awful, he understood why. If he seemed to have gone crazy ever since finding his wife with another man, he probably was. Losing Aegina would destroy him. Was destroying him. She was his wife. His only love. His heart was shattered.

She emerged, his oldest son in tow—his seven-year-old, Evan.

Ryker slid down in the seat. He was far enough down the street not to catch her attention. After waiting for them to get in the car and drive out into the street, Ryker followed. He took a different route to the doctor's office, saw her car already there and waited.

An agonizing hour later, she and his son approached. He walked to the car and met her there. She stopped short.

"Daddy!" Evan ran to him.

A brief shot of joy penetrated his grief. He crouched and took the boy into his arms, hugging with tears threatening his manhood.

"Why aren't you at Grandma's with us?"

How could Aegina do this to them? Through the maelstrom of his sorrow and pain, their children were suffering this split right along with them.

"I have to work."

"When are we going to come home?"

"I don't know."

"I miss my room. Grandma and Grandpa's house is cold, and she won't let us touch anything. We can't play when we want."

"You can come home." He looked up at Aegina. "I'll stay with my mom for a while."

"Grandma Harvey lives in the backyard," Evan said.

"That's right. I'll camp out with her."

"Can I camp with you?"

"You sure can." He gave the boy a mock punch on the arm. "That other boy leaving you alone?"

Evan's face fell. "He called Judy another name and I told him he better not do that anymore. He hit me and I fell."

Ryker searched for signs of harm and saw none.

"He's okay," Aegina said.

"Did you talk to the principal?"

"I had to. They called me in. The other boy got detention. It will be worse if he hits Evan again. They'll suspend him."

As Aegina talked, Evan grew more and more burdened.

"Why didn't you tell me this?"

She put her hand on her hip. "And when was I supposed to do that?"

"I don't know. Maybe you could have canceled one of your meetings with my mechanic."

Her lips pursed together, and she kept quiet. Neither one of them wanted to talk about that in front of the kids.

Ryker turned back to his son. "It's okay, buddy. That kid'll leave you alone now."

"He keeps calling me a girl! And now all his friends are doing it! Everybody thinks I'm a girl!"

He refrained from smiling at the way that sounded. "No, they don't. You hardly look like a girl." He wasn't as big as the bully, but he wasn't a small boy. He had a dense, athletic body.

"Want me to teach you how to punch him?"

His eyes brightened. "Yeah!"

He chuckled. "Okay. Next time you come over, I'll show you how to knock him on his butt."

"Cool! Thanks, Dad!"

"Ryker," Aegina warned in her annoyed tone. He'd heard that tone so much over the past couple of years, it amazed him that he hadn't noticed it until now. He hadn't noticed a lot of things. And now his sweet, beautiful Aegina was a bitch, and he felt responsible for making her that way.

"Get in the car, buddy." He messed up his son's thick brown head of hair.

After kissing and hugging his dad, the boy ran to the other side and hopped in.

"What are you doing here?" Aegina asked. "Stalking me?"

"How did the appointment go?" he asked instead of engaging in her sass.

She opened the driver's door and dropped her purse inside. "That's not why you're here."

"No, you're right. I came here because I wanted to apologize for the other day."

"I should call the cops right now. You could be arrested for being this close to me."

"I'm sorry. I acted badly before. I couldn't take thoughts of you with another man. I lost control. I said some things I regret. You didn't deserve that. It won't happen again."

That calmed her some. "Ryker, I can't deal with this."

"Really, Aegina, I'm sorry I flipped out on you." She slept with his mechanic, of all men. Who wouldn't go nuts after discovering that? "Why him, anyway? You could have anyone. Why an auto mechanic? *My* mechanic?"

She sighed and couldn't meet his gaze. She looked across the parking lot, out into the street of traffic passing a line of old brick buildings and the bakery on the corner.

Inside the car, his son played a computer game on a portable player.

At last she turned to him. "He showed an interest."

And her own husband hadn't.

"A man hadn't hit on me since before I married you. When he did, it made me feel young again. I felt the way I did when you and I met."

Ryker lowered his head, the sadness that poisoned him thickening. "Are you still seeing him?"

"Not right now. I told him I needed some time."

While that eased a margin of his inner unrest, it didn't erase her infidelity.

A long silence hung between them.

"Do you think we can ever get past this?" he asked.

She looked into his eyes, really looked. "I don't think so."

She was that far gone. "What about the kids?" He missed them and it hadn't even been a week yet.

"We can make arrangements for you to see them."

"When?"

"You can have them this weekend. I'll drop the restraining order."

Now that he'd calmed down, and she had seen for herself that he had, she felt comfortable doing so. He didn't know how long it would take to drop the restraining order, but she'd let him see his kids. Ryker took that as a step in the right direction. "Why don't you move back home? I'll stay with my mother."

"There isn't enough room in the carriage house."

"It has two bedrooms."

"It's your mother's space. We're fine at my parents'."

"Aegina—"

"I can't live with you that close, Ryker."

The question he needed to ask but dreaded worked its way into his dry mouth. "Do you want a divorce?"

She looked away again. "Right now…yes."

Right now? "I love you, Aegina. I don't want to lose you. I didn't see what I was doing, but I do now."

That brought her head back to him. Had she heard the truth in the way he'd said it?

"I've been a fool. I was happy living in Vengeance because I was living here with you."

Tears moistened her eyes. "Don't do that, Ryker."

"Don't do what? Tell you what I've learned about myself? What I was too ignorant to see?"

"Why now?" she sobbed. "Why do you have to do this when it's too late?"

"Is it too late?" He wished she'd tell him. He didn't want a divorce, but he wasn't sure their marriage was salvageable.

Aegina didn't answer. She was as confused as him.

"You still love me."

"I love what we once were. There's no going back to that."

There was no going back to before she had slept with another man. There was no going back to them as a young couple, devoting their lives to each other, pledging to be faithful. New, exciting love. Gone. His Aegina. Gone. And he was gone for her. She didn't have to say it. They'd done a lot of their communicating this way. Without words.

In a weird way, they were still connecting. Even when they were contemplating divorce, their connection was still there.

"What if we start over?" he asked.

A flicker of hope crossed her eyes before it died. "Is that what you want?"

He was too raw from her affair. They were both in the same place in that regard. He loved her and she loved him, but the mistakes of their past might overrule.

There was nothing else to say.

She opened her car door; their oldest son was still fixated on his game.

Before lowering herself into the vehicle, she paused. "I had breakfast with Detective Zimmerman's wife this morning. He responded to a call from your sister and Brandon last night. Is she all right?"

What had happened to Eliza? "I haven't heard from her."

"Brandon's dad escaped from prison and apparently went to his ranch."

"To do what?"

She shrugged. "I was hoping you could tell me."

He couldn't. He rarely spoke to his sister. He'd gone to her at one of his lowest moments in life and regretted it.

"She's been getting threatening letters, too."

Worry crept into him. "She didn't tell me."

"So far the cops don't think it has anything to do with the murders."

"Who do they think is sending the letters?"

"They don't know. Zimmerman thinks Eliza wrote them."

"Why would she write them?"

"To take suspicion off herself."

"Eliza wouldn't do that."

"How do you know? You never talk to her."

Ryker felt the well-placed barb and sent his wife an admonishing look.

"You two should really make amends," she said in response.

"I don't need to amend anything with her." She was the selfish one.

Her mouth curved with disappointment. "That's exactly what brought you and me to this point, Ryker. You always assume it's someone else who's causing your unhappiness when the cause has always been right inside of you."

"Eliza has nothing to do with us."

With a sigh of frustration, she shook her head. "Goodbye, Ryker."

Damn it. As soon as he took one step forward, she sent him backward again. What confused him most was how she thought Eliza had anything to do with their marital problems.

Women…

Eliza's mother called. Ryker had gone after Aegina again. He'd told her where he was going and she tried to stop him, and now she was beside herself with worry. Eliza told Brandon, and he insisted on going with her to Ryker's house. When they arrived, his car was in the driveway and her mother opened the front door, her round frame accentuated by jeans and a tucked-in white T-shirt.

"I'm so sorry to make you drive all the way over here. He pulled up just a few minutes ago," she said, raking her fingers through her messy short gray hair.

Eliza and Brandon stepped inside. When she bumped into him, he put his hand on her back as though to steady her. Just that small contact triggered an array of sparks. She looked over and up at him and saw he'd noticed. He lowered his hand.

"How is he?" Eliza asked her mother, who'd seen the exchange.

"Better than I expected." She led them through the home. "He said Aegina used to ask him to clean the hot tub so they could start using it again and he was always too busy with the shop. He took some time off to take care of things like that. Has one of his managers in charge."

Outside, Ryker was bent over the hot tub. Hearing them, he straightened and faced them.

"Eliza." He sounded surprised to see her. "Hey, Brandon."

"Ryker," Brandon greeted, his deep voice keeping the sparks at a hot simmer.

"What are you two doing here?"

"I called them when you went to intercept Aegina at the doctor's office," their mother said.

Ryker scowled at her and then Eliza.

"If you aren't going to care that you're arrested again, then somebody has to care for you," their mother scolded in response.

"What happens between me and Aegina is our business."

"Oh, then maybe we'll leave you in jail next time."

"She's going to drop the restraining order."

Eliza's mother's head moved back in surprise. "Did she tell you that?"

"Yes. We talked. That's why I went to the doctor's office. To talk to her. Nothing more."

He did seem a little brighter today. He'd talked rather than yelled. "Are you getting back together?"

That brought his mood low and he turned back to the hot tub. "Sorry to hear about that fire, Brandon."

That must mean he and Aegina weren't getting back together. But something must have happened to ease his mind today. They'd talked. Made progress. Eliza wanted to see her brother happy. Maybe then he'd stop resenting her so much.

Whatever he and his wife had resolved today, it hadn't changed how he felt about his sister. He still had some things to work out then.

"Thanks," Brandon said. "Since we're in town we'll start replacing the things I lost."

He hadn't told her that when they'd left the ranch.

"It's terrible what happened." Eliza's mother poured four glasses of tea. "Everyone's talking about it this morning. I had to run down to the market and two people stopped me."

Ryker didn't stop working, ignoring them. Or Eliza.

If she weren't here, he might engage in the conversation. She wished there was a way to reach him.

"I had to set old Heloise straight when she asked if a relative of one of the murder victims had done it in retaliation, thinking my Eliza could be the killer. I swear some people have nothing better to do than spread their bad ideas around."

That's what happened when there were no facts. Speculation ran loose.

"And then when I got home, I saw on the news that an escaped convict was reported on your property," Eliza's mother continued.

"Already?" How had that news reached the media so soon?

"There's a lot of attention on Vengeance right now. Triple homicide, kidnapping, an escaped convict." She eyed Brandon warily. "Your father."

"He's no father of mine. That's biology."

"More than that's going around town," Ryker said. "Aegina told me she heard Eliza's been getting threatening letters."

Eliza saw the way her brother looked at her and felt the kindling of reconnection stirring. He cared whether she was all right or not.

"Isn't that why Brandon is with you?" her mother asked.

Hearing the leading tone, Eliza braced herself for an embarrassing moment.

"I wouldn't let anything happen to your daughter, Mrs. Harvey."

"Some things never change."

"Mother..." Eliza cautioned.

Her mother swatted her hand. "Oh, Eliza, you really should stop running from love."

She glanced at Brandon, who smothered a grin at her mother's word choice.

"Ever since her father died, she's been all curled up inside her shell, afraid to peek her head out. Ryker accuses her of leaving him behind when it had nothing to do with him."

"Mother…" Now it was Ryker who cautioned her.

"It's really so simple, you two. Staring you both right in the face. It baffles me how long you've carried this on. You." She pointed to Ryker. "Your entire situation is your own damn fault. And you." She rounded on Eliza. "You married the wrong man. The right one is standing next to you. I don't ever want to see you do something that stupid again, do you understand me?"

"Mother!" Had she actually just said she should have married Brandon? Expertly cloaking it with a reprimand.

"Well, it's true. It's time you both heard what's wrong with you. You and Ryker. You haven't listened to the more gentle approach."

She was too stunned to speak. Ryker had abandoned the hot tub to stare at his mother.

"I just hope it's not too late for both of you."

Ryker with his wife and Eliza with Brandon. She seemed to be forgetting a few details.

"Mother, Brandon is David's brother."

"He's also dead."

"And Brandon broke up with me, remember?"

"That was a long time ago. You were young. I've seen you two together. At Ryker's birthday party the room heated up just watching the two of you look at each other. I saw it again today, so don't argue with me."

"Mother!"

"We should get going," Brandon said.

"Good idea."

Her mother chuckled, eyes that were so similar to hers dancing. "I was going to invite you for lunch."

Eliza's stomach was growling, but she'd rather starve than endure more of her mother's bluntness. "We'll grab something."

"We have a lot of errands to run," Brandon added, ushering her toward the door.

Her mother smiled at them all the way there. She'd accomplished what she'd set out to, whatever that was. She made a terrible matchmaker.

Brandon was hungry, and he had already heard Eliza's stomach. Without consulting her, he drove to the least popular place in town and parked. The awkward silence was tortuous. If he didn't absolutely need to pick up some supplies, he'd have driven back to the ranch, where he could have put at least some distance between them for a while.

Eliza said nothing as she walked with him to the out-of-date restaurant on the edge of town. Too late it dawned on him that it was the burger joint where he'd started dating Eliza.

She glanced at him, curious as to why he'd taken her here.

"I forgot," he said simply.

"I didn't," she replied just as simply.

"It's just to eat."

"I'm starving."

They were seated, and Brandon read the menu, unable to stop looking over the top at Eliza. She caught him just before the waiter appeared for their drink order.

"I would have thought you'd prefer lunch at my brother's house than here."

"With your mother? I don't think so."

She smiled, a relaxed, genuinely amused smile that was full of affection. Evidently, she'd recovered faster than him from that grilling.

"So hunger and my mother draw you out into public settings? I'll have to remember that."

He lifted his eyebrows. Was she teasing him? Why did he have to enjoy it so much?

"I go out in public."

She kept her gaze on her menu. "Before or after I came to town?"

"Both." He put his menu down and leaned back on the creaky old chair.

"Only out of necessity. Have you ever done it for fun?"

"I went to your brother's birthday party."

"For fun?"

"Not necessity." Well, not completely. He'd gone to make sure Eliza was all right, but he'd had a good time.

Her blue-green eyes lifted, and their playful light arrowed right into him. This was why he couldn't keep his hands off her. She looked at him and logic was pulverized.

"I'm not that boring," he said.

"Eliza Harvey, is that you?"

Brandon felt like leaving. A woman he didn't recognize appeared at their table.

"Veronica?"

Then he remembered the woman. She was Eliza's high school friend, now married to a carpenter. He didn't keep up on the town's social dynamics too much, but even he knew the woman was a talker. It would be out that he had lunch with Eliza.

While the two chatted about old times, Brandon glanced around. The restaurant was full, and he recognized many faces. He raised his hand to a few.

Figures, the oldest, crappiest restaurant in town would still draw a crowd.

"I was so sorry to hear about your brother," Veronica said to him. And then to Eliza, "Will you be going back to Hollywood after your husband's funeral?"

His body hadn't been released from the coroner yet.

"Yes…I think so…" She faltered. How could she not be sure about that anymore? She looked across the table at Brandon.

"I am so sorry. At least you have his brother. I remember when the two of you dated. Everybody thought you'd end up together." She shook her head. "My, how things change." Then she looked closer at them both and something clicked. "Well…I should get back to my table. The girls and I are out for a lunch break."

Brandon saw the table of three women Veronica indicated. They whispered to each other, smiling with a few chirps of laughter.

The waiter returned and got their order while Veronica rejoined her friends and the whispering continued.

"Do you think they remember this is where we came in high school?" Eliza asked.

"Probably." Anything was possible in this town.

"And you thought it was bad with my mother."

He half laughed at that. "What did she mean about the shell comment? After your dad died."

The light dulled in her eyes. "Nothing."

Yeah, something. "You aren't a turtle-in-a-shell kind of woman to me."

"I'm not."

Except when it came to her father's death? "I remember when he died." Eliza had mourned so deeply. After she grieved, she'd started her Friday parties. Now that he thought of it, that's when he'd begun to think she was too wild.

"I didn't think my mother was going to survive it."

Brandon had only seen what it had done to Eliza.

"She loved my dad so much. It nearly killed her when he was gone."

That's why Ryker had taken care of her. "She seems fine now."

"She isn't as fine as you think. She isn't as happy as she was when he was alive. She gets through her days. She told me she would never remarry. My dad was her only love."

He would have said she was lucky, that most people didn't find that kind of love, but losing it wasn't lucky.

Absently, she unfolded her napkin and put it on her lap. "I never want to feel that way."

Coming from her, that took him aback. The Eliza he knew charged full force into life. Was he actually hearing that she feared the kind of love her mother had for her father? It made sense. It explained so much. Why he backed off when they were young. Why she left Vengeance and became a famous event planner.

Why she married David.

He should have seen it back then. He chuckled, deep and low; his amusement showed and he didn't care. He adored her right now. "Eliza Harvey has a soft spot."

"What?"

He'd jarred her from heavy thought.

"You're afraid of love."

"I am not. I just don't want to ever be that dependent on a man."

Dependent? That's the label she had for it? "You think love is a dependency?" Like an addiction? He chuckled some more.

"What's so funny?"

She was getting insulted, and he couldn't help himself. "The idea of you being afraid of developing an addiction to a man."

Her mouth dropped open.

He'd walked right into that one. "I mean…" What the hell did he mean? Once they'd started having sex in high school, Eliza had encouraged him for more. Like an addiction. He'd been the same way. Had to have her. Every time they were together. And then her dad had died.

"You were addicted to me." He spoke the revelation aloud.

"It was called love." She threw her napkin onto the table.

He held his hand up before she bolted. "Dependency was your word."

That flustered her. *Good.*

Reaching across the table, he took her hand. "Eliza, I had no idea your father's death affected you so much. I didn't have a good relationship with mine, and my mother died when I was a young boy. I'm sorry."

She clearly wasn't ready to face that gigantic hole in her heart. He was very familiar with holes.

Her whole body relaxed, and her eyes warmed with appreciation. "Oh, Brandon. I'm sorry, too."

Sorry for his losses. Losses that were very different from hers.

The pull between them heated into an unbreakable bond. She seemed to have rooted herself into him. Or maybe the roots had always been there and only needed water to bring them to life again.

Resistance eased the draw of unwelcome attraction, deep attraction that perhaps had managed to grow into more than that. A word he dare not name. Not with his brother's body yet to be buried. He was ashamed. Slipping his hand free, he sat back and looked past her to the window, where he spotted Jillian.

An unexpected shock hit him. She just stood there, watching him, standing in a calf-length, black-and-white floral pattered dress, long, dark hair freshly brushed. She appeared normal except for her dejected and sad face and the way she watched him with Eliza. She'd witnessed a deep and personal exchange.

"What is she doing here?" Eliza asked.

That's what he'd like to know. Had she followed them? Brandon hadn't paid attention on the way here.

When both he and Eliza saw her, she started moving. But instead of moving on, she entered the restaurant.

"She's coming in here." Eliza sounded breathless. Incredulous. Maybe even a little alarmed.

He was, too.

"Is she armed?"

"I hope not."

She whipped a glance his way.

"Hello, Brandon," Jillian said, blue eyes duller than he remembered. "I was walking in town and saw you in here." She glanced at Eliza.

Brandon didn't respond, wondering if she was on drugs. What the hell was she doing? Was he overreacting? Or was she stalking him?

"I heard about the fire," she said. "I'm glad you're all right."

Her attempt at casual conversation felt skewed with his apprehension.

"How did you hear about it?" Eliza asked.

"Did the horses make it out okay?" She ignored Eliza.

"Yes. Thanks for asking." He wondered if he was being

too nice to her. Maybe if he was more of a jerk she'd leave him alone.

"I was going to call you. Do you have any plans for dinner tonight? With everything going on, you must be so frazzled."

He had a bad feeling about this. "Eliza and I have to pick up some supplies and then I'll have a lot of work to do. I don't think I'll have time tonight." Or any other night.

"Oh, darn it. All right. I'll catch you later then."

"Great." She waved in a cute way that was disturbing.

"Something is really wrong with that woman," Eliza said.

Chapter 12

The headlights from Brandon's truck chased a swath of darkness away as he drove along the narrow, winding dirt road. Eliza kept going over the afternoon in her mind. Gathering supplies had taken longer than she'd anticipated. He'd made a big order at the feed store and farm and ranch supply store, spending time talking with the general managers. He'd also had to meet with his insurance agent, who was a friend. She'd been pleasantly surprised at how social he'd been. He was well-liked in town.

Why that amazed her was what had her so quiet and lost in thought. As solitary as he was, how had he become so popular? And if he was social, had it really been her partying that had driven him away? Was still driving him away? Granted, socializing with ranch supply store managers wasn't the same as a night out on the town, but she'd narrowed her definition of him far more than she should have. He wasn't such a hermit after all.

All afternoon and into early evening, she had struggled with the warmth that had found a nest inside her heart, the glow of new discovery. The respect he had from everyone he encountered was obvious. It wreaked havoc on her fight against an already persistent attraction. Every movement he made stoked the reaction, every word he said, and the way he said them.

The farm and ranch supply store manager had taken a particular interest in her. He'd introduced himself, smiling and studying her closely in a *Magnum, P.I.* sort of way. He looked like the star, too.

"My daughter went to school with you. You're the one who went off to become a famous entertainer."

"Event planner. I'm not so sure about the famous part." She wasn't a movie star.

He turned to Brandon. "We were sorry to hear about your brother."

"Thank you."

Back to Eliza, "How long will you be staying with Brandon? Have you decided to move back home?"

"Oh…no." It came awkwardly off her tongue. Like it was a lie. Strange…

"Well, my daughter's right." He looked back and forth between them. "You do seem to belong here. She said you and Brandon were the only couple she thought should have stayed together. Most young loves don't last, but yours stuck with her for some reason. She's a very insightful girl." He fixed his attention on Brandon. "Eliza suits you."

Why was he being so personal about this? He must know that she had been married to David.

"Thanks for all your help," Brandon said shortly.

"We've been friends a long time, Brandon," the man persisted, stopping Brandon from turning away. "I can't help agreeing with my daughter."

"It was a pleasure meeting you." Eliza took his hand

and smiled her appreciation. If she decided to stay in Vengeance, he'd be one person she'd keep for a friend.

"Likewise, Eliza. You come back now."

She couldn't promise that, so she'd followed Brandon out of the store without further comment.

Brandon drove over the hill where the strange car had been parked. It wasn't there now. Darkness swallowed the trees until they reached the driveway. Ahead, the area where the stable had been was black. Headlights shone on what was left of the corral fence. But the big ranch house was well lit. The porch light brightened the entrance, and windows glowed on the lower level.

Had they left all those lights on this morning? They'd left late, well after sunrise. She glanced over at Brandon as he drew the truck to a halt. He stared at the house, puzzled.

"Did you leave some lights on?"

"No."

A shot of apprehension put her on high alert as they left the truck. What now? Had someone broken in? Brandon's father?

She took out her cell phone, ready to call for help if necessary.

At the front door, he paused and said in a low voice, "Stay behind me. Don't call anyone until I tell you."

Why had he told her that? Zimmerman had felt as though he'd wasted his time with his last visit. Maybe that was why.

"I won't." She could do without more judgment from Zimmerman, too.

He opened the door, and she entered quietly behind him. If there was anyone here they'd probably heard them pull up.

Noises from the kitchen made Brandon look back at

her. It smelled good in the house. Dinner cooking. Was someone in there?

"I thought your housekeeper only worked days," she whispered.

"She does."

Seeing his worry, Eliza's escalated. "Do your ranch hands help themselves in your house?"

"No." He stopped. Clanking dishes sounded. "Maybe you should wait here."

Eliza looked behind her down the dark hallway leading to the guest room and then out the front window to meager lights shining on the driveway and nothing else.

"I'll go with you. You have the gun."

After a moment's hesitation, he moved forward again. Eliza stayed behind him, hand on his trim hip, peering around him as he neared the kitchen entry.

Her heart beat with the fear of unknown. What lay beyond the wall?

She moved into the kitchen with him, stepping cautiously around his tall frame to the sound of boiling water. A kettle steamed, and spaghetti sauce simmered in another pan. No one stood in front of the stove.

Eliza looked at the same time Brandon did to movement on the far side of the kitchen. A woman turned from the far cabinet with plates in her hand.

Jillian.

She saw them and beamed a wide, unnatural smile. Her Cinderella strides were eerily animated.

Putting the plates down on the counter beside the stove, she sang, "Surprise…"

"What the hell are you doing here?" Brandon demanded.

Eliza swallowed a dry breath. Jillian acted as though this were an everyday, normal occurrence.

"When you said you were busy replacing what you lost, I thought I'd help out by making you both some dinner," the woman flippantly explained. She lifted the spoon in the sauce for a taste and closed her eyes. Buttery French bread warmed in the oven, and the sauce bubbled up into the air. But the delectable smells might as well be propane gas.

"Mmm. As you'll soon discover, I make the best Italian sauce this side of the Mississippi."

This was a horror scene. Eliza watched Jillian put the spoon down and waited for her to find a knife. Any moment she'd charge them with hand raised and eyes crazed.

"How did you get in here?" Eliza asked.

"The door was open," she said to Brandon, smiling softly now, all adoration. "I told your manager that I was here. Trevor."

Eliza shivered and gripped Brandon's arm. This was going to end badly.

"Jillian—"

She put up one hand, the other stirring the sauce. "I know what you're thinking. I've had a hard time accepting how fast you decided to call things off between us, and I reacted badly. I'm here to apologize, Brandon. I'm over it. I understand your choice, and I respect it. So, consider this a peace offering. You're going through a lot right now, and I don't want to make things harder on you. I just want to be friends." She looked at Eliza. "To both of you."

Friends? Eliza was too stunned to say anything. Jillian had entered Brandon's house uninvited and made herself at home in his kitchen.

To make him dinner.

As *friends...*

A silence heavy with anticipatory dread permeated the

kitchen. The delectable smell of buttery, garlic French bread and the spicy Italian sauce did little to entice her appetite. Jillian wore jeans and a white T-shirt with long, bulbous strings of turquoise and green beads around her neck and wrist. She stirred the pan of simmering sauce, looking across her shoulder at them, a soft smile on her glossed lips, slyness in her eyes. Eliza saw right through her. She was a witch disguised by beauty made ugly with feigned humility. Wicked insanity.

"You should have told me," Brandon said.

Eliza moved from behind him. Jillian had spied on them when they'd had lunch. And the way she'd acted when she'd come inside…

Eliza wasn't sure what to do. Should she call the police? Brandon was equally undecided beside her, both of them standing there staring at Jillian.

Jillian's smile expanded, and she laughed. "I guess I really did surprise you."

"Why are you here, Jillian?" Brandon asked, his tone deep and stern.

Jillian lifted the pot of boiling water and took it to the sink at the island, pouring it into a waiting colander. "I mean no harm, Brandon. Just one less dinner you'll have to make while you're dealing with burning stables and your brother's death. Most people don't ask for help in hard times. I've always found that a more proactive approach works best."

Eliza refrained from letting her anxious doubt show. Playing along might be smart right now. As soon as Jillian felt threatened, she might come after them with a raised knife or something.

"Did you get all the supplies you needed?" she asked as she began scooping noodles onto three plates, the pasta dangling like snakes on Medusa's head.

"Jillian..." Brandon trod carefully. "This is nice of you, but—"

"Have a seat, you two. Wait until you taste my sauce. I use two kinds of sausage that give it a great flavor." She moved, quick and efficient, carrying the plates to the stove and spooning the chunky, mouthwatering sauce over the noodles.

"Go on," Jillian urged. "Go sit down."

Eliza glanced at Brandon. His brow had grown more shadowed with anger.

Jillian carried the plates to the table, looking at them once before returning to the kitchen she'd commandeered to remove the bread from the oven. If she wasn't so crazy, Eliza would devour the meal. Whacked-out as she was, Jillian could cook spaghetti.

With the bread on the table, Jillian filled wine goblets with iced water from a pitcher. Then she straightened, finished rushing about, placing a hand on the back of one of the chairs and looking at Brandon with a hint of desperation in her eyes, smile faltering now.

"I did this for you," she said.

"I didn't invite you, Jillian."

"I thought you'd appreciate the help."

"I want you to leave now."

"But...I..." She lifted her hand to indicate her hard work.

"I'll reimburse you for the food. I do appreciate the gesture of good intent, but you should have called first."

Seeing the desperation expand, drawing Jillian's eyes down, Eliza moved away from Brandon, lifting her phone and pressing 911.

Jillian watched her, desperation intensifying with rage.

Eliza waited before sending the call.

"I did come here with good intentions," Jillian said.

"And we appreciate that," Brandon said. "But you weren't invited."

"I wanted to surprise you."

"You came into my house uninvited."

"To surprise you." She moved toward Brandon, pleading.

"I've tried to be nice about this, Jillian. You're going to gather your things and leave now. Don't call me anymore. Don't speak to me when you see me. Don't follow me. I want nothing to do with you anymore. Do you understand?"

Her mouth opened, and her eyes widened. "Brandon… why are you doing this? I only meant to make you dinner and show you that I can be a friend."

"You want more than that. You won't stop, Jillian. You keep bothering me even though I've told you it's over between us."

Jillian's head cocked. "Bothering you?"

Eliza felt the energy change and wondered if she should press Send on her phone.

Brandon sighed. "Stop, Jillian. I'm not interested in you anymore. And after tonight, I don't even want to be friends."

That shocked expression remained, her head jerking back. "This is the thanks I get for going out of my way to help you out?"

"I don't need your help."

"But I bought all this food and cooked this dinner."

"No one asked you to do that. And I'll remind you, you came into my house uninvited."

"I didn't break in. I told your ranch manager I was here."

"If you don't leave now, Eliza is going to call the police."

Jillian turned chilled eyes to her. "Do it and you'll regret it."

"What will you do?" Eliza asked.

Instantly, Jillian caught herself. Temper in check, she turned back to Brandon.

"Let's just have dinner. Talk. You'll see that I mean no harm."

A sound brought all of them turning to the kitchen entrance. A man stood there in worn jeans and a cowboy hat. Bright blue eyes stuck out from weathered skin.

"I told you I'd be watching you," he said to Jillian. "Mr. Reed asked me to keep an eye on things around here. Looks like it's a good thing he did."

"This is none of your business," Jillian retorted.

"I listened to everything you just said." He looked at Brandon. "She told me you were expecting her."

"Thanks, Trevor."

"Do you need me to do anything?"

"No. Jillian was just leaving."

Jillian ran her gaze over all three of them. Then with a furious glare to Eliza, she marched to the kitchen island counter and snatched her purse.

Trevor moved out of the way as she passed.

Eliza didn't relax until the front door slammed shut. Clearing her phone, she put it down on the table and slumped onto a chair, the plate of spaghetti still steaming in front of her.

Trevor strode into the dining area. "She's gonna crack."

"We'll be ready if she does."

Eliza looked wearily up at him, not as sure as him. He sat next to her and Trevor sat at the opposite end of the table. Brandon lifted the glass of water in front of him and swirled it, inspecting.

"Smells good," Trevor said.

"Do you think she poisoned it?" Eliza asked.

"No," Brandon said.

Why would she? Her motive was to win Brandon, not kill him. Eliza maybe, but not him. If the food was poisoned, Eliza wouldn't be the only one to suffer.

Jillian thought preparing a dinner for both him and Eliza would soften his regard toward her. She'd pretend she was satisfied with being friends, and then when the time presented itself, work her way into more. Maybe she hoped to play that role until Eliza left town. She felt threatened by Eliza.

"I wouldn't eat anything else she makes you." Trevor picked up a fork and dug into the spaghetti in front of him.

Laughing, Eliza picked up her fork and started eating with him.

Exhausted, Eliza crawled into bed, sighing at how good it felt to finally lie down. She'd stayed up with Brandon and Trevor, talking about the fire and their strategy for rebuilding. Though disturbed about Jillian, she'd never felt safer or more settled. The farm and ranch store manager's comments kept returning.

You do seem to belong here....

She snuggled down on her side, head sinking into the soft pillow, curled into a ball, thoughts keeping her awake. She slid her hand under the pillow, trying to get comfortable. Something coarse touched her fingers. Opening her eyes and leaning up on her elbow, she drew it out from under the pillow.

A card.

Chills of alarm prickled her skin. Someone had put it there. Jillian had been in the house.

Scared, Eliza switched on the light beside her bed and sat on the edge of the bed, looking around the room. The windows were locked, and the blinds were closed. She hadn't checked the closet.

Had Jillian come back while they were in the kitchen eating the meal she'd prepared?

Not wanting to open the card, she stood up and left the room.

Climbing the stairs, she went to Brandon's room. The door was open. He lay with his arms folded behind his head, the television flashing in the darkness. She couldn't see his eyes from here, not through the darkness, but she sensed he'd seen her.

She lifted the card so he'd know it wasn't him she'd come for.

His arms lowered and he threw the covers off, standing in one lithe movement. She was momentarily frozen with the sight he presented. In only underwear, his strong legs and six-pack abs added to the spectacle. Purposeful dark eyes sexy and ominous. He towered over her as he took the card from her limp fingers.

"You haven't opened it."

"I..." She was still entranced by him.

He tore open the envelope and took out the card with furious movements, flipping on a light with the same flair. He read it, then handed it to her.

She took it, reluctant to read.

"David got what he had coming. You're next."

None of the notes previous to this were this threatening. And this one she could believe came from his father.

"Where did you find it?" Brandon's tone was short with anger.

"Under my pillow."

Whoever had left it had been in his house. Jillian had already been here. His father had already tried to kill Eliza. Which one was leaving the notes?

Swearing, Brandon went to the wall by the door and punched. The drywall gave. Frustration made him do it. He felt helpless defending her, a man who couldn't keep his woman safe. Except she wasn't his woman. Why those thoughts had come she wouldn't examine now. More likely he meant to protect her from his father.

"It could be Jillian," she reminded him.

He jerked on a pair of jeans and went to the table beside the bed for his phone. She moved to him, putting her hand over his phone, gently taking it from him before he could make the call to police.

"They'll only assume I wrote it."

Indecision ravaged him, the desire to protect her high. But there was nothing he could do. Not right now.

"We have to give them the card."

"We can do that in the morning. I've had all I can take of Zimmerman."

His guardian instinct calmed. She marveled that she had the ability to do that. They stood in silence for a while, the mood changing, taking on its own intent.

He slid his hand along the side of her face. She stepped closer, and he kissed her. Eliza kissed him back and the kiss grew in fervor.

He'd remember this, that she was safe with him no matter how many holes he put in the wall or how much patio furniture he threw. She also knew that once his dad was back in prison that he'd have his peace back.

The logic made it easier to keep her head while he kissed her. She carefully let herself savor him, answering his gentle, searching tongue.

Drawing back, she saw his confusion and felt a surge of satisfaction. She'd accomplished exactly what she desired. Wafting like the fragrance of a bed of flowers on a hot summer day, the desire didn't stop there. If he kissed her again, she wouldn't be in control of her faculties anymore.

"I need to check the house."

She let him go. The house was locked tight. Jillian had left the note when she'd entered the house when no one was here and made them dinner.

She climbed into Brandon's bed, wary of the danger but unable to spend the rest of the night alone.

When he returned, he hesitated at the door. Then he removed his jeans and lay beside her.

A silent understanding eased the tantalization of being so close. He needed to protect her and she'd rather not be alone after reading a note that threatened her life.

Workers were everywhere, beginning to rebuild the stable. After changing into shorts and a sleeveless cotton blouse, Eliza dug in with them. She worked beside Brandon, digging through the rubble and throwing it into huge trailers that would haul it all away. Materials to rebuild would arrive in the next day or so.

That morning they'd dropped off the next card to Zimmerman and told him about Jillian's uninvited visit.

"How did she get into the house?" Zimmerman had asked.

"One of Brandon's workers let her in," she answered.

"So, she didn't break in. The worker didn't think she was there with criminal intent."

"She wasn't invited. She just showed up to make us dinner."

"Helping out during hard times. Your husband was murdered, Brandon's stable burned down and his father escaped from prison. You two are dealing with a lot. She offered to help in the best way she knew how. I've seen it before. Seems a normal thing to do."

"Ted Bundy seemed normal, too."

Zimmerman had studied her in a long silence, and then in a noncommittal tone said, "I'll check into it."

"Are you going to question her?"

"So she can tell us she went to help you out during a rough time?"

Eliza had grown overwhelmed with frustration then. "What about the notes? Are you sending them to a lab?"

"There were no prints or other evidence to use for DNA analysis."

Jillian was being careful.

Now a few hours later, Eliza threw a piece of charred wood into the trailer bed with more zeal than necessary, venting her angst.

The sun was hot. Sweat dampened her skin. She didn't attribute all of that to the sun. Watching Brandon added a fair amount of heat. He'd removed his shirt like a lot of the other men. She stopped what she was doing to get some water from a big cooler. A man already there handed her a towel from a folded pile on the table. She thanked him as he left to go back to work and wiped her face and neck. Drinking more water, she unbuttoned another button on her light and airy blouse, all that she dared to do.

Turning, she saw Brandon again. A sheen of sweat glistened as his muscles tightened and relaxed. His butt was just as tight in those jeans. She remembered how it felt under her hands.

He took in the neckline of her blouse, and she ached to go to him and wrap her legs around him. She could not get enough of him. Never could. Always she was left yearning.

It's what made her take another bottle of water from the cooler and walk over to him.

She handed him the bottle.

"Thanks." He grinned, sexy and flirtatious.

She couldn't stop from feasting her eyes on his bare chest, lightly haired and fit.

That sheen of sweat…

She would love to be on top of him, and for the cause of his sweat to be from her.

The heat that tormented her radiated as she met his gaze, her own eyes shaded by her hat, a much more feminine one, blue-and-white and wide-brimmed.

She wanted him so much. The only thing stopping her was respect for David. And even that was beginning to weaken.

He stepped toward her, the lure too great to ignore. At least she wasn't the only one suffering.

"Hot today." His small talk gave him away further.

She drank some water, seeing his gaze drift hungrily down the front of her.

He had to stop doing that. She powered the bottle, and their gazes drank each other instead.

Temptation was too much. She breathed her anticipation as he stepped even closer, angling his head to dip his beneath the brim of her hat, his bumping hers as his mouth touched hers. The fact that a dozen or more men worked around them didn't matter. She had a fever for this. For Brandon.

Gently, he caressed her, tasting and savoring, satisfying a gnawing urge. Eliza trembled with desire for more, like an itch that never stopped itching. It felt good to scratch, but it wasn't enough to ease the irritation.

She pressed him for more. He kissed her harder. Their hips came together. She clenched his hair in her hand. Parting their mouths, his plundering eyes bore into hers.

"I want you right now," she whispered.

He actually began looking around for a place to take

her. The camp table would do just fine for her. Hell, the ground.

But he saw with her that several of the men had stopped to watch them.

Flustered, she stepped back, knees shaky, sweatier than she had been before, an ache between her legs.

Spinning around, she put the bottle of water on the table and walked briskly toward the pasture. She'd seen Willow there before. The mare saw her and walked to the fence, eager for food or a ride. A ride she'd get. Eliza had to get away from Brandon.

All the new tack she and Brandon had picked up was in a temporary shed that had been delivered yesterday. Seeing Brandon back to work, she contemplated going for a ride. She could use the break.

Going to the shed, she found a bridle and decided against a saddle. That would take too long.

Hopping the fence, she fit the bridle on Willow's pretty head.

"What are you doing?"

The terse demand could only be from Brandon. He stood on the other side of the fence, arms dangling over the top, cowboy hat shading his handsome face.

"Going for a quick ride."

"I'll go with you."

"No," she answered sharply. "I need a break. I won't be long."

He hesitated. The fire hadn't died. If he went with her, she'd take him to the yurt where she could be alone and naked with him. And they'd lock the door this time.

He didn't stop her as she climbed up onto Willow's bare back. She reined the horse toward the open pasture and sent her into a canter. She was so hot she might have to go for a swim in the stream.

At last she was out of sight of Brandon. Her nerves began to loosen. Tension eased from her back. Breathing the fresh air helped, too.

As she came upon the yurt, she wished Brandon had accompanied her. But then she saw an all-terrain vehicle parked there. Someone was there, using the yurt for shelter. In an instant, she realized it was the ATV she'd seen in the stable. It hadn't been there when she'd gone to free the horses from the fire.

Who could it be? Everyone was working on the stable.

Just as fear sprang up in her, the yurt door opened and Brandon's father appeared. He was using the yurt as a hideout.

He chuckled, low and dark. "This isn't how I had it planned, but I can be flexible. How nice of you to come alone."

Eliza reined Willow around and gave her an urgent tap with her heels. The horse charged into a run. Eliza stayed low on her back, tapping her again.

Willow strained into a full run, eating up the ground.

The sound of the ATV put a ball of panic in Eliza's throat. She'd have rather dragged Brandon into the house with all the men watching than risk this.

The ATV caught up to her. Brandon's father veered toward the horse, frightening the animal. Willow jerked in another direction, nearly throwing Eliza. She clung to the horse, kicking her harder. The horse needed no urging. Willow was as frightened as she was.

The ATV came up on Eliza's other side, getting ahead of Willow. The horse dug into the ground and headed in another direction. Brandon's dad was herding her.

The stream curled through the pasture, and she and Willow were coming up on it. Eliza reined the mare to run along its bank. Ahead, there was a fallen tree. Brandon's dad would have to go around it. She'd gain some ground if she could jump it.

"Come on, Willow." She urged the horse to give more.

At the tree, the horse shied a little, running into the water, splashing wildly with her speed. She lurched with the jump.

Eliza lost her balance on her back.

"No!" She sailed off the horse's back, landing hard on her backside, her feet in the stream.

The buzz of the ATV circled the tree as she'd anticipated. Struggling to breathe, Eliza crawled to her hands and knees.

Dizzily, she saw Willow galloping away. She was heading for the house. The ATV stopped on the other side of the stream, and Brandon's dad climbed off.

"It's tough to do a jump like that bareback."

He walked with slow confidence toward her, heedless of the water.

Eliza pushed herself up and stood, unsteady, head swimming. "What do you want?"

"I think you already know."

"Brandon's done nothing to you that you didn't deserve." She stepped backward as he reached the other side of the stream.

"I deserved?" He stopped, putting his fingers against his chest. "I deserved to live without my wife? I deserved to be sent to prison?"

Eliza kept quiet. Jillian wasn't as crazy as she thought. This man was far more dangerous. She should never have underestimated Brandon's suspicion.

"David got off easy. Brandon won't be as lucky."

"Brandon isn't here." Why was he after her? Clearly he'd been the one to send her the notes. He'd targeted her all along. But why?

"I'm going to take from him what he took from me."

What was he talking about?

As he reached for her, she pivoted and ran up the slope. He was taller and had longer legs. He caught her in a tackle.

The sound of a gunshot got him off her quickly. He sprinted to the still-running ATV.

Eliza looked upstream and saw Brandon on a horse, charging for her. He fired his gun again.

The bullet spat up the dirt right beside the ATV's rear tire. Brandon's dad looked back and then revved the motor, racing across the stream and up the bank toward the protection of the trees.

Brandon fired again as he reined his horse to a stop beside her. He jumped off.

"I couldn't let you go alone." He breathed hard and his eyes were wild with worry.

She touched his face, so glad to see him. "He was in the yurt."

"We don't keep it locked."

He'd been staying there all along.

"Oh, Brandon. He's the one sending the notes. He's after me." It wasn't Jillian. "He thinks killing me will hurt you."

His breathing stopped for a few seconds. Then he said, "It would."

Chapter 13

This time when Zimmerman came to talk to Eliza, he believed her. The marshal was with him. Brandon led them all into the living room, where Eliza sat on the sofa and Zimmerman took his seat on the chair. Marshal Dodge stood opposite the coffee table, and Brandon went to sit beside Eliza. He felt drawn to her now. Not only to make sure she was safe, but in other ways he hesitated to explore.

His attraction to her had nearly resulted in her demise. Kissing her at the pasture fence had driven her to get away from him. That was a mistake. He chided himself for not considering the possibility that his father would be watching, that he'd be near. He never imagined he'd use the yurt to hide. And wait for a chance to pounce.

Brandon still couldn't accept how his father thought killing Eliza would be the worst possible punishment. Anyone dying because of his father would be devastating, but why did his father think Eliza mattered to him enough to single her out as his victim? His next victim, if he had killed the others.

Brandon turned to Eliza, finding it more and more impossible not to. She was poised and equitable despite the detective's opinion of her up to this point. Her long hair was draped over her shoulder, her shorts and blouse dirty from her struggle. Slender and neither too large nor too small in the chest, she had a flat stomach and filled out her clothes perfectly. She wasn't short, but she wasn't tall. And her profile captured him the same as it had when he was eighteen.

Physically they'd been compatible. That hadn't changed. Or had it?

Listening to her talk to Zimmerman about his kids revealed her prowess in communicating with people and her integrity. Zimmerman had targeted her as a possible suspect in David's murder, and yet she didn't hold a grudge. She was confident. Self-assured.

The way he'd felt when he'd seen his father chasing her stayed with him. No matter what, he couldn't leave her alone. Not until his father was captured. That's why he hadn't complained when she'd crawled into bed with him last night. He just had to find a way to keep his hands off her.

Kissing a woman had never felt so all-encompassing. Afterward, he only craved her more. Each taste fueled a deeper desire, one he feared to let out of his control. He felt pulled in a direction he shouldn't go.

"Enough about me." Zimmerman grinned in admonishment. "I came here to talk to you."

"I'm just trying to soften the blow. You were wrong, and I was right."

Zimmerman chuckled. "Jack Reed is trying to kill you. Yes, you do win that one. I still need more on the rest."

Eliza gave him a charming answering smile, though her brow line said she felt time would tell.

"We searched the yurt." Zimmerman looked at Brandon. "Reed wasn't expecting anyone to come along when you did. I doubt he was expecting Eliza to show up when she did. In fact, I doubt he expected anyone to catch him at the yurt. He left some personal items behind. Toiletries. Snack food. Water. That sort of thing. But we also found a business card from the man who tried calling David on his cell. The one you gave us."

Brandon exchanged a look with Eliza, as stunned as her by this news. How else could his father have gotten the card if he hadn't been in contact with David?

"Then you think it's possible Jack killed David and the others," Eliza said.

She wanted so much for him to believe her. Brandon wasn't sure if she really worried she'd be charged with a crime she didn't commit or if she was determined to win. Her social etiquette worked in her favor, but only because Zimmerman had proof she'd been attacked. Witnesses had seen her ride off, and there was real evidence inside the yurt.

"We're still not convinced on motive for the other two."

Ryker had forgotten that he'd been looking at colleges when he met Aegina. All of the application forms were in a box. None of them filled out. In lieu of going out of his mind and chasing after her again, he'd come up to the attic to go through their old photos, the ones they had from before they'd bought a digital camera. He'd been thinking a lot about the day he met his beautiful wife and the months that followed, and he began to wonder when he'd taken the bitter path of resentment.

Had it been when Eliza left Vengeance? He'd just met

Aegina and fallen madly in love in a matter of days. So had she. He remembered how they'd matched each other that way. He didn't think he cared all that much when Eliza left. It wasn't until after his two sons were born that he began to feel stagnant, and thoughts of her abandonment had injected him with negativity. He didn't like taking care of his mother. He loved her, but he didn't like the responsibility.

He and Aegina had talked about where they'd live. She'd expressly stated she wouldn't leave her family. She'd also told him that she wouldn't fault him if he decided to go to college. His heart had been so full with her that it hadn't taken any thought at all. His place was wherever she was. He'd given up his dream for her. He'd stayed in Vengeance for her. And it had been worth it. If he had a chance to do it all over, he wouldn't change a thing,

A new kind of purpose compelled him. He felt refreshed. Alive. Ready to start over. With Aegina.

He took the blank application forms with him downstairs. As he picked up his keys, the doorbell rang.

Jillian was here…at his house?

"Hello, Ryker. I'm sorry to bother you at home." Her long, dark hair swayed as she brushed past him to enter.

He shut the door as she removed her sunglasses to reveal her pretty blue eyes. "How did you know where I lived?"

"I looked you up."

"What are you doing here?"

"I need to talk to you about Eliza."

What the hell...?

"I need your help."

"My help." This had a bad feel to it. What could he possibly do to help her?

"Yes. I know that you aren't happy with her for leaving you to take care of your mother. And with her husband dying and all, it doesn't look good for her to be with Brandon. I was wondering if you'd talk to her for me. Tell her what a mistake she's making being with him. Tell her she belongs in Hollywood."

She actually thought he'd go talk to his sister about that? "Eliza made a mistake marrying David, Jillian. She also made a mistake leaving Vengeance. Not just because our mother needed us, but because she loved Brandon. She walked away from that love. She ran from it. If she and Brandon end up together now, it's because it's meant to be. You need to leave them alone. Move on. Find a man who loves you the way I'm starting to think Brandon has always loved Eliza. Love isn't something you have to fight to get. It just happens."

Her face was white with what Ryker could only call fear, and that was weird. Why did losing Brandon matter so much to her?

"But…you told me Brandon would love no woman."

"He wouldn't love any woman who ran from him. And Eliza ran." Saying it gave him a nudging thought that he'd been a little too harsh with her. If that was the real reason she had left, he should have been more understanding.

"Then why is she trying to get him back now?"

"Why are you trying to stop her?"

Her head moved back as though shocked by the question. "I'm the right woman for him. We have a lot in common. More than Eliza has with him. She's all wrong for him."

"And you aren't?"

"Why are you on her side now?"

Whose? His sister's? "Look, Jillian, I meant it when I told you that you are a beautiful woman. You can have any man. Just not Brandon. If there is any woman he'll ever let down his guard to love, it'll be my sister."

"No." Jillian stepped back. "That can't be."

"Let it go. He doesn't want you."

She shook her head. "You're wrong." Moving backward again, she had to catch her balance when she came to the porch step. "He'll love me, not her."

She couldn't make Brandon love her. Ryker saw the crazed look in her eyes. "Are you all right?"

"You're all on her side."

"Do you need me to call someone to help you?" Like a van from a mental institution? He'd be sure and call Eliza after this. There was no telling what the woman would do next.

Ryker knocked on Aegina's parents' door after no one answered the doorbell. No doubt her mother had seen him and ignored it. At last the door opened and Aegina appeared. He took her in. She was wearing jean shorts and a Dodge T-shirt he'd given her. He'd kiss her if they weren't having so many problems right now.

"Ryker."

"Can I talk to you? It won't take long. Just a few minutes." Behind her, her mother scowled at him from the living room.

She glanced back and stepped outside, closing the door. He went to the swinging bench on the front porch and sat down, the application forms rolled in his hand.

Aegina sat next to him, eyeing the papers and then his face.

"You look good," he said.

"Thanks. So do you." She pointed at his Dodge T-shirt with a smile. It was different than hers, but it was still Dodge.

It warmed him that she'd noticed.

"How's Eliza?" she asked.

"Good." He supposed. He hadn't talked to her.

"You heard, didn't you?"

"About what?"

She sat straighter on the bench, facing him some more. "You haven't heard."

"What happened?"

"Brandon's father attacked her."

He listened while she told him the details and what was going around town. Her mother was one of the queens of gossip in Vengeance. Anything that happened at the police department quickly spread. Brandon's father blamed his sons for their mother's suicide, but he had particular hatred for Brandon.

"Does he mean to kill her?"

"He told Eliza that he'd make Brandon suffer the way he had."

His sister was in a lot of danger. "Has Brandon's father been caught?"

"Not yet."

And then there was Jillian. Ryker would call her as soon as he left.

"You should really talk to your sister more, Ryker."

"I will." She may have left him with the care of their mother, but she was still his sister.

"I can't believe she didn't tell you what happened."

"She's dealing with a lot right now." Loving Brandon. Jillian. And now Brandon's father. "I haven't exactly been a brother to her lately." He recalled the last time he'd seen her and felt ashamed.

Aegina's soft regard spared him further angst. "You're different."

Was he? How? He was afraid to ask. He couldn't afford any mistakes with her.

She eyed the papers in his hand again. "Why did you really come here?"

It wasn't to talk about Brandon's father. "I was going through some old pictures of us when I found these." He handed the rolled pages to her.

She took them and flattened them on her thighs. Then she looked at him curiously. "They're blank."

"Exactly. They're all blank. I never applied to any of those colleges."

"But you wanted to."

"I wanted you."

After a moment of wavering hope and despair, she shook her head. "Ryker, you can't change the past."

"I don't want to change it. That's what I came here to tell you. I wanted you from the start, Aegina. From the first conversation. College would have been a challenge for me. I needed challenge. I got that with you and the kids, and I got that with the shop. We've made a great life here, honey."

"But…you complained all the time about giving it up."

"I was a fool. I didn't understand why college was so important to me. Now I do."

The challenge.

He saw her register that.

"I love you, Aegina. I always have. I'm sorry for not making you feel like I did. And I promise you'll never feel that way again if you give us another chance."

Fidgeting with her hands, she averted her eyes, facing the street. Then she returned them to him. "What about…"

"Your affair?"

She nodded as he sighed. That was a heavy burden.

"Are you going to keep seeing him?"

She shook her head. "He left town yesterday."

"How do you feel about that?"

"I…" She faced the street again. "I don't really care. He had to go because he was offered a job."

She didn't really care, but part of her did care. That didn't sound good.

Her hand slid onto his thigh, something she'd always done when they sat together. "I don't love him."

That eased him a bit.

"And the sex wasn't all that great."

He wasn't sure he needed to hear this.

"Not nearly as good as it was with us."

Now that was more like it. "It's hard to beat perfection."

That made her smile but only halfheartedly. "He was a placebo, Ryker. I thought you didn't love me. I needed to feel loved. I didn't with him. I feel more loved right now than I ever did."

The sex had never been about love. He understood that. Many affairs weren't. Any affair in his marriage couldn't be about love. Their love was too strong.

"If you're willing to try, I am," she said.

That was the best news he'd had in a long time. "I do, Aegina. You're my wife. You're the only wife I ever want to have. There's nothing wrong with starting over. In fact, I think that's what we should do."

A smile of deep appreciation slowly spread on her mouth. "Start over."

"I'll take you to dinner for our first date. Are you free tomorrow night?"

Her smile strengthened. "I'll ask Mother to watch the kids."

Drawn to her, he leaned over and tipped her chin up to kiss her. "I love you." He kissed her again.

She kissed him back, and then heat took over, a familiar heat that had gone away for a while, heat that he had missed.

He moved back, soaking in the softness of her eyes, drugged with passion. "Until tomorrow then."

"Until tomorrow," she whispered back.

He stood and went down the stairs, turning and walking backward to see her, happier than he'd been in years.

On their first date, he'd taken her home with him and they'd had amazing sex. He hoped tomorrow would be a repeat of that.

As he headed for his Charger, he wondered if he'd be able to make love to her knowing another man had been where only he belonged. Then again, the longer he waited, the longer he'd allow that man to destroy his marriage.

He'd make love to his wife, all right. Tomorrow and every chance he got after that. He'd make love to her until it was just the two of them again.

For now, he had to concentrate on his sister. He had to warn her about Jillian. He tried calling her, but she didn't answer.

He began to worry. What if Jillian acted on her irrational emotions?

"Ryker!"

He looked over the top of his car. Aegina was rushing toward him. "The school just called. Evan was in a fight."

She climbed into the Charger, and he drove down the street.

"He's in the principal's office."

"What happened?"

"That bully started teasing him again and Evan hit him. Gave him a bloody nose!"

Ryker grinned and chuckled briefly.

"You think that's funny?"

"I showed him a few self-defense moves."

"Ryker Harvey, you didn't!"

"Oh, yes, I did."

Aegina tried to be mad, but he could tell she wasn't. She was proud as hell for their boy. So was he.

"Guess that bully will be leaving him alone now," Ryker said.

"Yeah. Guess so."

It was another shining example of how much alike they were. They agreed about everything. Ryker just hoped they found new ground to rebuild a new foundation. The one they'd started with was rock-steady. Now… he couldn't predict where they would end up. All they could do was try.

Chapter 14

Eliza received a call from a woman in town who had a Halloween party to plan. She claimed to have gotten her name from the senator's daughter, which raised a red flag. Brandon was angry with her for agreeing to go. She wasn't even sure why she had. It was business here in Vengeance. She'd always maintained her ties here. Vengeance was her hometown. But why now? Why agree to work now? For a distraction. David was dead and she couldn't stop thinking about Brandon.

Did she hope he'd changed? Dread almost made her tell him to take her back to the ranch. She should not be feeling the way she was for him. Not with David murdered. His brother. Her husband. But they were already here, at the building where the woman had instructed them to meet. The parking lot was empty. The building had foreclosure stickers on the window of the front door.

"This was a used car lot. Old man Flanders went to live with his daughter in Tucson," Brandon said.

He knew about everyone in town. "How did you find that out?"

"Someone at the market told me."

"You sure are chatty around here."

It struck her as both odd and charming at the same time. He wasn't the surly recluse she had him pegged for.

He opened his truck door. "Are you sure this is it?"

She checked the address again. "Yes."

"Who would want a party here?"

It was a little run-down. Abandoned. Movement in one of the windows gave Eliza a chill. Someone had peered through the glass from the protection of a wall and then retreated.

"Maybe you should wait here while I go check it out," Brandon said.

"No, I'll go in with you."

She got out of the truck as her cell rang. She checked who it was. Ryker. She answered.

"Eliza, thank God." He was breathless with urgency.

"Ryker? What's wrong? Are you in trouble again?"

Brandon came to stand before her, the argument over whether she'd go with him tabled for now.

"No. Listen, I had a visit from Jillian. Whatever you do, don't go near her."

"What?" She caught sight of more movement inside the building. A shadow went through an open doorway leading to a back room.

"She's insane over Brandon."

Eliza pointed to the building and Brandon twisted to look, but the shadow was gone.

Brandon looked there and then at her in question.

"Yeah, I know," she told her brother. "She broke into his house and we caught her making dinner the other night. Imagine our surprise." She walked with Brandon toward the building. The closer she got the more disrepair she noticed. Weeds had taken over the border and grew in cracks in the parking area.

"She made you dinner?"

"Yeah. Spaghetti."

"Why?"

"Why would any crazy woman make the man she's stalking and his girlfriend dinner?"

"What happened after you caught her?"

"Brandon's ranch hand helped us get rid of her."

"Where are you now? Are you alone?"

"I'm with Brandon." She stepped onto the cracking sidewalk that led to the entrance.

"Good." He sighed his relief. "Stay with him or come to my house where I can watch you, okay?"

Her brother genuinely cared about her. "I will. Thanks, Ryker."

"Hey. Aegina and I have a date tomorrow night."

They were patching things up? "That's great news."

"Why don't you come over in the morning so we can talk?"

Her brother was ready to talk. Eliza was thrilled. "I'll be there. Tell Mom to make her veggie omelets."

"Will do. Did you say you were meeting someone for a possible job?"

They reached the front door. "Yeah. It was the weirdest thing. A woman called about a Halloween party, and she gave us this address to a foreclosed building."

"Huh. That is weird." He seemed to take time to think. "Be careful."

"Stop worrying. I'm with Brandon, remember?" When she reached for the door handle, Brandon stopped her, removed a gun from the waist of his jeans and looked around for anyone who might see them. There was no one other than a passing car.

"Yeah. That is a comfort. Give me a call later."

"I'll check in." She disconnected, smiling, feeling like she had a family again but too aware of Brandon's gun and the creepy building to enjoy it.

Brandon pushed open the door and entered with his gun drawn. The hardwood floor was dusty. Cobwebs were thickest in the corners of the open showroom, not a large room but big enough for one or two cars. There were no desks or tables, and the light fixtures were broken.

Eliza stayed behind Brandon as he moved to the back room. "I think the woman went back there. Maybe she saw you and left." Maybe Jillian had hoped Eliza would come alone.

The creak of a door sounded from the back. Brandon pushed through the door and they entered what once had been an auto repair shop. One of two overhead garage doors was open. A breeze flowed inside. Whoever had been here was gone.

Brandon went outside. Overgrown shrubs and grass and weeds swallowed the fence bordering the property.

A car engine started. She looked with Brandon and caught a glimpse of a tan car backing up to turn around near the end of the building. Half the car was visible beyond the swaying branches of a large lilac bush.

"Wait!" Brandon ran, waving at the person driving as he passed the shrubbery.

Eliza ran after him. When she reached the lilac bush, she stopped, close to the car but out of sight.

Through the branches of the bush, Eliza saw Jillian behind the wheel of the car, face wet from crying. She had braked the car to a halt as Brandon approached. Eliza held back.

Brandon bent to the open window, hand on the frame. "What are you doing here, Jillian?"

"She was supposed to come alone." Eliza heard her wail, an eerie sound in the breeze.

"What are you doing here?" he repeated.

"I..." She sniffled and struggled to regain her composure. "I was going to plan a party."

"Here?" Brandon straightened and looked toward the building, seeing Eliza by the bush.

Jillian glanced at the side of the building with him, dazed now that her crying had ended, lethargic. Eliza had a feeling that if she approached the car, she would stop talking to Brandon. She had a connection to him in some sort of way, some bizarre way that no one other than she understood.

"Jillian?"

His voice brought her head turning back to him, pitiful eyes meeting his.

"What is it about me?" she asked.

"What do you mean?"

"Why can't you love me? Why can't anyone love me?"

"You'll find someone. You can't force it, though."

Jillian shook her head rigorously back and forth. "There's no one. No one will ever love me."

Brandon didn't respond. Really, what could he say? Eliza almost felt sorry for the woman. She was so insecure that it had driven her mad.

"What is it about me?" she repeated.

Again, Brandon didn't reply. Jillian had emotional problems that needed to be addressed. She hadn't done anything violent yet, but maybe she'd reach a threshold and break. She was broken now, but she hadn't tried to kill anyone.

Or would she have tried if Eliza had arrived alone?

"I thought you were different," she said, off in her own world. "You were like me."

"Like you?"

As in crazy? Eliza marveled over that one.

"You know how it feels to be raised in a strict house, by strict parents. And your mother died."

"Jillian, what are you talking about?"

Now suddenly flustered, Jillian shook her head. "I should go."

"Wait. What are you talking about?" Brandon pressed, putting his hand on the frame of the car window again.

His nearness seemed to relax Jillian, as though she clung to every stolen moment she could be close to him. Sad and disturbing.

"Your dad, of course."

"What about him?"

"We have that in common. Your dad and mine."

Her voice came in patches with a gust of wind, making it difficult for Eliza to hear.

Jillian slid her hands up the wheel and gripped it at the top, facing forward, lost in her topsy-turvy world. "I dreaded walking home from school every day. I'd take my time and go the longest route. At first my dad would punish me for being late. Then he got used to me getting home late all the time. I always hoped by the time I got there, he'd be too drunk to…"

Her face was a window into the past, all the pain and suffering gathering into a frown of desensitized horror. She'd lived through hell, and hell wasn't such a scary place anymore. It was the place where Jillian dwelled most of the time.

Eliza stepped forward, feeling pity she couldn't grasp. She stopped when Jillian looked up at Brandon. "I could tell you were living the same life as me. Different punishments, but the same."

Different punishments…

Had she been sexually abused by her father? Brandon had been beaten. Jillian had been molested.

Eliza's stomach soured.

"How could you tell?"

Again, Jillian elapsed into history. "Your face."

"That was a long time ago. Things have changed now."

"No, they haven't." Jillian looked up at him. "You and I are the same. Why can't you see that?"

"We aren't the same. I got past what my father did."

That wasn't entirely true.

"You can't erase the past, Brandon. You need me. We're the same."

"Maybe you should go talk to someone. You and I are not the same, and I am not interested in you the way you want me to be. It's time you accepted that."

"You mean I need a psychiatrist?" Jillian scoffed. She wiped her face angrily, mood shifting trigger fast. "You'd like that, wouldn't you? You can have any woman you please. You don't stop and think about the consequences of your carelessness. You think you can engage and disengage whenever you have the whim. You didn't stop to think about how it would affect me."

"Jillian, we hadn't been seeing each other long. We never even had sex."

"That's what made me think you were special. You didn't rush. And your father was…"

"My father is a dangerous man."

"Yes. Dangerous. You and I belong together, Brandon." She turned and looked at Eliza, who was no longer hidden by the shrub. "You're just confused right now."

"I'm not confused, Jillian. You have to stop this. There is no future for us and never will be."

Jillian remained silent for a while, looking up at him, not accepting what he said.

She put the car in Reverse. "You'll see." Driving in reverse slowly, she forced Brandon to step away from the car.

Eliza moved to stand beside him as Jillian backed out onto the street and then drove out of sight.

That's when it struck her. "She's driving a tan car."

Brandon turned to her. "Is it the same model?"

Eliza wasn't sure. "It could be."

He thought a moment. "Jillian was with me when you and David saw the one at the ranch."

So it was impossible that Jillian had been driving the same car. "I sure hope she leaves us alone now."

"That makes two of us." He started toward the road where his truck was parked. "Come on. Let's go grab some dinner."

Walking with Brandon down the street toward their burger place, they heard Irish music drift out of O'Neil's. People spilled out onto the small enclosed patio; the two tables were full. Laughter and conversation blended into unified jollity.

"Looks like Roger is having another celebration."

"Someone else you know in town?" She supposed that shouldn't be so amazing to her. Vengeance wasn't a big city. Still, she wasn't ready to let go of her fifteen-year perception of him. It kept her safe, after all, believing he was too isolated to keep up with her social pace.

They drew closer, and a few people turned their way.

"Brandon," a round-bellied man with a bald head greeted from among the crowd.

"Roger." Brandon veered toward the entrance to the patio. "Eliza, this is Roger O'Neil. Do you remember Tory?"

"Yes." She was a grade behind her in high school. A pretty Irish girl who was popular with the boys. "Are you her father?"

"That I am. We married her off last year. She moved to Boston with her husband. We miss having her around, but I suppose you can't expect everyone to stay in this town."

Not unless you were Ryker.

"Where are you headed?" Roger asked.

"We were going to have dinner at that burger place," Brandon answered.

"Come and join us," Roger waved them onto the patio. "The Bradleys' girl got married today. Plenty of food inside."

"Put it that way..." Brandon stepped onto the crowded patio.

"I'll find you a table." Roger led them inside, where the band blew horns and beat drums to a lively jig. It was dim in here, more of a pub than a restaurant. That along with rustic tables and green accents belied its Texas address.

A waitress quickly cleaned a booth for them at Roger's bidding. Eliza sat next to Brandon on the bench seat so she could see the band.

"Heard all about the stable," Roger said. "Sure sorry to hear about David, too. Such a shock."

Neither she nor Brandon said anything.

"Those agents in town any closer to catching the killer?"

"No, not yet," Brandon said.

Another waitress dropped off two glasses of water. "What will you two be drinking tonight?"

"Water's fine with me."

"Two Foster's," Brandon said, grinning at Eliza's protesting glance. "Live a little."

It would be nice to forget about Jillian for a while. His father. David. Why did bad news always have to happen in threes?

"I was glad to hear the task force working the murders has eliminated you as a suspect, Eliza. I knew your dad back in the day. Nice family. He was a good man."

"Thank you."

"There's a buffet over there." Roger pointed to the corner next to the band. "Or you can order from our menu."

Someone interrupted Roger, and he made an excuse to leave them.

Eliza turned to Brandon. "Did I hear you say 'live a little'?" Brandon Reed, encouraging her to party?

"We aren't kids anymore."

What did that mean? That living a little now was different than partying as a teenager? She looked around at all the smiling faces. People danced. Drank. Laughed. A celebration. It was more than getting together as friends and partying. This was a celebration of life. Brandon did live that way. He never wasted a moment. She'd wasted them every Friday.

"You never stop surprising me."

"Don't let it go to your head."

She laughed and scooted closer to him on the bench seat, not caring how it appeared.

Their beers arrived, and they ordered dinner. Eliza lifted her beer and held it out to Brandon. He lifted his, eyeing her peculiarly, but with affection in his eyes.

"To life."

"Life." He clinked his mug with hers.

It felt too good to sit close to him and share a long look. She turned to the celebration.

"How many of these people do you know?" she asked.

"Just about everyone. I do get out every once in a while. I think I actually got an invitation to this wedding."

A lot had happened to cause it to slip his mind. "It's nice."

"It meets your Hollywood standards?" he asked dubiously.

"Well." She took in the plain white cake and tiny vases of red roses on the tables. "I'd have spruced it up a bit." Not much, though.

"Chandeliers, big floral arrangements, linens?"

She looked around the Irish pub. The style spoke for itself. "No. More color on the cake and maybe a banner or something."

"Casual for you. I would expect more extravagance."

"Really?"

"Aren't those the kind of parties you plan in Hollywood?"

"Yes, but..." She missed doing casual.

"Small-town charm getting to you?"

She smiled and breathed a laugh. "It sure is." And so was he.

They shared another long look. The waitress arrived with their sandwiches.

Eliza watched a little girl in a white dress dance with the groom. The bride danced with an older gentleman who must be her father. A table of men laughed boisterously, well into their beers. A couple sat at another table, deep into a quiet conversation. Newly acquainted.

She looked at the little girl again.

"Cute, isn't she?" Brandon said.

"Very."

"Do you want kids someday?"

"I don't know." She hadn't thought about it much. Her

business had taken the front seat in her life. Even her marriage had been secondary to that.

"Do you?"

"No."

His terse response reminded her of his hang-up with his father.

"I think you should. You'd make a great dad."

"No, I wouldn't."

Curious, how adamant he was. "Why do you think that about yourself? You aren't your father."

"No, but he's mine."

So, he had violent blood running through him, and that was why he didn't want kids. "Give yourself a little credit."

"Don't ruin the night, Eliza."

They had created this patch of tranquility in the middle of chaos. She didn't want to end it yet, either. Still, she couldn't let it go just yet.

"If I were your wife, I'd show you what a good man you are."

Rather than threaten to ruin the night, what she said softened the mood. Brandon looked at her with growing heat, heat kept at a low simmer, pleasantness, contentment, delight. Now she'd triggered something else, brought out a match that was ready to light.

The waitress reappeared. Her timing was impeccable.

Brandon ordered two more beers. She already felt the first one.

Out on the dance floor, the bride and groom danced to a slow song. The bride's parents danced nearby, each watching the couple, proud and happy.

The tune picked up in tempo, back to a jazzy, horn-blowing beat.

"Let's go dance." Brandon gave her a nudge to slide out of the booth.

Levity renewed. Excited over the prospect of him cutting loose, she stood and went to the crowded dance floor. He turned out to be a good dancer. Another surprise. She boogied closer to him. He took her hand and swayed with her to the snappy beat. She loved the smile in his eyes.

Nothing mattered but this. Lively music, the crowd, the happy celebration. An escape from all that was happening outside of it. No one judged them. No one gave them disapproving looks. No murders. No threats. Everything fell away except sharing this night with Brandon.

She danced in his arms through three vivacious songs. Then a slower, romantic tune began to play. With her arms over his shoulders, she looked up at him, at the match that was ready to light, and stepped back. Talk about ruining the night. All they needed was another round in bed. They sat out the slow song, drinking beer well into the next faster one.

She was beginning to feel the alcohol quite a bit.

"I've had enough. How about you?" he said.

Right in tune with her. "I was just about to say something like that."

Normally, Eliza could stay the entire the night, but strangely, now was different. This wasn't her party. She hadn't planned it. She was a guest.

Leaving the pub, Brandon took her hand as they walked along the street to his truck, a silent message that he was enjoying this as much as her. Being together. Forgetting all that stood in the way.

She inhaled deeply. It was a quiet, clear night. This didn't feel wrong.

At his truck, she stopped. Instead of opening the door for her, he pulled her to face him, pulled again and had her against him. Her hands were on his chest. He angled his head and kissed her.

The kiss quickly fanned into more. He cupped her face with one hand, his mouth mashing with hers. When he lifted his head, she stared up at the fire in his golden-brown eyes. The past was nowhere near her heart now. Only the rightness of this night burned in her.

He opened the door, and she got in. It was a wordless acknowledgment of what would come. As he drove toward the ranch, she was so aware of him. He glanced over once, eyes flaming, drifting down her body. Then he drove faster on the two-lane highway leading out of town. The fifteen-minute drive felt like an hour. It was long enough for the magic of the night to wear off.

When they reached the driveway, she'd already decided to refuse him if he tried to finish what he'd started. Judging from his now tense profile, low, shadowy brow, tight line of his mouth, he'd drawn the same conclusion.

The flame was officially doused when another car appeared on the road, heading for them.

"Who's that?"

Brandon didn't answer. The headlights drew nearer. As it passed she saw it was tan in color. Jillian's car.

"Does that woman never give up?"

"It wasn't Jillian." Slamming on the brakes, Brandon whipped his truck around and revved the engine to give chase to the car. But the car had sped up and now raced a good distance ahead.

At the highway, it disappeared as it turned.

Brandon reached the highway. By then there was no sight of the taillights of the other car. Brandon drove fast. He didn't lessen the pace until the next town over from Vengeance popped up on the horizon.

He drove through town, searching side streets. No sign

of the tan car. Finally, he turned and drove back toward the ranch.

"Are you sure it wasn't Jillian?"

"It was my dad. I saw him driving."

"Jillian's car?"

He didn't comment.

"Do they know each other?"

"I don't see how. He's been in prison for ten years. And Jillian didn't know him when he was here."

She was about thirty years younger than him, too.

"Weird that they drive the same car."

"Dad probably stole the one he's driving."

They reached the ranch, Brandon keeping a vigilant eye as they made their way to the front porch. Inside, Brandon stopped her from going to the guest room.

"Sleep with me."

Chapter 15

Brandon told himself he brought her to bed with him to protect her from his father. The night they'd had couldn't be topped, but the enchantment had faded the moment he'd driven onto his road. It had ended altogether when he'd seen his dad. What had he been doing here? He hadn't seen any signs of a break-in. All the windows and doors were locked. The stable was void of mischief. Had he just waited for them to come home and given up when the hour grew late?

What would he have done if they'd been home? Tried to kill Eliza? Brandon had no doubt. He also wouldn't put it past him to return before morning. Which was why Eliza was sleeping in the same bed as him.

She emerged from the bathroom. The light beside the bed was on, dim light illuminating her long sleep T-shirt. She hesitated in the doorway before stepping to the other side of the bed and getting in. He was in underwear with the covers drawn to his waist, pretending to be into an *American Dad* episode.

He was hard as stone. Growing harder with her lying so close. It was the night. It had been so easy to be with her. So much better than when they were kids. He didn't understand how it was possible. And he resisted the nagging reality that there was nothing about her that would keep him away. He'd broken up with her because he'd known she would fly away. She wasn't ready to settle down. Nor had he been. Now…

Now it was so different.

Talking about family had disturbed him. As with the rest of the night, even the talk had felt right. She was right for him. She was his girl. Always had been.

That made him go cold with dread. Had he ever been this close to a woman before? He didn't think so. Now that he was, he was out of his realm. Tempted to be with her, terrified to allow it to happen.

Rolling his head, he saw her gaze was already on him, thinking the same thoughts. She was a runner because of the way she'd lost her dad. She accused him of being the same way because of his. The abuse he'd suffered.

Whatever dynamics worked on them, this night wasn't over, and it might be his undoing if he gave in to what his heart urged.

"Does tonight scare you?" she asked.

"No." It was a lie. It scared him to death.

She smiled. "Liar."

How had she gotten to know him so well? Maybe she always had.

She rolled onto her elbow, her face close to his. Her nightshirt drooped and gave him a glimpse of cleavage. Naked cleavage.

"This doesn't scare you?" She traced her finger along the side of his mouth.

"Does it scare you?"

Her smile softened. "Yes."

"It should."

"Why, because you won't be there for me if I fall in love with you?"

No, because a future with him would be risky. A woman like Eliza would push him at every turn. He couldn't predict where that would lead. He needed predictable.

She leaned down, hovering above his lips. "I think you have it all wrong."

"Yeah?" He was too hard to stop her.

"Yeah."

"How so?"

She kissed him tenderly. What had made her so brazen, he couldn't guess. But it sure felt good.

"You need to be pushed."

"What about you?"

"I need to be the one doing the pushing."

"Eliza..." She sounded a little too serious. Was she talking about a future? That would mean she'd have to give up her company in Hollywood. Was she really prepared to do that? To move back here?

The thought increased his dread. It was a wave inside him. He tensed.

But she kissed him again, and all he could think about was how hard he was. Tossing the covers off him, she straddled him. Feeling her bareness against his groin, he lost all other coherency but the feel of her right against the length of him, the only barrier his underwear.

She must have decided this was where the night was going to go before she left the bathroom. What had changed her mind from the drive home?

"I don't want this night to end," she said, leaning down to kiss him.

He couldn't disagree. Putting his hands on her bare hips, he lifted her T-shirt and flung it over the side of the bed.

She was a vision sitting on top of him, full breasts, trim waist, slender thighs spread for him. Rolling her onto her back, he pushed his underwear down and kicked them off his legs.

Kissing her, he probed for her. He'd slow down as soon as he sank inside her. As he did, sensation overtook him. She was wet. He slid so easily, buried himself deep. He shuddered with the pleasure it gave him. He held still. If he didn't, he'd lose control too soon.

"Make love to me, Brandon," she murmured between kisses.

Looking down at her, he began to move. Each stroke brought him closer to oblivion. He feasted on the sight of her, her round breasts prone to him, her nipples hard. He took one into his mouth, rewarded by a sultry sound from her. Her hands were on his shoulders, toned arms reaching for him. He kissed her and then rose up so he could see her body, those breasts and the juncture of her thighs where he disappeared inside her. It was his undoing.

He moved faster. Seeing her flushed face, he knew she was close. He held off just long enough, until he heard her guttural cry. She was the most beautiful sight in the world. He stayed immersed her as he came with an intensity that awed him.

The incredibleness of it made him uncomfortable. He didn't remember feeling this way when they were young. While he'd been disappointed to realize she'd choose her parties over him, he hadn't been irrevocably connected to her. The infatuation, the chemistry, had been hard to walk away from, but they had been too young to place any permanence on it. That's how it had been for him, anyway.

Now it didn't seem to matter that she'd been married to his brother. And his brother was dead.

Except it did matter. It mattered a great deal to him. Maybe that was what made him feel so hollow right now. Instinct would have him getting off the bed and leaving the room. Sleeping on the couch downstairs. He needed to get away. The urgency was so much more powerful with her than it had been with any other woman.

The why of that had him spinning inside. Why did he need to run? Was Eliza's assessment accurate, or was his conscience at work here? Going with the former would suggest he had strong feelings for her, strong enough not to be denied, strong enough to put a four-letter label on it. And that he could not do.

He couldn't forget his brother. Even as his feelings for Eliza overpowered that decision, he refused to give them further credence. For the first time since his father had escaped, he wished Eliza wasn't here at his ranch.

Eliza woke facing Brandon sometime later in the night. Watching him sleep, she wondered if she'd imagined the withdrawal she'd sensed in him, his silence and the anxiety in his eyes. If he'd only overcome the tragedy of his past, let it go, come to terms with the abuse and his father's violence.

His eyes opened then. They gazed at each other for a while. In the soft moments of waking, none of his demons haunted him. She reached to touch his stubbly face, wishing he could forget them forever. Moving closer, she kissed him before the moment vanished.

Gradually, he took over the kiss. His arm moved under the covers, his hand cupping her breast. Then he rolled onto her.

She opened her legs.

"Eliza," he murmured, part passion and part protest.

If she gained nothing more from this night than to give him something heavy to ponder, something that might alter his course, it would all be worth it.

He slid into her slow and gentle, packed with lots of meaning as he looked right into her eyes.

He moved back and forth, only closing his eyes when he kissed her. She sank her fingers into his hair, holding him to her mouth for a deep one. Only a few more poignant thrusts brought her to her peak. She came looking into his eyes, and he came with her. Prolonged seconds passed while they still looked into each other's souls.

He kissed her sweetly and then lifted his head to whisper, "Stop doing this to me."

"You do it to yourself," she whispered back.

Eliza woke the next morning to the recollection of the previous night. Lifting her head, she saw that his side of the bed was empty. An unwelcome premonition turned her stomach over. Why had he left her? He wasn't in the bathroom, either. He'd find a reason to bolt now. Just like with all the other women in his past. And her when they were kids. Except, he'd never admit it. That last joining hadn't been enough. Or maybe it was too soon to tell.

She was going to be so mad at him if he treated her like another woman who got too close. As if she didn't matter.

Getting up, she put on her nightshirt and went downstairs. He was in the kitchen drinking coffee. He saw her and his eyes held none of the tenderness that was there last night. Yep, he was cornered. Damn it, she should have thought of that last night. She should have waited until she was sure where his head was in regard to them.

"You got up," she said casually. She was leaving as

soon as she could pack. Damn him! She began to stew over his stupidity.

"I didn't want to wake you."

Fool. She deliberately moved close to him, sliding her hands up his chest. "I wish you would have."

The aloofness she saw intensified. Putting his cup down, he stepped back, taking her wrists and pushing her hands off him. "I've got a lot of work to do in the stable today."

While her heart shattered, she remained outwardly collected. "I'll help you." Push him. He needed a good pushing. Or a good clobber across the side of his head.

"No. You should stay in here today."

"Why?" She kept her tone playful. "Are you afraid you're going to take after your dad right now?"

"Eliza..."

"Brandon, you're running. From me."

"Have you forgotten that you were married to my brother? He's dead. Doesn't that mean anything to you?"

His stinging words, spoken so harshly and with such blame, pierced her deeply. Guilt returned. She may not ever be able to get over it. David would always be there between them. "That was a mean thing to say. Of course I care."

"Doesn't look that way to me."

She tried to stop her flush. She'd crawled on top of him. She'd initiated their lovemaking.

"I didn't hear you complaining," she retorted.

With a gruff sigh, he ran a hand down his face. "This can't continue. I won't marry you, Eliza. You were my brother's wife."

"You self-righteous bastard!" She stepped closer to him and slapped him. "You can turn this all on me if it makes you feel better, but we both know the truth is you're *afraid!* You'll never marry anyone because you're afraid. You accuse me of running when you're the only one running now."

"Eliza—"

"Shut up." She wasn't finished. "I climbed on top of you last night because I believed there was a reason we had such a good time together, why it always feels so right when we're together. I know you felt the same. But you refuse to open your heart, to me or anyone who gets too close. I feel sorry for you, Brandon. You'll never find happiness if you keep pushing people away."

He stared at her in silence for a while. "How can we ever be happy with David between us?"

More stinging hurt inundated her. He was right, but there was no denying what they had, what they'd always had ever since they were young. She and David had made a mistake marrying. It should have never happened. Did that mean she and Brandon had to punish themselves the rest of their lives?

Brandon would, and he'd use his brother as an excuse to keep running.

She marched to the guest room, hearing him follow.

"Eliza."

She jammed her clothes into her bag, all the while berating herself for allowing him to do this to her again. No other man could have done it.

She froze as that realization led to another. She hadn't meant to love anyone the way her mother had loved her father. Now that she did, it was strangely freeing.

Slowly closing her bag, she turned to Brandon. "You were right about me. I did run from love after my dad died. I didn't want to feel that intensely about anyone, only to lose them and endure the heartache I watched my mother suffer. But I was wrong, Brandon. I was wrong to think never feeling that way was better for me. I love you, and I'm losing you. I can't fight that. I can't fight my love for you anymore, and I'm not going to."

"You were married to my brother."

That was his excuse. A good one, but an excuse nonetheless. "I made a mistake marrying him. I'm sorry he's dead, but I didn't kill him. I didn't coerce him into marrying me, either. It was as much his fault as it was mine. I married the wrong brother."

She grabbed her bag and headed for the front door.

"Where are you going?"

"My brother's." He could take care of her just as well as Brandon could. "I need to spend more time with him anyway."

When he didn't stop her, her heart broke even more. Even the threat of his father didn't compel him to try and make her stay. She was no different than Jillian to him. Not crazy, but a woman who made him feel cornered. Eliza embraced the pain. It wouldn't last. Soon it would fade to something she could live with. She'd done it before, she could do it again, damn him.

Chapter 16

With her carry-on bag in tow, she stepped into Ryker's house. All the furniture was still there. Aegina was still living with her parents.

Ryker walked into his renovated kitchen. "You okay?"

"I hate how similar our lives are right now." She left her luggage by the door and followed.

Sitting at the snack bar, she accepted a glass of water from him. He put his own in front of the stool next to her and sat.

"Thanks for taking me in."

"You're my sister." He drank from his ice-filled glass.

"I don't feel like I've been much of one over the past several years."

He put his water down. "I've been meaning to talk to you about that. With everything going on between me and Aegina, and Evan getting into a fight, it's been a ride lately."

"Evan was in a fight?"

"A bully has been roughing him up at school. I showed

him a few moves and he used one of them. He was almost suspended. It took some fancy talking with the principal."

"You taught your son how to fight?"

"Some parents might think that's unconventional. Violent, even, but that bully wasn't going to leave him alone. Evan only tried to defend a girl. I didn't want him to lose that instinct. If he's afraid of being bullied, he might not do the right thing next time. He might not defend a girl."

"So now he's a tough guy at school." She breathed out a laugh. "He wouldn't be the first."

"Brandon was like that with you. If my son turns out like that, I won't complain."

"You're a good father, Ryker."

"And a terrible brother."

She shook her head. "I should have been there for you more."

"I should have been there for you more. We both lost our dad. I should have given you more slack."

"I should have helped you with Mom more."

"Let's leave it at we both could have helped each other more."

"Okay." She beamed.

"I told you I didn't need any help," a voice hollered from the other room. Their mother was listening.

"Yeah, I know, Mom," Ryker yelled. "Mind your own business now. Eliza and I are becoming brother and sister again."

"'Bout time!"

She and Ryker laughed.

The sound of the news program made them both stop and turn to the small television on the snack bar surface. Not so much the sound of it, rather, the name she'd heard.

What is believed to be the body of Harlan Marks...

"Yesterday, construction workers uncovered the mummified remains of a human body during the demolition of an old house that was sold to a commercial developer late last year. What's even more interesting is the house once belonged to Harlan Marks. Marks was reported missing by his daughter nearly twelve years ago. His wallet was found buried with him, along with a gun believed to have been used as the murder weapon. Then eighteen, his daughter, Jillian Marks, lived in the home until its sale last year. She is so far unavailable for questioning."

"Jesus," Ryker breathed.

"Do you think she killed him?" Her teary confession to Brandon ran through her head. She'd been abused. Sexually molested by her father. But that wasn't in the news. It must never have been reported.

Someone knocked on the door.

Eliza froze as she wondered if it could be Brandon, then chided herself for even entertaining the notion. He'd stay as far away from her as possible now.

Ryker went to answer and moments later returned with a woman in tow. It was Willa Merris, the senator's daughter. Eliza hadn't seen her since the night she and Brandon had found David at the Cork.

"She said she wanted to talk to you," Ryker said.

Willa came closer. She was on the tall side for a woman, with reddish-blond hair and blue eyes that were as beautiful as her debutante past, but filled with soft sweetness that lent her an air of fragility. "I called the ranch and someone told me you were here."

"Brandon?"

"No, I think it was his housekeeper."

He'd already told everyone on the ranch? More likely they'd asked where she was.

More curious than ever, she indicated the woman to sit beside her.

Willa did. "Have you heard the news about Jillian Marks's dad? They've been talking about it all morning."

"Yes."

"I heard her say something to David that night you and Brandon came and tried to get him to go home with you."

Willa had heard what David and Jillian had talked about. *Of course!* Eliza should have thought to go talk to Willa and the woman who had been with her that night.

"What did you hear?"

"I've debated on whether or not to go to the police. It didn't seem important at the time. But now I'm not so sure."

"If it will help solve the murders, it's worth a try."

Willa nodded. "That's why I'm here. I wanted to talk to you first, to see if you knew anything more."

"More about what? Willa, what did David say to Jillian that night?"

"Not much. Jillian was afraid. I could tell. He must have said something to her before they arrived at the Cork."

Eliza's enthusiasm sank a little. She hadn't heard everything.

"Jillian asked what he wanted after they sat down. And David said she better leave Brandon alone or he'd tell him about the affair she'd had with my father," Willa said.

"She had an affair with the senator?"

"Yes, but I couldn't help thinking there was more. His threat scared her."

"Why didn't you go to the police? Jillian had clear motive to kill David, and possibly your father," Eliza said.

"She kept saying it was more than an affair, that she loved my father. I never suspected she could have killed all three men."

No one could seem to find a suspect who fit that bill.

"Now I hear on the news that her own father was murdered, and Aegina said she's been stalking Brandon."

"Yes."

"There could be more that David knew about her," Willa said.

Eliza looked up at Ryker. "We have to go talk to Zimmerman."

He nodded. "Willa, too."

"You don't need to be involved," Eliza said. "Willa and I will go to the station."

But he was already picking up his keys. "I'll take you."

Eliza stood. "Are you sure?"

"Very sure. I won't let you go anywhere alone right now."

His declaration warmed her and eased her worry that he may never forgive her. He was here for her. All the way.

Like the brother she had missed, he raced them across town, no longer bitter, on her side now.

At the police station, they walked past reporters. None of them bothered her. She was no longer a person of interest. They didn't know Jillian was stalking Brandon.

Inside, Ryker asked to speak to Detective Zimmerman.

"Send them back," he called from the middle of a roomful of desks.

They were allowed inside.

Another man stood beside Zimmerman, towering in height, dark hair combed and green eyes perceptive and smart and right now intense with something on his mind, something that had obviously brought him here. Gabe Dawson, looking every bit the billionaire oil baron he was. His ex-wife had disappeared and ever since, he'd allegedly been sniffing around Vengeance, hunting for information.

"Gabe." Willa sounded surprised.

Zimmerman passed questioning eyes over Willa, and then to Ryker and Eliza and he said, "Let's go somewhere to talk." He led them to a conference room, where they all sat. He shut the door.

What did Gabe have to do with this? He'd been nosing around town about Melinda, of course, and he and Willa looked at each other as though they had some kind of connection.

Zimmerman made sure everyone was introduced before beginning. "Gabe here has come across some information that may prove instrumental in solving this case. In his search for Professor Grayson, he's uncovered some things that could be useful."

When Zimmerman turned to him, Gabe spoke. "I discovered Sheriff Peter Burris threatened Jillian Marks before she started seeing Brandon."

Because of her affair with the senator. "Was she stalking him?" Eliza asked.

"It would appear so," Zimmerman said.

"A friend of the sheriff told me he bragged about it one night over a few beers. He said Jillian wouldn't dare go against him. He said she had no choice other than to do as he said, and that was to stop stalking the senator."

"He ended their affair?" Willa asked.

Eliza wasn't sure if this was difficult for her to hear.

"Yes," Gabe answered. "And the sheriff set her up to look like she had possession of drugs. If she didn't stop what she was doing, he was going to arrest her."

Eliza sat back with a whoosh. Jillian had motive to kill all three men. The senator for dumping her. The sheriff and David for threatening her.

"Thank you, Willa, Mr. Dawson," Eliza said. "I'd like nothing more than to catch David's killer." And right now that was looking to be Jillian Marks.

"I won't stop until I know what happened to my ex-wife," Gabe said.

That earned him an uncertain look from Willa that Eliza didn't understand. Was there something going on between these two?

"Willa, Gabe, I need to stay to take formal statements from you." Zimmerman interrupted her musings in time to catch him direct another order to Eliza and Ryker. "You two are free to go."

They left the police station and walked to Ryker's Charger.

"What are you going to do once this all settles down?" her brother asked.

She thought for a few seconds. Going back to Hollywood didn't have the appeal it once had. She'd feel like she was running again.

"I think I'm going to move back to Vengeance."

Ryker stopped short. "No. You aren't."

"Yeah. I am." The more she voiced it aloud the more certain she became. "I belong here."

"What about Brandon?"

"I'm not moving home for him. I've spent enough time away from you and Mom."

"You don't have to move back for us, Eliza, I was a fool before now."

"I'm moving back for me. To spend more time with my family. It's for me, no one else."

Ryker chuckled. "That's more like the Eliza I grew up with."

They climbed into the Charger.

"I'm also moving back for you," she confessed.

He only chuckled again, knowing exactly what she meant already. Eliza smiled back at him, happier than she'd been in a long, long time.

A tan car passed them as they turned onto Ryker's street. There weren't many houses here, and no one was out.

She pointed. "That car! There's Jillian!" Where was she going? Why was she here? Had she followed them?

"Are you sure?" He drove faster, going after the car.

"Yes!" She couldn't tell who was driving.

"Call the police."

Eliza took out her cell phone and started to call 911 when a truck slammed into the back of Ryker's. The tan car slowed. Ryker was sandwiched between them. He tried to swerve out, but the two cars worked in tandem.

They'd passed Ryker's house. It was more deserted here.

The emergency operator answered as the truck from behind slammed into them again. The phone flew out of her hand, bouncing off the open window frame and falling outside.

"Damn it!" She twisted to see the driver of the truck.

Jack Reed.

Sick with fear, she saw that Ryker wasn't doing much better.

He stopped his vehicle. They were trapped.

"Get out and run, Eliza!" Ryker yelled.

Eliza got out, intending to find her cell phone, and gunfire exploded. She screamed and huddled near the Charger.

Ryker swore and went down. Was he shot?

Jack Reed walked slowly toward him. Eliza jumped up onto the hood of the Charger and scrambled to the other side.

Jack aimed his pistol at Ryker, who must already be shot or he wouldn't be lying on the ground.

"No!" she yelled.

Jillian opened the door of the tan car and stood. She and Jack Reed had been working together, but why?

Chapter 17

After Brandon had seen the news, he'd raced into town. Eliza wasn't at her brother's house, so he called Zimmerman, who confirmed she'd been there, and proceeded to reveal what he'd learned from Gabe Dawson.

Brandon should never have let Eliza go. He'd told himself that she'd be safe with Ryker, but all the while another kind of terrible feeling denied that as the whole truth. If Eliza wasn't the woman for him, what woman would be? He could tell himself he needed a meek and mild woman, but none of them had ever worked for him. Was that his phobia of ending up like his father at work?

His phone rang.

"Where are you?"

It was Zimmerman again.

"At Ryker's house. Eliza isn't here."

"She's near there. We just got a 911 call."

Apprehension geared up his pulse. *No. Eliza.* Something had happened to her. His father had gotten to her.

"Where?"

"Must be right up the road. Help should be arriving any second."

He shaded his eyes. There was nothing on the two-lane county road that bobbed up and down over the hilly landscape, wide-open spaces and no houses.

Hearing sirens, he ended the call and ran to his truck. A police car passed, then another. Brandon followed. Over the first hill, Ryker's Charger was parked, and Ryker lay outside the open driver's door.

A policeman exited his cruiser, armed. He aimed into the cab and then knelt by Ryker.

Brandon reached them.

"Stay back," the second officer said.

"I know him. It's Ryker Harvey." Brandon went to Ryker, who struggled to breathe and pressed his hand to a bullet wound on the right side of his chest.

"Brandon," he managed to say. "Eliza…" He coughed.

Fear as he'd never experienced before cauterized him and made it difficult to remain calm. "Where is she?"

"Jillian…and J-Jack…"

"Jack Reed?" the officer kneeling beside him queried.

"Jack and Jillian are together?" Brandon asked, his mind reeling. He tried to ignore the comedy of their names.

He should have guessed something wasn't right when Jillian drove the tan car to the empty car sales building

"Yurt…" Ryker barely got out.

Yurt. His yurt? His dad would try to take Eliza there. To kill her. He'd kill her right under everyone's noses.

Cursing, Brandon looked down at the officer. "How did you know to come here?"

"Got a call. Eliza called for help just before she lost her phone."

"Phone's here." The second officer approached, holding a cell phone.

Brandon snatched it from him and ran to his truck, calling over his shoulder, "Get him to a hospital. Now!" As if they didn't already know what to do. Urgency ruled him.

He drove onto the field along the road. He knew this land better than anyone. He'd get to that yurt. Maybe before his dad did.

And Jillian…

How was it possible that the two knew each other?

Eliza.

The thought of her at his father's mercy crippled him. What would he do if anything happened to her? If she were killed…

That would be his ruin.

In that instant, he understood what had made Eliza run. Her mother had felt the kind of love he felt for Eliza. She'd shied away from it, and Brandon had been her first lesson.

He couldn't keep running. He ran for different reasons than Eliza. He ran from his heritage, from what ran through his veins. Ever since he was old enough to think about it, he couldn't come to terms with how he could be his father's son and not be like him.

His father was a horrible man. His father had an uncontrollable temper. His father had loved deeply, as deeply as Eliza's mother had. And his father had lost that love. As a child, Brandon had thought losing love was what had driven his father mad. But the abuse had begun before that. Not as severe, but there. Brewing. Waiting to erupt. His mother's death had been the catalyst.

All the women Brandon had pushed away had been the result of seeing his father go mad from loving and losing. Just like Eliza.

Brandon wasn't a violent man. He had a temper, oh, yes, when provoked for good reasons. He had a temper. But he was not the violent man waiting to erupt like his father. Eliza had been right about most of that. She'd missed the most important one, though, the one that had them both avoiding love because of what they'd seen as kids.

He was Brandon Reed, his own man. One who answered to no one, followed no one and feared no one. He was a man who made his own way in life, because he hadn't had the fortune of having parents to guide him.

Least of all his father.

He stepped on the gas, sailing over a hill, taking a little air as he rushed to save the woman he loved. He had to tell her. He had to get there in time.

That's when a memory dawned on him.

Eliza kicked the trunk over and over. Jillian had helped Jack tie her and put her here. The way they'd talked to each other was chilling.

I knew she'd follow me if she saw this car.

You should go now. The police will be looking for you.

What about you?

I've got it from here.

Tied and lying in the trunk, Eliza had watched them hug like father and daughter. Jillian had tears forming in her eyes.

I'll be in touch, Jack had said. *Like always.*

Like always…

The car stopped, and Eliza's pulse resumed a sickly beat of fear and helplessness. She tried desperately to think of a strategy. Jack intended to kill her. What was she going to do?

The trunk opened. Eliza struggled in her restraints,

tied tight and firm. She'd tried to wrestle her way out of them all the way here. Her hands and feet were numb.

Jack easily hauled her out of the trunk. She hated how she had to lean on him to stand.

"What are you going to do?" Besides kill her.

"I'm going to wait for him to find you here."

He didn't expect to get away.

"Brandon is going to kill you."

Jack laughed. "He doesn't have it in him. He's a boy in a man's body, an insolent little boy who never learned to be a man."

"What does that make you?"

"The boy's father." Before she could retort, he lifted her and slung her over his shoulder.

He strode toward the yurt as though nothing in the world would stop him. Dread sickened her more and more the closer she came to her place of death. Knowledge of death was bad enough, knowledge of when and where was infinitely worse.

How would he do it? Would he strangle her like David and the others?

He kicked open the door and stopped.

He didn't move.

Eliza tried to look around but in her upside down position, she couldn't see much. She did see a pair of boots, though.

Brandon's boots.

"Brandon?"

"Put her down," he said, cool and calm, the sound of his voice almost foreign. He could be starring in a modern-day Clint Eastwood movie. And his dad was about to make his day.

She twisted and lifted her body with her abdominal muscles just enough to see him. Leaning against the far wall, he propped a big, long-barreled pistol on his forearm.

Jack slid her off his shoulder. Her feet landed on the floor and she stumbled, unable to feel her feet. She fell and rolled to her rear, scooting to the wall next to the door.

"I remember when you used to go to that old corner bar every night," Brandon said.

"Yeah? So?" Jack shifted his weight, looking bored.

"I saw you there once. With Harlan Marks. I didn't place him as Jillian's father until I remembered that. It was so long ago that I almost forgot."

This time Jack didn't have a remark.

"Did you help Jillian kill him?"

"Since when did you get so interested in who I spent time with at a bar?"

"Why did you do it?"

Why had Jack helped Jillian kill Harlan?

Eliza waited with Brandon. Jack didn't have anything to lose. He'd resigned himself to going back to prison. He'd only escaped to punish Brandon once and for all.

"He had an affair with my wife."

"Did she kill herself when you found out?"

Jack stormed toward Brandon. "What do you know about anything? You—"

Brandon pushed off the wall and punched Jack once, square between the eyes. Jack stumbled and regained his balance, but not before Brandon stretched his pistol out, inches from his left eyeball.

"I saw you in the bar with him after that!" he roared.

"Jillian came to me," Jack relented. "When she was eighteen. She had a plan, and I liked it."

To kill Harlan.

"You've been in contact all this time?" Eliza asked, incredulous. The two must have fed off each other's anger and insanity.

"I was the father Jillian never had." He kept his gaze on Brandon. "And she was the daughter I never had. She was the *child* I never had. She honors me. Loves me. *Respects* me."

"It was hard to respect you when the only thing I ever saw was your fists and bloodshot eyes."

"Insolent! You see? You never listened to me. You drove your mother to her grave."

"You drove her there. You and Harlan both."

The sound of sirens broke the tension, creating a new breed of it.

Two abusive men had driven Brandon's mother to her grave. Had she thought Harlan was better? A safe haven? Until she'd discovered he molested his daughter. He hadn't laid a hand on her, but he had his own daughter.

Eliza grew infinitely sad. That poor woman. She'd seen what abuse had done to her sons. Imagine how she felt when she learned the next man she loved had violated his daughter.

Jack charged Brandon, who merely pulled the trigger on his pistol. Without so much as moving, he stopped his father with a bullet.

Jack landed on his knees, staring in shock at his son before falling facedown on the yurt floor. Full of purpose, Brandon stepped over him and came to Eliza.

He untied her knots, focused and wordless.

She worked her numb hands as he untied her feet. "How did you know to come here?" And why had he come after her?

"Ryker told me."

Oh, Ryker! Was he all right?

Brandon saw her face. "He was okay when I left him with the paramedics."

He helped her to her feet, which were prickling from lack of blood flow. When she took a step, she swayed against Brandon.

Outside, the sound of vehicles approaching alerted her to the arrival of police.

Brandon lifted her, cradling her in his arms.

"You don't have to carry me." Why had he come for her?

"Be quiet, Eliza. After we deal with the police and make sure your brother is okay, you and I have a lot to talk about."

Chapter 18

When they reached the hospital, Aegina and the children were already there. She paced in front of her boys, the youngest curled up on a chair sleeping, Evan staring at his mother. Aegina saw her, and Eliza hugged her.

"He's in surgery." Aegina covered her mouth, fighting frightened tears and glancing at her kids. She was trying to be strong for them.

Eliza refrained from asking if he'd be all right. It was clear Aegina didn't know. Brandon's hand on her back provided a modicum of comfort. Whatever he wanted to talk about would have to wait. She didn't have it in her anymore to hope he'd come to his senses. And she was too worried about Ryker to pay much attention.

A doctor approached. Nothing in his expression revealed the outcome of the surgery.

"Mrs. Harvey?"

"Yes," Aegina replied shakily.

"Your husband's going to be fine. The bullet grazed his lung and passed through. We've removed bone fragments from his ribs and he's lost a lot of blood, but he'll recover fully."

"Oh, thank God!" Aegina exclaimed.

Eliza nearly collapsed with relief herself. And then Aegina began crying. Brandon put his arm around her and held her close to his side.

"Mommy, where's Daddy?" Evan asked, tugging at her shorts.

Eliza knelt to his level. "They're going to take him to a room where we'll be able to go see him, okay?"

The boy nodded, worry he didn't quite comprehend aging him beyond his seven years.

The doctor left them and Aegina turned. "He said Ryker will be asleep for a while."

"Do you need anything?" Brandon asked Aegina. "Something to eat or drink?"

"I've got water. The boys and I will go up to Ryker's room and wait for him to wake up."

"Okay. Eliza and I will be back in a little while."

Eliza shot him a look. None of the withdrawal she'd picked up on this morning came from him now.

"Let's go," he said.

He wasn't going to accept no from her. Aegina smiled. "Go on. I'll call you when he wakes up."

Eliza went with Brandon outside, only to be greeted by a throng of reporters. Questions were firing at them.

"Did Jillian Marks kill your husband?"

"Is it true you shot your own father? How do you feel about that?"

"Is your brother going to be okay, Mrs. Reed?"

"Yes," Eliza answered that question with a smile.

"Did Jack Reed or Jillian shoot him?"

"Were they working together?"

"How did you know he'd take Eliza to your property?"

Brandon ushered Eliza to the truck without comment. She wasn't in the mood for this, either.

"Did your father work with Jillian in the triple homicide?"

Brandon shut the passenger door and went around to open his, reporters clustering around him.

"Take me to Ryker's so I can get cleaned up." Then she'd go back to the hospital. She wasn't all that dirty, but a shower would feel good after all she'd been through today.

"You might as well bring all your things with you when you're finished," he said.

"Why?"

"Because you're going to live with me now."

"I am, huh?" He was sure acting different.

"I pictured this differently. No reporters. You and me somewhere a little more romantic."

"You? Romantic?" She had a feeling she was about to get her wish.

"I can be romantic."

A hardened, loner rancher who everyone in Vengeance loved. "Prove it."

Chuckling, he drove another way that took them into town. In front of an old, historic church with sandstone exterior and a steeple, he parked.

"Come on."

"What are you doing?" Too curious, she got out.

He took her hand and led her past the church. There was a park next to it, the same park where she'd stripped to her underwear and her teacher had seen her dancing for him. She held on to the stop sign pole and circled around it, sending him a sultry look.

He stood there grinning at her.

"This isn't romantic."

"Not yet, no."

She took another turn around the pole, seeing people walking up and down the street and gathered in the park, picnicking, or in the playground. They didn't have the cover of night or the late hour to offer at least some privacy.

She stopped circling the pole and just looked at him.

"I'm sorry about this morning," he said.

"What changed your mind?"

"The thought of losing you." He was no longer grinning. "I watched my dad lose touch with reality after my mother died. Loving her made him go crazy."

Kind of like her with her parents. Without realizing it until now, they'd both shared the fear of loving someone so much that losing them destroyed them. But not loving destroyed, too.

"I always thought that about my mother. Except now I see she's fine. She misses my dad, and will always love him, but she isn't broken. Not the way I always imagined."

"I'm glad you see that now."

"I'm glad, you do, too. About your dad. You're nothing like him, Brandon."

"I never would have if it hadn't been for you."

They stood there staring at each other, Brandon with satisfied affection and she teetering on the brink of utter delight. He'd come to his senses. Brandon loved her.

Then his expression sobered. "Promise me we'll never forget David."

That would be easy. "I promise." David was a good man. She'd remember him from their youth, before he got embroiled in all his trouble. She'd help Brandon do the same. Remember the good, not the bad. Together they'd celebrate his life that way.

She moved so that her back was against the stop sign pole.

He moved forward, leaning one hand on the pole above her head.

"Let's get married."

"Okay."

He grinned again. "That was a lot easier than I expected."

"It must be your lucky day."

"Lucky. Yeah, I'm lucky all right." He bent and kissed her, still with his hand on the pole.

"Is this romantic enough for you?"

"It's getting there."

"I'll have flowers delivered later."

"That's better."

"To the ranch. Where I want you to be every day."

"Yes." She ran her hands up his chest and kissed him, savoring every liberating, delicious moment of it. She'd be free to kiss him anytime, anywhere, without fear of losing him until death took either one of them from each other. He was hers. Finally.

"Eliza Harvey, is that you?"

Brandon pulled back, lowering his hand and turning with Eliza to see a woman approach. At first she didn't recognize her.

"Mrs. Thompson?"

"Are you all right? You're the talk of the town right now." She looked from her to Brandon and then up at the stop sign. "But I didn't hear anything about this."

Brandon looked from Eliza to the woman, and then dawning made him grin. "The pole dance."

"It's good to see you've settled down," Mrs. Thompson said to Eliza.

"I'll invite you to the wedding." Especially after the teacher who'd seen her strip for Brandon had seen them kissing in the very same spot.

"You're getting married?"

"Yes. Something we should have done a long time ago."

"No more than a year after high school," Brandon said.

"Life is funny that way. Sometimes you have to grow into things. Or out of them." She directed her attention to Eliza. "I never did understand why you married David. It's sad and all how he was killed, but the truth has a way of coming out one way or another."

A woman with two kids waved from a blanket in the park and Mrs. Thompson saw her. "I'm meeting my daughter and grandkids. Congratulations, you two."

Brandon took her hand. "Come on. Let's see if we can find a place to eat without being hounded by reporters. Then I'll take you to Ryker's."

She could take a shower and change and then they could go back to the hospital to check on Ryker before going back to the ranch. They walked up the block to a pub and went inside.

After being seated at a table and ordering a couple of burgers, Eliza heard the tail end of a news story on Jack and Jillian. No one in the pub paid them much attention.

The next news story began. This one was about Melinda Grayson. Another video of her had been released by her captor. The timing was impeccable. Could Jillian be behind it? Were the murders connected somehow?

Vengeance might be closer to solving the murders, but there was still plenty of scandal to go around. Eliza looked across the table at her new fiancé. She was glad it wouldn't be about her anymore. She was going to spend the rest of her life cherishing every moment. She'd yearned for this so long, to be with the man she loved, to live in peace and happiness and not have to struggle so hard to make them on her own. Force it. Now she didn't have to try at all. Her happiness would come naturally with Brandon.

The news program ended, and she focused on the man across the table from her, the man of her dreams, the only man for her. She almost couldn't believe he was hers, that he'd come around.

There was one area that he hadn't faced, yet, however.

"How many kids do you want, Brandon?"

His head jerked up. "What?"

"Kids. You and me. What do you think? Two?"

"Woman, you're going to drive me to an early grave."

"You're going to be an old man with me. And you're going to watch your kids grow up and have kids of their own."

What had begun as apprehension smoothed to acceptance. "We can have four if you want."

"Really?"

"I'm not my father. I'd love the chance to raise kids the way they should be raised."

She smiled, certain now that he'd come full circle. He wasn't a violent man. Never would be.

"And you said you were the one who was lucky."

"I am."

"So am I. I love you, Brandon."

"I love you, too, Eliza."

She laughed, thrilled and overjoyed. Yes. This was the beginning of something really special. She couldn't wait to start her life with him. As he reached across the table and cupped her hand in his, she decided that she'd start right now.

* * * * *

Don't miss the next story
in the VENGEANCE IN TEXAS *series:*
A BILLIONAIRE'S REDEMPTION
by Cindy Dees, available March 2013.

Available February 19, 2013

#1743 WHAT SHE SAW

Conard County: The Next Generation
by Rachel Lee

When Haley Martin poses as Buck Devlin's girlfriend to help solve a murder, she never imagines that he's putting her life, her dreams and her heart at risk.

#1744 A BILLIONAIRE'S REDEMPTION

Vengeance in Texas • by Cindy Dees

Willa Merris may be off-limits, but Gabe Dawson is a billionaire and can break all the rules to keep her safe... if she'll let him.

#1745 OPERATION REUNION

Cutter's Code • by Justine Davis

Will family loyalty ruin Kayla Tucker's chance at a true, lifetime love, and will past secrets destroy everything she holds dear?

#1746 COWBOY'S TEXAS RESCUE

Black Ops Rescues • by Beth Cornelison

Black ops pilot Jake Connelly battles an escaped convict and a Texas-size blizzard to rescue Chelsea Harris, but will he also lose his heart to the intrepid small-town girl?

A rattle came from the trunk lock, and she tensed. *Oh, please, God, let it be someone to rescue me and not that maniac killer!*

The lid rose, and daylight poured into the pitch-dark of the trunk. She shuddered as a stiff, icy wind swept into the well of the trunk, blasting her bare skin.

"Ah, hell," a deep voice muttered.

Her pulse scampered, and she squinted to make out the face of the man standing over her.

The gun in his hand registered first, then his size—tall, broad shouldered, and his fleece-lined ranch coat made him appear impressively muscle-bound. Plenty big enough to overpower her if he was working with the convict.

A black cowboy hat and backlighting from the sky obscured his face in shadow, adding to her apprehension.

HRSEXP0213

"Are you hurt?" he asked, stashing the gun out of sight and undoing the buttons of his coat.

"N-no." When he reached for her, she shrank back warily.

Where was the convict? She cast an anxious glance around them, down the side of the car, searching.

She jolted when her rescuer grasped her elbow.

"Hey, I'm not gonna hurt you." The cowboy leaned farther into the trunk. "Let me help you out of there, and you can have my coat."

His coat... She almost whimpered in gratitude, anticipating the warmth. When she caught her first good glimpse of his square jaw and stubble-dusted cheeks, her stomach swooped. *Oh, Texas!* He was a freaking *Adonis*. Greek-god gorgeous with golden-blond hair, cowboy boots and ranch-honed muscles. He lifted her out of the trunk, and when he set her down and her knees buckled with muscle cramps, cold and fatigue, she knew she couldn't dismiss old-fashioned swooning for at least some of her legs' weakness. He draped the coat around her shoulders, and the sexy combined scents of pine, leather and man surrounded her. She had to be dreaming....

Will Chelsea find more than safety in her sexy rescuer's arms? Or will the convict come back to finish them both off? Find out what happens next in COWBOY'S TEXAS RESCUE

HRSEXP0213